THE
MISADVENTURES
OF
MARTIN HATHAWAY

THE
MISADVENTURES
OF
MARTIN HATHAWAY

⚙ BOOK ONE OF THE MISADVENTURES TRIOLOGY ⚙

KATHRYN CLARE GLEN

W.J.
★CREATIVE★
PUBLISHING

ISBN 13: 978-1-945769-26-9
eISBN: 978-1-940014-80-7

Library of Congress Catalog Number: 2015947308
Printed in the United States of America
First Printing: 2016

20   19   18   17   16   5   4   3   2   1

Cover design by Jessie Sayward Bright
Interior design by Kimberlee Morehead

Published by W.I. Creative Publishing, an imprint of Wise Ink Creative Publishing.

W.I. Creative Publishing
837 Glenwood Avenue
wiseinkpub.com

To order, visit seattlebookcompany.com or call (734)426-6248. Reseller discounts available.

For my sister,
who believes in Martin Hathaway
and, more importantly, in me.

❂ CHAPTER ONE ❂

GLASS SHATTERED AND rained down throughout the library, followed barely an instant later by the sound of wood splitting. A man in a gray suit with a red cravat looked up from his book to discover that another man in a sweater and corduroys had crashed through the skylight and lay upon the remains of what had once been a very lovely coffee table. He shook his head and resumed his reading.

Footsteps could be heard running up the stairs. A young woman dashed into the room, blaster drawn. The man did not look up from his book.

"Ah, Daisy," he said, licking his thumb and turning a page. "Someone here to see you."

Exasperated, Daisy placed her blaster back in its leather holster.

"Basil," she asked, "why is there a man on my coffee table?"

"He appears to have fallen through the skylight and landed there."

"Why haven't you done anything about it?"

"It's my day off."

"You don't get days off."

"I know." Basil glanced up from his book and smirked. "That

is why I had to take one."

Daisy sighed. Basil's smug half-smiles were significantly more enjoyable when one was not the object of their derision. Though they both knew she had every right to press her point, this was one battle Daisy Fitzgerald McNamara chose not to fight, at least not at this moment. Ever the woman of action, she knelt beside the fallen man and checked for signs of life.

"He's breathing," she said with her ear above the man's mouth, "and I don't see much bleeding. Help me take him to Sick Bay."

Having been Daisy's First Officer far too many years to any longer be impressed by the graceful manner with which she flung herself into any given fray, Basil had already resumed his reading.

"As he's likely suffered a head and possibly a neck injury," he replied dryly, "do you really think it a good idea for us to band together for the purpose of jostling his spine?"

"Fine. Go get Melody and bring her here."

"I'd love to, but the day off and all."

Daisy drew her blaster. Basil put down his book.

"Alright. Alright. I'm going."

As Basil retreated down the stairs and out the front door, Daisy examined their visitor more closely. She rummaged through his pockets and discovered several small metal discs with indentations around their circumference, a rectangular object that appeared to be made of some hard substance and glass, and a leather envelope. She opened the last item and pulled out green papers with pictures of men and bizarre icons. These she pocketed to see what Basil could make of them. The envelope also contained a calling card made out of the same strange material as the rectangular object. The calling card bore a picture; if it was the same man, the card indicated that Martin Hathaway now lay on her floor.

Daisy held it by the unconscious man's face for comparison. It was not particularly alike. Perhaps the picture was taken when the man was under some duress. Daisy waved her hand, physically dismissing the conjecture from her mind. No. Even with allowances made for the dilation of the pupils and the shocked expression, the man in the picture's chin was a little too long and his nose was much too prominent for him to ever be described as attractive. But the man on the coffee table . . .

Daisy palmed the calling card and turned her head to the side, considering the figure sprawled upon the wreckage. Attractive was not the proper word, she concluded. This man was . . . familiar. Rapidly, she searched through her memory for some connection to her person. The effort proved fruitless. Perhaps one of Sophie's sketchbooks might shed some light on the mystery. Daisy rose to consult the archives but was stopped by one of the most pathetic sounds she had heard in over a twelvemonth.

Martin groaned and blinked his eyes. His entire body ached. For a moment, he thought he had gone blind, but he realized he was staring directly into a bright light. Suddenly, a woman's face appeared in the light. No, not in the light. The light was radiating from her. It was woven in her auburn hair; it encircled her head like a halo. She was saying his name.

Oh, no.

"Am I dead?" Martin asked the vision.

She laughed; it was the sweetest sound Martin had ever heard. He was definitely dead, but he was not certain how he had merited a place in heaven.

The laughter subsided, and the woman's expression sobered considerably.

"You're not dead," Daisy replied, pulling her blaster from its holster and pointing it at his face. "Would you like to be?"

"What?" Martin gave a start and tried to push himself away from the intimidating brass gun that now filled the space where the beautiful woman had been. "No! No, thank you. Alive is fine. Alive is good."

"Excellent." She withdrew the weapon and Martin breathed a sigh of relief. Gingerly moving to cause the least amount of pain and touch the fewest bits of broken glass and splintered wood, he sat up and looked about him. The walls of the room were lined with chestnut bookcases, all filled with leather-bound books with brilliant gold lettering on the spines. The intact furniture appeared beautiful but uncomfortable. Martin had seen pieces like them when Hailey had drug him out to antique stores in search of fabulous little items she could up-cycle and list for a fortune on the Internet.

"You probably shouldn't try to move yet," Daisy advised. "Our CMO should be here soon and she can give you an all-clear."

"Your what?"

"Our Chief Medical Officer."

"Oh, right." Martin rubbed the back of his head. He could feel a very nasty knot forming. "Actually, I think I'm okay. Just a little sore. But I don't remember hitting a house. I mean . . . I remember slipping . . . and the air was cold and I thought I was going to die . . . but now it's warm and I'm on the floor."

"You might have lost consciousness during the fall."

4

Martin nodded. "I must have. How long have I been out?"

"Maybe five minutes."

That couldn't be right. It was night when he had . . . well, he was pretty sure that his condition required more than five minutes' recovery time. Judging by the amount of sunlight pouring in through the hole in the ceiling, Martin guessed it was nearing noon now.

He tried to stand but could not find anywhere to put his hands for support that was not covered in broken glass. Daisy took his arm and put it around her shoulder. She wrapped one of her own around his waist and helped him to rise and slowly make his way over to the sofa. The sleeve of her dress was soft in Martin's hand. He realized it was silk and wondered who on Earth wore silk in the middle of the day.

"Are you a reenactor?" he asked as she lowered him into repose and adjusted a pillow under his head. She smiled, but she did not reply. Martin did not mind. It was a sweet smile. He thought her mouth might have been a little too small for her face, but when she smiled she seemed . . . enchanting.

"I didn't realize they had a historical house at Eagle's Peak," he continued, trying his best to affect half the degree of charm this woman appeared to command. "I took my students to a couple for field trips. They always try to get the actors to break character, but of course you all are smarter than a bunch of smart-aleck kids. Not that that's hard to be . . ."

Martin knew he was babbling. He also knew he was blushing. He was quite certain the neckline on the woman's dress was not period-accurate, whatever period she was going for. The effect was enhanced by the woman's hairstyle, which was pinned high upon her head in soft curls, elongating the line of her white throat. Hailey's going to kill me if she has to pick me up and this lady is around, Martin thought between awkward stammers.

As the woman continued to smile at him and fuss over his comfort, he knew that if he were not stopped soon, he would continue saying things to her until he had thoroughly exhausted his vocabulary. Luckily, Martin was saved from further verbal embarrassment by the entrance of a man and another woman, this one with a much more acceptable collar.

"Look, darling," Basil said, ushering Melody into the library. "The fallen angel I promised you has risen."

Daisy turned from Martin and held herself as straight and tall as her petite frame would allow. "He's conscious, but I'm afraid he might have some brain damage. He's flushed and has been speaking nonsense."

Martin protested that his brain was fine, but he was ignored. Setting her leather bag on the table beside the sofa, Melody pulled out what appeared to Martin to be a brass circle covered in tiny lights. She set it on his head and adjusted the circumference until it matched his own.

"You shouldn't have moved, poor dear," she admonished. "Something might have been knocked loose."

"No really, I'm fine. If I could just use the phone, my friends can come and take me to the hospital. How is this crown supposed to help, by the way?"

"See?" Daisy shook her head. "Nonsense. Be sure you run a thorough scan of his temporal lobe."

SOON MORE FOOTSTEPS were heard on the stairs. Martin turned

his head in hopes that the footsteps might belong to someone, anyone, he recognized. Melody chided in a soft, lyrical voice that such movement was not yet worth the risk, and she was right. Two middle-aged men, neither of whom were the least bit familiar to Martin, stepped into the library. They looked like reenactors as well, and Martin reasoned they must be playing this bizarre family's servants, as their costumes were not as fancy as the other three.

Readers of a squeamish disposition are now warned that a lengthy description of appearance and finery is to follow. If this is not your particular cup of tea, or if you are the sort given to writing strongly worded but little considered Internet reviews pointing out minutia—like the fact that Martin had no time to make all of the observations that are to come between the appearance of the men in the library and the first man's salutation—then you are most welcome to skim the text until dialogue and our adventure resumes.

Martin noted as best he could from his position on the sofa that the two middle-aged men each sported a dark brown bowler hat, on which was a strange round insignia. The insignia was divided into two hemispheres, the top blue and the bottom green. Over this a large white daisy had been embroidered. The insignia was framed once in a deep purple and then once more with gold. This gave Martin the impression that the two men must be attired in some uniform. He was almost correct, as the men were dressed nearly identically in buckskin breeches held in place by brown suspenders. The sleeves of their cotton shirts were rolled up, a detail which, when coupled with the fact that both men were red of face and profusely sweating, indicated they were until recently engaged in some sort of physical labor.

The men certainly seemed well cast for their part. Though they appeared to be at least twenty years his senior, there was no question they were capable of more heavy lifting than Martin Hathaway had ever thought of doing in his life. The man on the left's bicep alone was the size of Martin's whole face.

Though slimmer and taller than the two workingmen, the sandy-haired young man whom Martin would come to know as Basil Underwood was hardly less intimidating. His gray jacket, waistcoat, and pants were all impeccably tailored, and as he stood leaning with one hand upon a dainty purple chair he looked like an action figure version of whatever historical figure he had been hired to portray.

Actors, Martin snorted derisively before turning his gaze much more agreeably back to the two women at his side. Taking them in as one unit, he nearly snorted again, though this time out of amusement. They reminded him of the good and bad angels that come to sit on cartoon characters' shoulders in times of moral crises.

Dr. Melody Underwood was undoubtedly the good angel, from her modestly coiffed golden hair down to her immaculately polished white boots. She wore a high-waisted skirt of light green, and upon the lace collar of her blouse she had pinned a brooch of the same insignia as the one on the workers' hats. Everything about her dress, manner, and voice begged the word lovely, and Martin Hathaway sheepishly realized that Hailey would not likely appreciate this woman's presence any more than the other's, neckline or no neckline.

As for the other woman, Martin concluded that, bad or good, an angel was still an angel. Daisy's blue silk gown had pick-ups of black lace sewn artfully around the ample skirt, raising the hemline to facilitate movement and highlight her black boots. Martin wondered how one person could look so soft and yet so powerful at the same time. The effect was mesmerizing, and Martin Hathaway would have found himself blushing and babbling again had not one of the new arrivals cleared his throat, commanding the attention of the room.

"Beg your pardon, Captain," the man said, removing his hat, "but there are Monitors in the Valley, and they say they have a message to deliver to you in person."

Daisy was poised but puzzled. "You mean there are Monitors at Communication Point, surely, Gilly."

"No, Miss. In the Valley." Gilly looked worried, as well he should.

"Then I better see them." Efficiently, Daisy addressed her other two subordinates with a slight inclination of her head in each direction. "Carry on, Melody. Basil, see what you can do to find out who our visitor is, where he came from, and how he got into my house."

Basil contemplated the cut of the fingernails on his right hand, his usual method of indicating the tediousness of the Captain's order, sighing, "I suppose you would not accept his name, that he came from the sky, and that he got into your house via the skylight?"

Daisy flashed Basil a smile that Martin would have thought sinister had it been displayed on a less angelic face.

"Don't think I won't stun you in front of your wife, Basil."

With that, Daisy exited the room followed by Gilly and his companion. Martin had listened carefully to this exchange and wondered if he did, in fact, have a little brain damage.

9

❁ CHAPTER TWO ❁

AN ASTUTE READER, or even a very dull one who has scanned the book summary, will be aware at this point in our tale that Martin Hathaway is not having what could be described in any sense as a typical day. This was odd indeed, as Martin's morning had given no indication that the events to follow would be anything other than mundane at best. Quite the reverse, Martin's day had started in the clichéd manner in which most days on Earth begin: the alarm rang.

Its shrill, electronic timbre jarred Martin out of what he vaguely remembered as a wonderful dream. He slammed his hand against the bedside table until he located the "off" button and wondered if falling back asleep would take him to wherever it was he had been. Even though he could recall nothing about it other than a general good feeling, Martin knew the dream-place had one distinct advantage over his current reality: there, it was not six in the morning.

He felt Hailey stir next to him. Reality was not without its perks. Rolling onto his side, Martin cuddled against her and gently placed three kisses on the back of her neck. Hailey murmured something.

"What's that?" Martin asked.

"I said, 'You're going to be late again.'"

With a sigh, Martin rolled away, sat up, and placed his bare feet on the floor. Excepting the bathroom and kitchen, every inch of floor space in his apartment was covered in a soft, white carpet, and yet his feet always felt as if they had turned to ice the second they were put into use. He scurried into the kitchen to prepare the coffee, relying on quick, rapid movements to keep himself warm.

Stepping into the shower, he rejoiced that it could be counted on to be hot, at least for the first five minutes. It could not be said that he enjoyed his ablution, however, as the following mishaps occurred: first, he stepped on Hailey's razor, which always seemed to find new ways to attack him in the mornings; second, he was required to bend and contort his spine in directions humans were not built to reach, as the shower head had been installed at exactly the right height for Hailey's comfort and the wrong for his; and third, he remembered that today was a Staff Development day.

Someone was always trying to develop Martin Hathaway. His father thought he should man up and make an honest woman out of Hailey. Martin would not be reluctant to do so if Hailey were not so insistent on his raising his ambitions beyond being a mere teacher. His friends were constantly bombarding him with recommendations for how he should invest his money, free time, and immortal soul. Even the concessions man at the movie theater would not get off his case, persuading Martin every time that he really did want to upgrade to the Mega Size for only a quarter more. No one with any degree of acquaintance with Martin Hathaway would accept his assurances that he was quite happy with his life. This was very perceptive of them, since he was not.

Undaunted by the relentless barrage of petty annoyances that comprised his every morning, Martin stepped from the now freezing shower, dried himself, and dressed for the day. He pulled a sweater over his cotton button-down while walking into the kitchen and, consequently, nearly walked straight into Hailey.

"Sorry, babe," he said as he kissed her cheek. "How's the coffee today?"

Hailey took another sip from her mug before answering. "Delicious. As always. I swear, Martin, if you have one talent it's for coffee."

Martin grinned. "It's because I make it with love."

She rolled her eyes. This exchange had been cute the first few times Hailey had slept over at Martin's, but having lived with him for the better part of two years, it was starting to get on her nerves. She studied him as he made his daily Pop-Tart and poured half of the remaining coffee into a travel mug. Earlier that month she had persuaded him to let his hair grow out a little. She had seen the cutest photos of his high school days at a visit to his mother's, and she had been convinced that if he let his hair curl like that again he would be perfectly acceptable to be seen with her at dinners with clients. Now she wondered if it made him look a little too much absent-minded-professor and not enough up-and-coming-administrator.

"You know your principal would take you more seriously if you wore a blazer instead of a sweater every day."

Martin laughed with the Pop-Tart in his mouth, spraying crumbs across the counter. "I don't want him to take me more seriously. Then he'd give me more to do."

"But that's just what you need. I know you, and you're bored. You need a challenge. Iron sharpens iron, after all."

"What does that even mean?"

"It means what you choose it to mean. Words are merely an outward expression of our inner monologue. When I saw that phrase on Pinterest the other day, I instantly knew it was speaking your voice. We both know you need more to do than lecture to snotty kids all day."

"I like to think I do a little more than that," Martin said as he slung his messenger bag full of graded papers over his shoulder. "Though, I won't today. Today, I'll have snotty kids for half, then mind-numbingly insipid PowerPoint presentations for the rest of it. Wish me luck."

Hailey did, and then reminded him that, if nothing else, he had something to look forward to after work.

"You're right," he said cheerfully, pretending not to catch her meaning. "It's Ryan's bachelor party tonight."

That was not what Hailey had in mind. Swallowing down her annoyance and speaking as one would to a child who refuses to put away his toys and come to the dinner table, she replied, "No, it's Nadya's opening at the gallery tonight, and then the after-party at The Garage. We talked about this all week."

"Right again." Martin's smile was fixed now in an expression of willful good humor. "And I told you all week that I'm not going, because I have plans with Ryan. He is my best friend. I am his best man. I planned this camping trip longer than Nadya's been an artist, and I'm not missing it."

"Ryan is a vulgar, classless loser. You haven't spent time with him in two years."

"All the more reason why I'm not letting him down tonight."

If Hailey were to make a list of all the traits she admired in Martin, assertiveness would not have been on it. His pliability was the strongest factor keeping them together after the initial rush of attraction had gone. It infuriated her to see a defiant Martin, mainly because she did not know how to handle him.

"Listen," she thrust a finger at his chest. "Tonight, I'm going to the gallery and drinking lots of wine. Then, I'm going out for dancing and cocktails. At 3, I'm going home with someone. You can be that someone, or you can snuggle in the dirt with Ryan."

Martin was not practiced in holding his ground. He was also late for work. "We'll talk about this when I get home," he said and walked out the door.

Hailey was going to talk about this now. She flung herself onto the couch, opened her laptop, and left an angry post on the Young Feminist Professionals Forum. Having vented, she poured herself a second cup of coffee and waited for the first response.

Damn it, she thought. *His coffee is delicious.*

"Mr. Hathaway, are we boring you?"

Martin gave a start and looked up. "No, Dr. Avery. Just concentrating on my notes." He moved his arm to cover the elaborate sketch of a wide-mouthed Principal Avery swallowing him whole, just in case the copiousness of his note-taking would be called into question.

"Excellent. Then can you remind us what the most important factor in classroom management is?"

"Engaged time?"

"Teacher presence, Mr. Hathaway. Teacher presence. Nothing is more important to the maintenance of order than teacher presence. And why is that?"

"Because if you aren't in the room the kids can run wild?"

Dr. Avery shook his enormous head and sighed as if every ounce of his compassion was at this moment engaged in pitying Mr. Hathaway. Luckily, Mr. Rice, Martin's Department Chair and mentor, came to his rescue.

"Teacher presence is who we are in the classroom. It's the nonverbal expression of our expectations for student behavior." Dr. Avery thanked him for his presence that day and began his summation of the importance of the preservation of order. When the principal had wandered sufficiently far as to be out of earshot, Mr. Rice leaned toward Martin and whispered, "It's also all we've been talking about since 1:30."

"Sorry." Martin genuinely was. Earlier that morning he had chastised a freshman for doodling instead of filling out the note-taking guide Martin had painstakingly prepared the day before. "My mind's not really been here today."

"Big plans for the weekend?"

"Several, actually."

Their conversation was interrupted when the principal strode back toward their table. He stopped close to Martin's side and said to the room, "Now, perhaps Mr. Hathaway can tell us what management technique I'm currently demonstrating."

"Proximity control, Dr. Avery."

"Very good, Mr. Hathaway. And I thought you had left for the weekend already."

MARTIN CLIMBED THE STAIRS to his apartment two at a time.

He had stopped by the florist's on his way home from work and picked up a bouquet of gerbera daisies that he intended to have properly displayed in a vase on the table when Hailey returned. If that did not get him out of hot water for abandoning her for the next forty-eight hours, he would have to formulate an escape plan.

Any hopes Martin still retained for reconciliation were dashed when he reached his door. There were two piles stacked in the hall. One was comprised of his overnight bag and camping gear. The other was the neatly folded clothes he typically wore when out with Hailey and her clients. An envelope bearing his name was taped to the door. Reluctantly, Martin opened it and took out the enclosed note. It read:

Dear Jerkface,

Guess who left his house keys in the apartment again today. Don't worry; I have them. They are in the handbag I will be taking to Nadya's opening tonight at 8:00. If you would like them back, I suggest you arrive suitably attired. If not, I hope you packed all your camping shit already, because you're only getting what's outside.

Hugs & Kisses,

Hailey

PS–If anything in the hall got stolen while we were at work, it's not my problem.

"Oh, MARTIN, you shouldn't have. These are so pretty. How did you know I love daisies?"

"Lucky guess," Martin smiled sheepishly. Perking up, he

asked, "Is our boy ready?"

"All set!" Ryan stepped out of the house and bid his fiancée adieu for the next two days.

She waved at them with one hand, the other clutching the bouquet. "Bring him back in one piece!" she called as they made their way to the car.

"Will do!" Martin promised.

He stuffed Ryan's gear in the trunk of his car alongside his own and those of their friends Kyle and Zac. Food and booze, the other staples of any great male bonding trip, were in the second vehicle driven by the aforementioned friends. Martin got into the driver's seat, backed out into the street, and set course for Eagle's Peak State Park.

"Aren't you a little overdressed for camping?" Ryan inquired of Martin's apparel.

"It was this or a velvet blazer."

"You own a velvet blazer?"

"Hailey found it at some vintage place. Apparently it looks cool because it's ironic." Martin explained the reason he had not changed out of his teacher clothes. Ryan rightly conjectured that his story also explained the presentation of flowers to his fiancée, though he was not one to look a gift-Martin in the mouth.

"Did you finally tell her about Tuesday poker night?"

Martin reddened. "No, she still thinks I'm taking classes to add endorsements to my license."

"Are you kidding me? You've been sneaking around for two years, and she finally kicked you out just because of a camping trip?"

"I haven't been sneaking around. I'm going out with the

guys, not other girls. And she didn't kick me out. We can get past this. She'll cool off by Sunday."

Ryan was not convinced. "Why do you even want her to cool off? Anyone who locks you out for having friends has to be batshit crazy."

"Hailey's the best thing that ever happened to me. We'll work it out."

"Dude, maybe it's time something else happened to you."

RYAN WAS A MAN of honor and principle. Even though it was technically his big night to drink too much and get into stupid shenanigans, he made sure that, after establishing camp and building a fire, Martin consumed the right amount of alcohol to curse Hailey but not enough to cry about her. Unfortunately, it had been a long time since Martin Hathaway had gotten good and properly drunk, and he responded to the feeling and the freedom much like a collegiate attending his first party. Initially he was hilarious, but shortly his friends found themselves stumbling after and yelling for him to stop climbing on things.

"Martin, you asshole," Zac called as Martin scrambled up the side of the naturally sculpted rock that formed the eagle's head of Eagle's Peak, "if you die I'm taking Hailey out."

"God, it's brilliant up here." Martin held his hands aloft and looked out over the great expanse of earth below him. "I'm going to fly."

"Shit, he is going to die." Ryan tried to climb up after him, but he was not nearly as fit and had never been as nimble as his friend.

"Eff you, Ryan," he slurred. "I'm not going to die. I'm going to fly."

"Dipshit, you can't fly. Hell, you can't even cuss right. How could you fly?"

"I can fly. You're the one who can't fly. You're—" But his friends never found out what cutting epithet Martin had devised to apply to Ryan. Martin slipped, tumbled over the side of Eagle's Peak, and disappeared with a scream. His friends scrambled to the edge in horror. It was a clear night, and they could see all the way down to the river that rushed below, but they could find no sign of Martin.

Suffice it to say, Martin Hathaway could not fly, and today really was not his day.

⚙ CHAPTER THREE ⚙

ONE CAN THUS appreciate Martin Hathaway's confusion upon finding himself not only alive, but also unscathed, relatively sober, and in the middle of what was increasingly reminding him of the set for a play by Oscar Wilde. He was also a bit embarrassed to be the cause of so much trouble for both his friends and the nice, albeit eccentric, troupe of actors he had literally fallen upon. Martin endeavored, as was his fashion, to compensate for these negative feelings with an onslaught of cheerfulness and conversation.

"So . . ." he ventured, smiling up at Melody. "I'm . . . um . . . I'm Martin."

"Oh, heavens!" Melody laughed, running her hands over Martin's scalp to check for structural damage. "We're getting as bad as Daisy in the manners department, darling."

"Hardly," Basil replied. He stood beneath the opening in the library ceiling, stroking his chin and staring up into the sky. "Martin, would you mind telling me how much you weigh?"

Martin did not mind, but he was not able to answer. Melody cut him off, admonishing, "Darling, not now. Mathematics can wait until after we've been properly acquainted."

With a dismissive wave of his hand, Basil turned from the

skylight and flopped into a purple wingback chair. "As you wish, darling. It's only the Captain's orders."

"Captain?" Martin interjected, glancing between the pair. "You mean that woman, right? The one who just left?"

Melody sang, "Yes, dear. That would be Daisy. I am Chief Medical Officer Dr. Melody Underwood, and this is my husband, First Officer Basil Underwood."

"Charmed," Basil smiled in the manner of one who is anything but. "Now. If we may continue. Your weight, Martin. What is it? Twelve, thirteen stone?"

"Stone?" Martin blinked, bewildered. *Geez*, he thought, *these people don't break character for anything.* "Look, guys, this is fun and all, but I think I should probably see a real doctor now."

Melody's hands ceased their gentle movement. Martin thought he might have heard a dejected whimper, but his attention was arrested by Basil, who leapt to his feet and crossed over to the sofa in two long, confident strides.

"Listen, chum," Basil growled, leaning over Martin with one arm upon the sofa. His other was at his hip, revealing that beneath his suit jacket he wore a leather holster and thus carried a brass gun very like the one Martin had been threatened with only moments ago. "I have been concussed, stabbed, blasted, poisoned, and otherwise broken on occasions so numerous they boggle even a functioning mind. I can assure you, there is no doctor on Arnica more capable nor—dare I say it—more real than the one sitting very professionally at your head. I suggest you thank your lucky stars that you have found her and pay very close attention to her advice, lest we be pressed to inform the Captain that you succumbed to your injuries while she was out."

If Martin had been able to sink farther into the sofa, he would have. He was far too intimidated to question the man's use of the phrase on Arnica. Instead, he nodded meekly, glanced up at Melody, and murmured, "Sorry. Go ahead with . . . whatever you're doing."

"It's alright, Martin," she returned, searching through her medical bag and retrieving a notebook. "It's quite possible you really have no idea what you're saying."

Basil smiled in a manner far too open and friendly not to be considered threatening. "Everything sorted, then? Good. Now, Martin, if the doctor would give you an all-clear for movement, perhaps you might join me over by the desk and answer a few questions about what you think your origins are. Or how much you weigh. We could start with that one."

With Melody's aid, Martin rose from the sofa and slowly made his way to the far side of the library where an ornately carved desk sat beside a large window. As he did, he mused, This is my own fault. I had this coming. I really should have just gone to the gallery.

THOUGH MARTIN MAY not have been in his element, Daisy Fitzgerald McNamara unquestionably was in hers. Stepping lightly down her front staircase, Daisy paused at the bottom to tighten the laces on her boots. She also grabbed her green felt trench coat from the hook on the wall, pulled it on, and popped the collar before walking out the door. It was not the most sensible outfit for a walk across the open Valley in midsummer, but she did not see much point of being an airship captain if one did not dress with a little flair.

The two men flanked her on either side and walked a pace behind. Gilly explained as they walked that patrols had cornered the Monitors as they crossed the bridge at the border between the Valley and the Neutral Territories and were holding them by the river.

The second man asked, "Captain, how did Monitors find their way into the Valley?"

"That, Gibson, is what we're going to find out."

As they neared the river, Daisy saw four of her crew surrounding three black-uniformed Monitors. Gilly's report was not in error. They had crossed the bridge, despite that being impossible.

She called to her crew, "Stand down. Blasters holstered. These are the Neutral Territories, or have you forgotten?" The four members of the patrol slowly backed away from the Monitors and fell in place behind their captain.

One of the Monitors stepped forward. "Greetings, Captain McNamara. I come with a message from The Principle himself."

"Then you should have gone to Communication Point. Or is your party lost?"

The Monitor smiled sinisterly. "We are not lost, nor do we intend to stand by for weeks while you arrive at your leisure. We have a Parley Pass written in The Principle's own hand."

"The Principle cannot issue passes into lands he does not own. You would do well to remind him of the respect he showed the Neutral Territories when he wanted Dwarvish chocolate for his wife's birthday."

"He has not forgotten, which is why we deliver the following message: You have a citizen of Anatamenwar in your home. You will return him to the Hall within a fortnight, or we will come and claim him."

"Since when does The Principle concern himself with individual Unpredictables?"

"He is not an Unpredictable. He is a Citizen. Taking him for your own is an act of war and will be treated as such."

"There is no citizen of Anatamenwar in my home. The Principle is welcome to come search for him personally. Now, I suggest you return and deliver my response before your presence here is also deemed an act of war."

The Monitor bowed. "Two weeks, Captain McNamara." He and his fellows turned and marched back over the bridge.

Daisy watched their retreat. "Gilly and Gibson," she said when the Monitors had disappeared down the forest path, "follow them. I want to know where they go, who they are, and how they found my Valley."

"Aye, aye!"

Gilly saluted and started on his way, but Gibson asked, "Why, Captain? Aren't the Monitors going back to the Hall?"

She shook her head. "They're not from the Hall. And those were no Monitors."

"Captain, what do you mean?"

"There were three things wrong with those men. Can you figure out what?"

The crew considered the encounter. One ventured, "Well, they were in the Valley."

"Good. That's one. Now, how would you describe their physique?"

"They were a little on the thin side. Smallish, too," Gibson said.

"And how would you describe the physique of a typical

Monitor?"

"Big, beefy, and scary, Miss."

"So there's two. Three: do Monitors usually make a ticking sound?"

"No, Miss."

"Exactly. Follow them."

MEANWHILE, THE THREE occupants of the library were engaged around a large desk in an excellent visual for teaching young children about prepositions. Martin sat on the desk, Melody stood in front of the desk, and Basil sat behind the desk. The latter had asked Martin a series of questions, reexamined the skylight and the damage to the table, and was now busy making calculations on several sheets of paper. Melody had not said a word to Martin beyond, "Does it hurt when I do this?" to which the answer was nearly always "Yes!" Occasionally, the brass ring on his head would go "ding" and she would examine it, frown, and write something in her notebook.

"Okay," Martin said when the ring went "ding" the twelfth time, "I'm sure what you're doing is very professional, but I really think I should call my friends now."

"How do you propose to do that?" Basil asked without looking up from his work.

"Well, on my phone. I always keep it in my pocket." Martin put his hand in his front left pocket. Then he checked the front right pocket. Finally, he checked both back pockets at once.

"Oh my god," he cried, "I've been robbed!"

Calmly, Basil responded, "Very likely by the Captain."

"What?!"

"Standard protocol. You may have been carrying weapons or

dispatches."

"Weapons or dispatches? Don't you all think you're carrying your characters a little too far? I didn't even pay admission!"

Melody rechecked the brass ring and chewed on the end of her pencil.

The door slammed downstairs. Daisy entered the library alone, still wearing her coat.

"How is our guest?" she asked Melody.

"I can't explain it, but he's fine. He has bruises and cuts and a nasty bump on the back of his head, but other than that he's perfectly healthy. I ran the brain scan twice now, and there's no damage at all. I even did a concentrated scan of the language centers. No abnormalities."

"He's perfectly healthy, you say?"

"Yes, Captain."

"Good." Daisy walked across the room, picked up a chair, and carried it back to the desk. She set it down in front of Martin and climbed on so that she now stood six inches above his head. Grabbing him by the collar of his sweater, she lifted him up to her eye level. Martin glanced down to see his feet dangling and kicking above the ground. He could not decide if he was more terrified or impressed by the woman's strength, though he was certain whatever Eagle's Peak was paying her for this role was not enough.

Martin looked up and immediately regretted it. Daisy's formerly sweet face was contorted into a horrifying grimace.

"HOW DID MONITORS GET IN MY VALLEY?" she thundered.

"I don't know," Martin squeaked. "Did you have them installed?"

"Now you mark me. I am Daisy Fitzgerald McNamara, Captain of the Airship *Nephthys*, Keeper of the Lost Valley, Friend of the Fair Folk, and Bane of Anatamenwar. Every man, woman, and child in a five-mile radius is under my protection. If one of them is so much as inconvenienced by the Hall, you will answer to me. Is that clear?!"

Martin was currently prepared to agree with any statement, no matter how ludicrous, this woman asserted, so long as it meant she would let him go. "Yes. Perfectly. But . . . but I still don't know what you're talking about."

Daisy's features softened. She cocked her head to the side and considered Martin.

"You really don't, do you?" she asked quietly.

He shook his head.

Daisy let go of his collar and he dropped onto the desk.

"Well," she said, gracefully hopping off the chair, "that's sorted, then. Basil, report."

Basil looked up from his calculations for the first time since he had begun them. Lightly tossing his pen aside, he leaned back in his chair and locked his hands behind his head.

"Oh, we've just had a lovely little time, Captain. We had a nice chat with our fallen angel here in which he began by insulting my wife . . ."

By this point in the proceedings, Martin had formed the firm conviction that he was the only person with any degree of sanity in the room. He chose to assert this position by arguing with his obviously deranged counterpart. "I didn't mean to insult her! All I wanted was—"

Basil interrupted, "A real doctor. Yes, your request has been noted. Now, subsequent to having solved the existential crisis provoked by the appearance of a female doctor, little Gabriel here flirted with both of us—"

"I was just making small talk!" Martin protested.

"—and tried to pass it off as small talk. Apparently, asking two people if they really are married in real life is par for the course in Eagle's Peak polite society."

Daisy knew Basil was enjoying provoking the intruder far too much to report anything useful without redirection. This she gave, curtly. "Basil, what did you learn?"

"Our little Lucifer says his name is Martin Hathaway. He comes from a land called Eagle's Peak—"

"No," Martin protested again. "That's not what I said. Or meant . . . or . . ."

Daisy stepped in front of Martin. "Did I say, 'Martin Hathaway, report'?"

Martin shook his head.

"Then don't. Continue, Basil."

Basil cleared his throat. "As I was saying . . . he comes from a land called Eagle's Peak which I cannot find on any chart. There's a Swan's Peak south of West Ironton, but he insists upon the Eagle. He says that he was out with three companions when he became intoxicated, climbed a large rock, and fell off an even larger cliff."

Daisy giggled.

"Yes, that was my reaction as well. Though, of course, I made a manly chortle. I am now in the process of calculating the trajectory of his fall based on the angle and force with which he destroyed my favorite coffee table, and if given a few more minutes of peace, I believe I can take us to the point from which he began what must have been his hilarious descent."

"Excellent. Carry on." Daisy paced back and forth across the room while Basil calculated. Martin coughed once to test if it was time for him to report, but a single glance from Daisy indicated continued silence to be his best course of action.

Suddenly, Daisy stopped and exclaimed, "Eagle's Peak!" She took one of the papers she had confiscated out of her pocket and showed it to Martin. "This eagle. Is it the key to finding your land?"

"You did rob me!" Martin snatched the dollar bill from her hand. "Now this is the last straw. I don't care what money looked like in the 18-whatevers, there's no way you people can get me to believe you don't recognize George Washington."

Melody checked the ring again and sank into a chair. She looked as if she might cry.

Basil glanced up from his work. "May I see that?" he asked Martin.

"NO!" Martin clutched the bill to his chest. "Look at your own!"

Daisy pulled the remaining bills from her pocket. "Here, there's plenty more."

"And they're all mine! Give them back! And my wallet!"

"There's Common Script on all of them, but also another language I can't make out."

"Nor can I." Basil rose slowly, studying one of the bills. He looked out the window, up at the skylight, and back at the bills again.

"Do you think it's a code?" Daisy asked.

"No, I would have broken it by now." Basil smiled, stuffed the bill in his pocket, and gathered up his papers. "But I do think my work is done. If you'll all follow me, I'll explain the mystery of our Morning Star."

"I'm not going anywhere with you people." Martin picked up the chair on which Daisy had stood. Holding it as if he were a lion tamer surrounded by three particularly unruly beasts, he continued, "You're all crazy and probably overworked. I want my things back. I am going to call my friends and I am going to wait here for them. You let me do this, and I won't call the police."

Thoroughly disgusted, Daisy drew her blaster. Martin closed his eyes and hid his face behind the chair, but he did not back down.

"Put that thing away, Daisy," Melody intervened. "If he's gone into shock, stunning him will only exacerbate the condition. Better give him his things and see if they calm him."

Basil agreed. "There's been enough violence against furniture for one day. Give him what he wants before he holds the vases hostage as well."

Reluctantly, Daisy holstered her weapon and searched through the rubble for the items she had removed from Martin's pockets. She crossed the room and presented them to him, open palmed to indicate that she came in peace. Ignoring the bottle caps, Martin grabbed his wallet and phone. He placed the former in his back pocket and shook the latter in Daisy's face.

"I don't care what the fines are for drinking on park property," he said. "I'm going to have a very long talk with the Eagle's Point tourism bureau about you lot when I get out of here."

He hit the power button on the side of his phone and the screen illuminated. Gasping, Daisy moved closer to get a better look. Martin rolled his eyes and waited for the signal bars to load. He smacked Daisy's hand away when she tried to touch the screen. Everyone in the room held their breath. Martin began to look worried. He moved to stand by the window. The trio followed. He put the phone back in his pocket.

Martin rubbed the back of his neck, focusing his gaze upon the library's breathtaking wood flooring. Rocking back and forth on his heels, he muttered, "No service."

Basil clapped his hands together. "That was fun! Now, as I was saying: if you will all follow me . . ." The trio went out of the library and down the stairs.

"Keep up, Martin!" Daisy called from the door.

For lack of a better plan, Martin followed.

⚙ CHAPTER FOUR ⚙

STEPPING OUTSIDE THE HOUSE, Martin Hathaway realized he was not anywhere listed on the Eagle's Peak hiking trail map. For one thing, at Eagle's Peak the leaves had just reached their zenith of autumnal splendor, but here it was unarguably summer. The lush, green ground rolled lazily on and on for miles, dotted periodically by old, gnarled trees and stone cottages. Off in the distance he could see they were surrounded on three sides by snowcapped peaks and on the fourth by a formidable-looking river. Children were laughing, birds were singing, and Martin was gaping.

"What is this place?" he asked breathlessly.

Daisy smiled. People were usually impressed upon first seeing her Valley, but Martin's was by far her favorite reaction. Even if he turned out to be a spy from the Hall, she was going to enjoy this moment. She made a formal curtsey with perhaps a little more flair than needed and said, "This is the Lost Valley. Welcome, Martin Hathaway."

Through years of awkward growth and emotional repression, Martin Hathaway had mastered the art of the understatement. What he wanted to tell Daisy was that the Lost Valley—its green, its open skies, its people—was exactly how he had always pictured Heaven. What he said instead was, "It's nice."

Daisy smiled at this notion. There were many words she would have employed to describe her Valley, but nice had never made the list. Nonetheless, she recognized the compliment and responded with the graciousness of a true hostess.

"You should see it in the spring," she said, "when the sweet-breath first come into bloom."

Martin pointed to a cottage. "What's that?"

"It's one of the Free People's homes. I told you every man, woman, and child in a five-mile radius is under my protection, but you didn't think I'd have them all under my roof?"

"How many people is that?"

"104. The Jeffersons had twins last week."

He was about to congratulate the Jeffersons when he saw it. Anchored half a mile away was an enormous red balloon. Underneath, Martin thought he could see a boat made of wood and held together with iron. He stopped in his tracks.

"What. Is. That?!"

Calling over his shoulder, Basil informed him that it was the A.S. *Nephthys*, of which it had been firmly established that Daisy was captain. "And for the record," he added, "that is the grass. That is the sky. Those are mountains, and that thing running past is a rabbit. Now, if we could hold all further questions until the end of the tour, that would be smashing."

They had walked around and behind Daisy's home in the direction of the airship. Martin grew more excited the nearer they got to it, and he hoped Basil would let him see it up close before they moved on to wherever they were going. Thus were his thoughts when, abruptly, Basil stopped walking and declared that they had arrived.

Daisy looked around and said, "Basil, we're ten feet from the house."

"Fourteen, to be exact."

"Why did we walk out here? We could see this spot from the library window."

"We could have, yes. But standing here illustrates my point much more effectively."

"What point? There's nothing here."

"Precisely. At this exact spot, there is not a 325-foot cliff."

The good will that had swept through Martin's soul upon seeing the Valley was beginning to give way to panic. "Then why the hell are we here?" he demanded. "I thought we were going to where I fell."

"We were, and we are." Basil was clearly enjoying himself. "You see, Martin, your fall should have begun at a point approximately 325 feet above us, give or take five for wind resistance and your body weight, which I admit I approximated. Now, as we all have noted, there is nothing 320 to 330 feet above us but sky. From this, and other evidence, we can conclude that Martin here somehow managed to slip the bonds of Space and Time and fell from another universe into our own via an opening directly above Daisy's ill-conceived skylight."

Melody cried out with joy and threw her arms about her husband's neck. "Oh, darling," she exclaimed, "you're wonderful. It's the only thing that makes sense."

"THE ONLY THING THAT MAKES SENSE?!" Martin roared. He did not concur. "Not a word of that made any sense. There's plenty of things that make more sense. Why couldn't I have fallen from one of those mountain-looking things?"

"I'm sorry, Martin," Basil said with all sincerity, "but it's not mathematically possible."

"Well, then, maybe your math is wrong."

The women gasped. Basil stepped away from his wife, walked up to within inches of Martin's person, and stared him directly in the eye.

"My math," he said in a low growl, "is impeccable."

Melody pulled her husband away with assurances that Martin was not in his right mind now and nothing he said should be taken seriously. Martin would have protested, but a sudden horror had seized him.

"Not in my right mind," he moaned and held his head. "Oh, God, I know what's wrong. I know why I'm here. Don't you see? No, of course, you can't. You can't see it because you don't exist. I'm in a coma. I'm in the hospital in a coma and you all are the fevered ghosts my brain's inventing for who knows what purpose."

Daisy put a hand on his shoulder. "No, Martin. It might be hard to accept, but Basil has a point. We've all existed before you came."

"No, you didn't! You just think you did. My brain's created elaborate back stories for all of you but hasn't bothered to tell me about them yet. Think about it! You're all speaking English, for Pete's sake!"

"I don't know who Pete is," she said soothingly, "but we're not speaking English. We're speaking the Common Tongue. Though, Basil, why can Martin speak Common Tongue?"

Basil was pouting, but Melody had a suggestion. "If we accept the existence of an infinite number of universes, it follows that any given language would evolve an almost infinite number of times."

Martin was incredulous. "Oh, right. And given an infinite number of universes, I just happened to fall into the universe where the people look and talk just like me?"

"Yes," Basil said with his back to Martin. "Which brings me to my next theory: that God does exist, gets infinitely bored, and has a vicious sense of humor."

"No, no. That's not it." Martin began to pace in a circle, waving his hands as if to block the deviant brainwaves responsible for this mess. "We're not really here. I'm not really here. I just have to wake up, you'll all go away, and Hailey can kill me for going into a coma in the first place."

Basil turned and walked slowly toward him. He unholstered his blaster. The women, well versed in Arnican customs and Basil's temper, ran to intervene. The First Officer, however, did not fire his weapon, but rather turned it over in his hand and offered it to Martin.

"Would you hold this for a second?" he asked calmly.

Puzzled, Martin took the weapon. "Ok. Why?"

"Because if you remained unarmed, this would have been unsporting of me." With that, he punched Martin squarely in the face. For the second time that day, Martin Hathaway lay supine on the ground and writhing in pain.

"You hit me!"

"Yes." Basil flexed his hand, examining the damage. "Did it hurt?"

"Of course it hurt!"

"Ah. Then I think we can conclude that you are, in fact, physically present in this particular point in Time and Space."

As a good CMO should, Melody had carried her medical bag with her on their short walk. She knelt on the ground beside

Martin and tended to his now bleeding nose.

"Basil," she chastised, "that was not nice, even if he did insult your math. Think of all he's been through, falling through two universes."

"It's not supposed to be nice, darling. It's science." Basil also knelt to the ground. "Now listen, Martin, and I'll go through what we know. 1: You are physically here in Time and Space. 2: You fell with a force and, as you yourself admit, from a distance that should have resulted in severe injury. 3: Melody, the foremost medical practitioner in the land, can find no sign of major injury upon you. 4: My math is not wrong. From this, we can conclude that you must have only fallen from a slight distance above the skylight. Thus, some portal from your world—a world in which it appears to be acceptable to question people's mathematical prowess in front of their wives—must have opened directly above the library, depositing you at our infinitely patient feet. Q.E.D."

Martin wagged a finger at Basil. "Ah-ha! I've got you now. You said 'Q.E.D.' That's Latin. You couldn't read the Latin on the dollar you stole from me. You are a figment of my imagination."

"My dear boy"—Basil may have not overstated his patience—"it appears we have another proof of the coevolution of multiple universes. I don't know what Q.E.D. means to you, but those of us who grew up speaking Common Tongue know it is an acronym for 'Quite Enough Discussion.' Which, I believe we all will concur, we've had."

Even if Martin Hathaway had not been reeling in pain, he could not have countered such sound, disinterested reasoning. As Daisy, following the CMO's orders to facilitate blood drainage, lifted his head and gently placed it in her lap, he decided that, for the moment at least, his brain must know what it was doing.

"THAT'S YOUR PROBLEM, Gibs," Gilly whispered as the two men crouched behind a fallen log. "You always got to know why. The Captain knows why. That's enough for me."

"But she's just a kid. She's barely any older than my Annabell."

"She's a McNamara. She's ten times as smart as you or your Annabell will ever be and she's barely got started."

Gibson picked a centipede off his shirtsleeve. "She's smart enough not to be lying in the dirt watching Monitors march back to the Hall, that's for sure."

"You can march right back with them, you know."

"Bite your tongue."

Gilly did. Not because of the effectiveness of Gibson's curse, but because both men were struck in the back of their heads. Had they not been conversing, they might have noted that their assailant made a slight ticking sound as he approached.

⚙ CHAPTER FIVE ⚙

"Just once more," Martin said as he lay across the sofa in Daisy's parlor. Melody had left him to resume the work she had been in the middle of before his traumatic arrival. He had an ice pack on the back of his head and cotton stuffed up his nose. "Once more, and maybe I'll believe."

Daisy sat in the window seat looking at the river. She had said nothing since their return to the house, which left Basil to explain it once more.

"For the sixty-seventh time," he said with his head between his knees. "Infinite universes. Bubbles. Butterfly flaps its wings. Live dinosaurs."

"Every possible combination of events that could ever happen gets played out somewhere," Martin mused aloud.

"Exactly. Which means somewhere there is a universe in which I am stabbing you with a pen knife instead of really, really wanting to."

Daisy spoke up, "We don't stab our guests, Basil."

"But I really, really want to."

Silence fell upon the room momentarily, each person absorbed in their own musings. Finally, Martin sighed, "I guess I should be glad I didn't land in the universe where Hitler wins."

Basil lifted his head.

"I assume," he said, "that signifies a breakthrough. Can we ring for food now, Daisy?"

She nodded. "We can, but it won't do you any good. It's Cook's day off. You'll have to make yourself a sandwich. And rustle up something for Martin; goodness knows when his last meal was. Just coffee for me. And while you're at it, fetch the Captain's Log from my study. And my favorite pen. You know the one."

Basil rose, not to fulfill his Captain's requests, but rather to add the proper amount of drama to his protestation. Hands upon his hips to indicate the exact degree to which he had been put out, Basil thundered, "Daisy, I am your First Officer, not your personal assistant. And why does Cook get a day off but I can't have one?"

Daisy was unmoved. "You are and that's why. I can make a sandwich myself. I can't calculate the rate of fall of a man from another world or brew coffee, however."

"You most certainly can. You choose not to."

"Basil, are you hungry or not?"

He was. He asked Martin if he had any food allergies as he stormed out the door, but he did not pause long enough to receive an answer.

"Don't forget my pen!" Daisy called after him.

Silence filled the room. Throughout the exchange, Daisy had not turned her gaze from the river. Martin shifted so he could see her better and gave a tentative cough. Daisy did not move, so he coughed louder.

"Shall I send for Melody?" she asked without turning.

The acknowledgement was enough for Martin. "Can I ask

you a question?"

"Apparently."

"It's just . . . why do you let him talk to you like that?"

"Who and like what?"

"Basil. All the talking back and the arguing. Why don't you go all 'I'm Daisy Fitzgerald McNamara, look on my works, ye Mighty, and despair!' with him?"

Daisy made a soft sound that Martin thought might have been a laugh. "I imagine," she said, "that if I did that, the next morning I would discover I no longer had a First Officer."

Martin was impressed, but not entirely convinced. "Is he that good?"

Daisy turned and looked at Martin. After what he thought was a rather awkward eternity, she stood up and walked toward the sofa. Martin worried that he was about to be lifted in the air again, but she stopped before him and said, "Basil Underwood is many things. One of those is a pompous ass. Another is loyal. He may complain all the way, but he will follow me right up to Death's door. Would you, Martin Hathaway?"

Martin considered his response. "Are we going to ring Death's bell and run?"

This time, Daisy definitely laughed. It occurred to Martin that he probably would follow her into Death's kitchen for tea and scones. Daisy saw it in his eye, but she was not ready to believe it. She walked back to the window and resumed her watch of the river.

"What are you looking at?" Martin asked when he could stand the silence no longer, which is to say immediately.

"The river."

"Right. Going somewhere, is it?"

"Excepting from the sky or now a rift in Space and Time, the river is the only entrance to the Valley." This was almost true, but it would be true enough for Martin's purposes. Daisy continued, "There will be no sleep for me until I know how those Monitors found it."

"Those are the things you were yelling at me about?"

"Yes."

"What . . . um . . . what exactly are they?"

Daisy sighed. There would also be no peace for thinking until Basil came back. She turned away from the window and explained slowly, not as one would to a child, but as one practiced in storytelling.

"Five hundred years ago the realms of Men were in chaos—"

Martin lifted his head from the sofa and inquired tentatively, "Um . . . will this story eventually result in an answer to my question? And if so, could we skip to it?"

Daisy inhaled slowly before replying, "Fine. The Monitors are the guards of the Hall."

"And the Hall is?"

"The governing seat of Anatamenwar."

Martin contemplated this. "Sorry. You were right. Explain it your way." Noting the scowl that had grown on Daisy's face, he added, "If you don't mind. Please."

She began again. "Five hundred years ago the realms of Men were in chaos. They were scattered, leaderless, and vulnerable. Petty skirmishes and wars were regular. Eventually, several chieftains held a meeting, during which they established The Principle. Simply put: The Principle is Order. Everything, everyone, in its place and performing its function. Each of the chieftains pledged their people to The Principle, and they called their new alliance the Kingdom of Anatamenwar, or No Longer Shall Brothers Squabble in the ancient tongue. As the society grew and became solidified, the idea of The Principle eventually came to be represented by an actual man in office.

"Today, Anatamenwar runs like a well-oiled machine. Children are tested for their proficiencies in infancy and trained up by the Hall to know only what they need to perform the function for which they are best suited—"

Martin started laughing. Daisy was completely shocked. "Just what," she demanded, "is so funny about the destruction of the free will of mankind?"

"I'm sorry," Martin shook his head, "but it's all so ridiculous. The Principle. Order. Hall Monitors. Even high-stakes standardized tests. I'm definitely in a coma. Every word out of your mouth is clearly a thinly veiled allegory for how much I hate my job."

This was a big moment in the life of Martin Hathaway, as it was the first time he had ever admitted to himself, let alone aloud, that he did not like his chosen profession. Unfortunately, Daisy was unaware of this and did not appreciate having the history of her race dismissed as a haphazardly designed allegory for the problems of public education. She turned away from him and looked back at the river.

"Oh, now I really am sorry," Martin sat up, took the cotton out of his nose, and walked over to the window seat. Even if Daisy was a figment of his imagination, he did not like seeing her unhappy, and he liked knowing he had made her so even less. "It's been a really weird day. I take it back about the coma. See? I'm really heeeeeeeeeerrrrrrrrrrrrrrreeeeee!"

Martin had made the mistake of attempting to mollify Daisy

and prove his physical existence by taking her hand. She taught him the error of his ways by flipping and dropping him to the floor mid-sentence, all without breaking her watch on the river.

"Alright, Captain Lazy Pants. I've got your log and pen," Basil returned and paused in the doorway upon once again finding Martin lying spread-eagle on the ground. "Ah. Martin, a word to the wise: all of the flowers in the Valley are beautiful, but they are also quite dangerous. Best not to touch."

He gave Martin a hand getting back on his feet and presented Daisy with her requested items. "I'm off now to check on the kettle. Do try to remember your own rules about murdering guests while I'm gone."

Daisy accepted the pen with an open palm. Upon feeling its weight in her hand, she looked up and said in disgust, "Basil, this is my second favorite pen."

"I know," Basil smiled. "I couldn't find your third."

Having been left alone in a room with someone who has twice shown her capacity to cause major bodily harm, most people would surreptitiously meander toward the exit. Martin Hathaway was not most people, however, and took a seat opposite Daisy. She tolerated his presence as she wrote in the log but soon experienced the uncomfortable feeling of being watched.

"What is it now?" she asked, looking up to see Martin regarding her with expectation.

"It wasn't right," he asserted. "I said I was sorry."

Daisy blinked twice. "Excuse me?"

"You shouldn't have flipped me."

No one ever seriously told Daisy McNamara what she should not have done. Plenty of people told her what she should do;

that's why she had officers, after all. Largely their advice was ignored, because she was the Captain. But never, not even when she was a little girl, had anyone admonished her after the fact with any expectation of changing her behavior.

"What do you want me to do about it?" she asked, genuinely curious.

Martin crossed his arms. "Well, I think you should apologize."

"Sorry." It was difficult to determine if her response was declarative or interrogative, but Martin gave her the benefit of the doubt. He got up and sat next to her, choosing a space on the far end of the window seat.

"It's alright," he said. "You had a weird day, too. Men probably don't usually fall into your library."

"Not usually, no."

"So, do you have a plan?"

"I currently have nine. Of which are you inquiring?"

At this moment, Basil returned with an artfully arranged food tray. He was impressed to see Martin had conquered the window seat and yet retained all of his limbs. After handing Daisy her coffee, he nudged Martin to make room for him as well, so it was nice and cozy.

"A . . . um . . . a plan for getting me home." Martin tried to pick up what he assumed was his sandwich without knocking anyone with his elbows and eventually decided it best to wait for one of his companions to give up and move elsewhere. "I mean, I can't stay here forever. And I have to get home. I didn't leave a sub list, for one thing. Then there's Ryan's wedding. And Hailey. She's got to be worried sick about me."

"Who's Hailey?" Basil smiled amusedly.

"Hailey's my . . . well, she's . . . here, I can show you." He pulled out his phone. Few things other than this mysterious glowing device could have commanded Daisy's attention. She set the Captain's Log aside and peered over Martin's shoulder. He touched the screen and pictures of three men around a campfire appeared. It was mesmerizing.

"How does it work?" she asked.

"Electric circuits. There are these bits of metal inside, and the electricity goes through them, and then we see the pictures."

Both his companions nodded. Martin smiled to himself. They had bought it. He flicked his finger across the screen and eventually found a picture of Hailey at the gallery. Basil stood up and turned his back. Daisy raised her eyebrows.

"Is that Hailey?"

"Yeah. She's something else, right?"

"She's . . . umm . . . well . . ."

Basil knew what she was. "She's in her underthings," he said with disdain.

"No!" Martin quickly shut the phone back off. "That's just how the women where I come from dress. That outfit was really expensive and classy, actually."

"Just think of that, Basil," Daisy teased. "Women in Martin's world spend a lot of money on only a little fabric."

Basil shuddered. "No, thank you. I don't care to think of that at all. Now, Martin, if you've finished showing indecent pictures of your conquests to the Captain, we can discuss returning you to your land of debauchery."

"It's really very progressive," Martin protested, honor bound to defend his home planet, or at least those parts of it with which he was most familiar. "People used to dress like you, but now women have careers and voices in society."

Basil resumed his seat. "Just think of that, Captain. Women with careers and voices. Wait until I tell Dr. Underwood about how progressive Martin's world is. She'll probably burn her corset in glee."

"You guys do have a good sort of world here," Martin conceded, "but you can see why I'd like to get back. Do you have any idea how?"

Basil assured him that the problem of returning Martin to his own world had been foremost on his mind since Martin's arrival. Practical application of theoretical physics was a bit tricky, but he had thought of one possible solution.

"We can fling you back out the skylight with the same force with which you entered. I'll get the cannon!"

"Basil . . .," Daisy admonished.

"Alright, and a helmet."

"You're not firing a cannon in my library. Also, it would only work if we knew whatever opening Martin came through was still there. Seeing as how nothing from another world has fallen into the library before or after Martin's arrival, I think it's not likely."

"It would be worth a shot."

Martin looked back and forth at the people at his side. "Are you guys messing with me, or can I really not get back?"

"A little of both, I'm afraid." Daisy rose, picked up her Log, and refreshed her coffee. "This is how I see your situation, Martin. You have two courses before you. You can leave the protection of the Valley and search for a way back to your world. Having known you all afternoon, I wager within twenty minutes you'll be picked up by Monitors. You will then be taken to the

Hall, questioned, Reprogrammed, and assigned a function. You will toil at this function until you die. Or, you can sign up with the very nice airship captain you've had the good fortune to meet and cross your fingers that somewhere on her travels she'll discover a way to get you home."

Martin bit his lip. He glanced out the window across the open, rolling valley and then back up at its Captain. "Um . . . I guess the second one would work."

"Excellent." Daisy turned to Basil and issued her orders. "Martin has joined our crew. Interview him, find out what his talent is, and assign him a job. Orient him to the ship and give him a berth in the Bachelor's Quarters. Then ready the crew. I want to sail at first light." She informed them that she would be in her study and left the room.

"Wait a minute . . ., " Martin called after her.

Basil clapped a hand on his shoulder. "Well, Martin. Today you learned one of life's great Truths. Real freedom is the ability to choose which power-mad dictator you will serve. You chose a cute one, and I commend you. Now, if you'll wait here, I have a few questions for the Captain before we begin your orientation." With that, Basil Underwood exited the Parlor door hot on Daisy's heels.

Everyone he knew in the world now gone, Martin Hathaway had nothing to do but eat his sandwich. He bit into it and marveled that the taste was somehow both exotic and familiar. He gave up contemplating what the ingredients were, opened it to have a look, and discovered he had been served peanut butter and shellfish.

BASIL RAN UP the stairs after Daisy and followed her into her study. "Now, see here!" he cried along the way. "I may be your personal assistant, but I am most definitely not your babysitter."

"Of course not. You're Martin's babysitter." She shut the study door and pointed out the window toward the river. "Now, answer me this. How long would it take Gilly and Gibson to get to my house from the edge of the Valley?"

"Five or ten minutes, depending on how big of a hurry they were in."

"Exactly. That means at the same moment that Martin came crashing into the library, Monitors found and crossed the bridge. Even you shouldn't need to calculate the odds of those two events occurring randomly."

Basil scratched his chin. "It's possible whatever disruption in Space-Time that Martin fell into spanned the entire Valley and allowed the Monitors in as well."

"Possible. But they said we had a citizen of Anatamenwar in my home. They knew Martin was here."

Basil snorted. "Martin isn't a citizen. He's a human puppy."

For the first time all afternoon, Daisy allowed herself to look worried. It frightened Basil, though he would never admit to it in public.

"Martin," she said, "is either the unluckiest man in his universe, or he is the most cunning spy in ours. Until I know which, I want him watched at all times."

"I'll watch him, but I draw the line at sleeping in the Bachelor's Quarters."

"That's fine. Miss Smith will be on guard then."

Basil gave a slight shudder. Resuming his composure, he said, "Aye, aye, Captain. Oh, and since we're sailing tomorrow, do you have a location to give Westfield?"

Daisy nodded. "Fitzgerald House."

It was Basil's turn to look worried. "Are we evacuating the Valley?"

"We have a few days before we need to worry about that. Just the crew. I want to take Martin to see my uncle. If anyone can figure out if Martin's who he says he is, he can."

Relieved, Basil started to return down the stairs. Daisy remembered another loose end and called to him. "Oh, and get someone to repair the skylight."

He mimed tipping his hat and started out again.

Over her shoulder, Daisy added, "Someone not Martin."

He stopped. "Sometimes, Daisy," he said, "you can be a positive killer of joy."

✺ CHAPTER SIX ✺

BASIL STOPPED AT the bottom of the stairs and peered into the parlor. Martin had finished his allergen sandwich and was in the process of pouring himself a cup of coffee. The lid fell off the pot as he poured and landed with a plop into his cup, splashing the beverage across both the tray and his person. Cursing and shaking the hot liquid off his hand, he looked about desperately for something with which to soak up the mess. He settled on a doily that adorned one of the chairs. Realizing he now had nowhere to put the coffee-stained lace, he stuffed it into the pot and replaced the lid. He sat back, picked up his cup, took a sip, and burned his tongue.

Sometimes Daisy worries too much, Basil thought. He stuck his head into the room and called to Martin, "Well, hurry up then. We don't have all day."

Martin jumped at the sound of Basil's voice and spilled his coffee again.

"Just leave it," Basil sighed. "It'll give Daisy something to do besides brood."

Basil stepped outside into the sunshine and made his way to the ship. After taking one last dangerous sip of the coffee, Martin hurried out after him.

"So," he said when he had caught up with Basil, "thing is, I've signed up with the ship and all, but I'm still not sure what you lot actually do. Are you like freedom fighters or something?"

Basil hooked his thumbs on his vest pockets and pondered over Martin's question. "I don't think," he finally said, "we count as freedom fighters. We already have our freedom, so there's not much point in fighting for it. We do many things. Sometimes we explore uncharted or unreliably charted lands. Sometimes we smuggle contraband goods between the kingdoms. Mostly we make raids on Anatamenwar's cargo ships. I suppose we could be best classified as pirates."

"Pirates!" Martin was shocked but quickly recovered. "But you're like Robin Hood kind of pirates, right?"

"Who?"

"Robin Hood. You know, you rob from the rich to give to the poor."

"Give to the poor!" Basil was aghast. "Why ever would we do that? Then the poor would be rich, and we'd have to rob them. Sounds like an awful lot of repetitive work. No, we rob from the rich and give to ourselves. Freedom isn't free, Martin."

"That's not what that means."

"How do you propose we feed, house, and clothe 104 people, then?"

Martin shoved his hands in his pockets, momentarily defeated.

"Well," he concluded, "I guess that's ok. They're all refugees from Anatamenwar, right?"

"Excepting Daisy and those born in the Valley, yes."

"And Anatamenwar's a terrible place."

"The worst."

"I bet the people all live in squalor while supporting the elite."

"All live in squalor!" Basil stopped and turned on his heel to stare incredulously at his companion. "Don't be ridiculous. How could a society like that stand, with only the elite getting to be happy and have nice things? No, all citizens have very nice, clean living spaces. Nicer, and often cleaner, than the Bachelor's Quarters on the ship, I assure you."

"But why would there be refugees at all?"

"Genetic flukes, really." Basil resumed walking, tilting his head condescendingly in Martin's direction as he elaborated. "You see, Martin, for the most part the people of Anatamenwar are very happy fulfilling their functions and having their weekends off. But every once and awhile, someone is born who, quite frankly, gets bored. They start reading books written for other functions, go on walks, and tinker with things. These are called Unpredictables. The Monitors' main function is to watch citizens for signs of Unpredictability and recommend them for Reprogramming. For the most part, Reprogramming does the trick, but we few, we lucky few, find our way out of the equation and into the Valley."

"The Reprogramming, is that some sort of brainwashing or surgery?"

"Brainwashing or surgery?! Good god, Martin. What sort of twisted world do you come from? Reprogramming means you have to attend Saturday classes, and they're deathly dull. I went to twelve myself before I jumped out the window." Basil laughed. "Teacher never saw that coming. That's the thing about Unpredictables, of course. They're unpredictable."

Martin was quiet for much of the rest of the walk to the ship. They had nearly reached it when he said, "But that makes you the Bad Guys."

"And Girls."

"What?!"

"I was merely pointing out that several members of our crew are female. I had rather thought you noticed by now."

"I know there are girls. But you're not supposed to agree to being the Bad Guys."

"And Girls."

"And Girls!"

Basil gave Martin a wink. "Well," he said, "perhaps we're more the Morally Ambiguous Guys and Girls. Daisy would probably make some argument about the unchainability of the human spirit. Fact is, though, Anatamenwar has a very nice little society and we take their things because they're pansies."

That evening while lying awake in his hammock, Martin Hathaway would come up with two very clever replies to this statement, one of which insinuated Basil himself was a pansy. However, at that precise moment they had walked over the last hill and arrived in front of the ship. Martin was in awe, and it is difficult to be witty under such conditions.

The ship was larger than Martin had expected. So large, in fact, that he could not believe it was actually floating above the ground. Nonetheless, it did float, and was tethered to four great iron rings by ropes thicker than Martin's arm. He was able to walk completely underneath and had to jump up to touch the smooth hull.

"It's amazing!" he exclaimed as he ran about trying to take it all in at once.

"Yes," Basil conceded. "Old *Nephthys* is a sight to be seen."

"Was there an Egypt in your world?"

"A what?"

"Oh, nothing. I just wondered. In the past in my world, people thought *Nephthys* was a protective goddess of death."

Basil was amused. "Now that is something. '*Nephthys*,' however, happens to be ancient tongue for 'daisy.'"

Martin raised an eyebrow at him.

"That's right. Daisy Fitzgerald McNamara is captain of the A.S. *Daisy*. Says a lot about our lady and master, doesn't it? In her defense, her uncle was the one who built and christened the ship in her honor."

Basil walked to the stern and called up to a burly man sitting on some stairs. "Ahoy, Jameson! First Officer Underwood and a new recruit wish to come aboard."

"What's the password?" the burly man shouted in reply.

"Jameson, don't be an ass. We don't have a password."

Jameson tossed down a rope ladder. Basil scurried up it, and Martin followed with slightly less grace.

"Sorry, Mr. Underwood," Jameson said as he gave Basil a hand onto the stairs. "But you can't be too careful. I heard from the patrol that Monitors got into the Valley."

"You and the patrol had best keep that news to yourselves until the Captain issues an official statement," Basil chided professionally.

"Too late for that, sir."

"Yes, I figured it would be." He looked back over his shoulder to see Martin struggling to pull himself from the rope ladder onto the stairs. "This, Jameson, is our latest addition, a one Mr. Martin Hathaway. You might not believe it from the look of him, but he sat in the window seat with the Captain."

"No!" Jameson gasped, making no effort to conceal his shock and wonder.

"I know," Basil smirked. Glancing back down over the rail, he cupped his hands around his mouth and called, "Martin, if you're quite done fooling around on the ladder, we do have a lot still to accomplish before bed."

Out of a newfound respect, Jameson gave Martin a hand onto the stairs. Basil led him up and into the interior of the ship. Martin hardly knew where to look. The dark wood was adorned with intricately carved daisy chains. Glass tubes of every imaginable color were intertwined about the ceiling. Electric lights illuminated the hall in the exact glow to give the ship an air of wonder while still allowing you to avoid stubbing your toe.

"What? How?" Martin sputtered and turned in place.

Basil sighed. "Martin, please do us both a favor. Listen, follow, and for God's sake don't touch. Now, we are standing on A Deck."

"I know."

"No, not a deck. A Deck. 'A' as in animosity." He pointed to three large red doors in front of them. "Forward are the entrances to Starboard Storage, the Armory, and the Starboard Engine Room. The rooms on port side are identical, except substitute the Brig for the Armory and, of course, it's the Port Engine Room and Port Storage. Aft is an observation room. I wouldn't recommend you spending much time there, however, as it is an open-air observation room, and we both know your history with heights and propensity for plummeting from them."

"Noted. What are those?" Martin pointed to the array of colored tubes above them.

"Those are the Communication Channels. You can speak directly with any section of the ship using them, but it's best not to unless in an emergency. Tony, our Communications Officer, doesn't take kindly to people holding up the Channels with frivolous discussion about what we might be having for dinner or whether the Captain is ever going to let so-and-so out of the Brig."

"And how does it work?"

"You speak into them, and then you listen."

"No, not the Channels. The ship. The engines. The lights. The everything!"

Basil grinned and tapped a finger on his nose. "Steam, my boy. Steam is king."

"Steam?" Martin could hardly believe it. "All of this runs off steam power? How can you possibly generate enough?"

"That is the Engineer's problem, not mine. Now, if we may continue with the tour . . ."

Basil walked quickly, naming all the rooms they passed and any crewmember they ran into. Martin alternated between pivoting on one foot and jogging to catch back up with his guide, desperate to understand and explore every new place they passed. They zipped by a gym, Basil's laboratory, a theater, and a library, pausing only briefly at Sick Bay for Basil to give Melody a kiss and say, "Remember how you always wanted a puppy, darling? Good news: Daisy says we're keeping Martin! Guess who gets to housebreak him."

Melody waved to Martin and wished him the best of luck. He would not have minded to stay and chat a little, but Basil was off down the hall again. The Kitchen and Mess Hall were pointed out on the port side and the Control Room directly forward before Basil opened the last door on the starboard side and ushered Martin into the Enlisted Lounge. Four men were playing cards at one of the tables. They stood to attention when Basil entered, but he waved them off and opened another door. Ushering Martin inside, he shut the door and pulled a small brass lever on the wall, causing a faint electric light to glow overhead.

Martin Hathaway looked about in confusion. While the Enlisted Lounge had been spacious and open, this room was decidedly cramped and confined. The only furniture to be seen was a large red armchair, but this took up nearly half the space. Books were piled about the area, and Martin was afraid too much movement might send them all tumbling down upon him.

"Welcome," Basil said, flinging himself into the armchair, "to the First Officer's Lounge."

"This is your room?"

"One of them, yes. Well, technically, this isn't a room. It's a closet. I had to commandeer it. But you couldn't expect me to lounge with the enlisted, could you? Never be any peace. Now, have a seat anywhere, and we'll begin your interview."

Martin made a motion toward a small pile of books with the intent of using them as a seat, but the horror that spread over Basil's face when he did so prompted him to sit cross-legged on the floor. He looked up at the First Officer, waiting to be questioned. The two men stared at each other for a while before Basil finally broke.

"Well, let's start with what you already might know. Were you trained for any function in your world?"

"Umm . . . yes. I was a teacher."

Basil pressed his fingers together and considered this. "Hmm . . . strictly speaking, we don't have much use for teachers on the ship. The children stay mostly in the Valley, and, naturally, their education tends to be self-driven. But you might not be a total loss. Teachers are often experts in their field. Did you teach anything specific?"

"History."

"Ah. Presumably the history of your world?"

"Yes."

Basil nodded. "You do see the problem with that, don't you?"

Martin did. He suggested, "I could be your historian. I could read up on the history of your world and then advise. You know, if you need historical advice."

"No." Basil dismissed Martin's offer with a wave of his hand. "I already serve in that capacity, and it doesn't seem cost effective to feed and keep an Apprentice Historian. We could make you the new Bard and have you tell your histories as fiction, but I'm not sure Daisy's entirely over the tragedy of our last one."

Martin was intrigued. "Your Bard had a tragedy?"

"Was a tragedy is more like it," Basil snorted. "You see, he had created this character, Paxton Cambridge. Daisy simply loved Paxton. She couldn't get enough stories about him. Then one fateful day, Will—"

"Wait. Your Bard's name was Will? Like Shakespeare?"

Basil squinted at Martin, unsure as to whether his latest non-sequitous remark merited reporting to Sick Bay. "No, Will like William. Anyway, Will spun a beautiful tale in which Paxton sacrificed himself most bravely for the sake of his friends. It was inspiring, but poor Paxton was toast. Naturally, Daisy was upset about this and demanded Will bring him back. He refused on artistic grounds, and Daisy marooned him on an island."

Martin really should not have been surprised by this story, but he still found it difficult to believe that anyone named Daisy was capable of being the least bit despotic, especially when the name had a soft pair of eyes and a silvery laugh attached to it.

"Wasn't that a bit harsh?" he asked. "Marooning someone for artistic integrity?"

"Artistic integrity, my foot. Personally, I would have marooned him sooner. The man split one too many infinitives and dangled far too many participles to retain my favor. The point is, Martin, Will refused to comply with the Captain, so the Captain refused to continue being responsible for him. Life on the *Nephthys* is simple that way."

"But you refuse to comply all the time. At least you have all afternoon."

"No," Basil smirked, "I put up a fuss. There's a vast difference. You do understand: it's Daisy's ship. If I don't want to follow Daisy, there's no reason for me to be here."

"You could take over."

"What?"

"Well, if she's such a hard Captain, the crew could mutiny and take over. You don't have to follow someone just because the ship is named after her."

Basil leaned forward and considered Martin's countenance. He inquired slowly and cautiously, "Tell me, Martin, is everyone in your world a violent revolutionary?"

"What?!" Martin gave a start. "No, of course not!"

"Just you then?"

"Me?! I'm not a violent revolutionary!"

"You have thus far today suggested that not having a nice home is a fair reason to attack an established government, surgery is an effective tool against social unrest, and overthrowing Daisy is an appropriate response to not wanting to fetch her favorite pen."

"No! I didn't! I mean, I did, but I was just saying—"

Removing a notebook from a pocket inside his jacket, Basil flipped it open and said, "All the same. I'm going to make a note here not to issue you a blaster." He took Daisy's favorite pen from his jacket pocket and began to write.

"I can handle a blaster!"

"Delusional as well . . ."

"I'm not delusional!"

"Defiant. Possibly homicidal. Let nowhere near the Captain…"

Martin had enough. He got up and demanded Basil give him the notebook. Basil refused and insinuated he would send his written report to the Captain posthaste. Naturally, a scuffle broke out. Unnaturally, Martin managed to hit Basil just above his left eye and would have emerged completely victorious had Basil not been in possession of a blaster. This he aimed at Martin, who held up his hands and slowly resumed his place on the floor.

"Now," Basil said, catching his breath, "this is how you choose to prove you are not a violent revolutionary, is it?"

Martin hung his head. "I'm sorry. It's just . . . it's a brand new world. I don't know what's going on. I don't know how to act. It's all very confusing, and I just want to make a good impression. Can we start over?"

Though it would never appear in any of his medical records

or personnel files, Basil Underwood had a soft spot in his heart for hopeless causes. With one eye on Martin, he flipped to a blank page in his journal.

"Alright, Martin. Let's try this one more time. You say you were a history teacher, which I noted is not especially needed at the moment. Do you agree?"

"Yes."

"Good. Now, you must have some other talent. Everyone on the ship has at least one, which is why Daisy agreed to keep us. So, Martin, what would you say is your talent?"

Martin tried desperately to think of a talent other than the one that popped readily to mind. He never was particularly good with interviews, however, and he knew that the longer he pondered, the more convinced Basil would become that he had no talent at all. Reluctantly, Martin admitted, "I make very good coffee."

Martin expected Basil to laugh or say something sarcastic. Instead, Basil nodded and seemed to be thinking this information over as if it were a perfectly rational thing to say when essentially bargaining for your life, as Martin was. Little by little, a smile crept over his face.

"Martin, all island marooning aside, what do you think of our Captain?"

With no idea how one should answer such a question, Martin opted for honesty. "Well, she's amazing, isn't she?"

"Hmm." Basil scribbled something in the notebook. "Define amazing."

"I mean . . ." Martin bit his lip, unsure if it was proper or even possible to define all the subtle nuances that had gone into his word choice. He ventured, "You know. She's all tiny and soft and delicate and she smells like springtime, but she'll kill you with her bare hands and then you'd probably thank her anyway."

Knowing but ultimately dismissing Daisy's fears concerning Martin's identity, Basil hesitated for a moment before saying, "Strictly speaking, Daisy won't kill you."

"That's good news. Not even after I'm no longer a guest?"

"No. Daisy won't kill anyone. She finds the taking of human life morally reprehensible. Don't misunderstand me, she will make you wish you were dead if it comes to that, but no one on this ship will end your suffering."

"But the first thing she did when we met was point a gun . . . or 'blaster,' I guess . . . in my face and offer to kill me."

"Well, the Captain will have her little joke. And, of course, you were right in thinking the blaster could kill you, as everyone else's in the world will. Daisy's modified all of ours to stun only. I suppose if we stunned you enough times in rapid succession that might kill you. Shall we try?"

Basil drew his blaster.

"No!" Martin cried, shielding his face with his hands. "No more science!"

"You're no fun," Basil sighed and returned his blaster to its holster.

Lowering his hands, Martin started to laugh. He laughed until tears came into his eyes, at which point he wiped them away and laughed harder. Basil wondered if he had gone insane or if the condition was pre-existing and finally rising to the surface.

"Ask me . . .," Martin said as he recovered the capacity for speech, "ask me again what I think of the Captain."

"I'm game. Martin, what do you think of our Captain?"

"I think she's simply stunning." He erupted into fits of gig-gles. It had been a long day.

Basil sat composedly until Martin had finished, only the left corner of his mouth giving the impression that he was anything other than long-suffering. When Martin grew silent, Basil re-joined, "She put the fist in pacifist."

Martin fell into giggles anew, and this time Basil allowed both corners of his mouth to betray his amusement. Several terrible puns at Daisy's expense later, he closed his journal and announced, "Martin, my boy, I think I know the perfect job for you."

⚙ CHAPTER SEVEN ⚙

BASIL AND MARTIN were still laughing when they opened the door to exit the First Officer's Lounge, but they quickly stopped. Where they had left four men playing cards, they now found twenty people all smiling and watching the door.

"Didn't I give you all jobs?" Basil demanded of the collective.

Martin poked his head into the room. "What's going on?" he asked.

"No idea." Basil gestured toward the gathered. "Everyone, this is Martin. Martin, mostly everyone. You'll learn their names as they become important. Now, follow me and we'll begin your training."

Martin waved at mostly everyone as he exited the Lounge. A few of the women giggled. A thought occurred to him, and he ran up and whispered to Basil. "Umm . . . do you think . . . you know, everyone staring and smiling . . . do you think it's because two men were in the closet together?"

"Why would that be at all amusing?" Basil inquired over his shoulder.

"You know . . . we just came out of the closet."

"I don't understand you. I'm in and out of the closet all the time. That never interested anyone before."

Before Martin was able to explain the joke, a stressed baritone voice bellowed from the Control Room, "I DON'T CARE IF HE TOOK HER OUT FOR DINNER AND A SHOW, THE COMM CHANNELS ARE FOR OFFICIAL COMMUNICATIONS ONLY!"

"Ah." Basil shook his head and climbed the starboard staircase to B Deck. "That's what all the fuss is about."

"What is?"

"We learn yet another of life's Truths today, Martin. Add a dash of fact and a pinch of mystery to a pot of boredom and—hey, presto—we have the makings of an instant celebrity."

"Celebrity? What, me?!"

"Apparently so," Basil smirked. "Try not to do anything noble for the next few weeks like rescuing a kitten or solving a crossword, and it should all blow over."

They reached the top of the stairs and turned toward the stern of the ship. Basil remained the consummate tour guide, informing Martin, "Forward is another open-air observation platform. Starboard we have the Bachelor's Quarters with which you will soon become intimately familiar. Port are Married Quarters with which, if I have any say in the matter, you will not. Mine are, naturally, further aft . . ."

Basil stopped speaking when they reached the middle of the ship. Here, there was a rotunda culminating in a stained-glass skylight. On the port side was a ladder leading outside the ship, and on the starboard sat a little old woman knitting. Martin marveled at it all and waved to the woman. Basil walked stiffly through the port side of the rotunda and then began where he had left off, ". . . nearest the Captain's Quarters. Now, on the starboard are the Women's Quarters, as you can tell by the giggling we now hear."

"Who was that?" Martin asked.

"It sounded like several women, actually."

"No, the old lady. The one knitting."

Basil shuddered and ducked behind a wall. He pulled Martin beside him and peered around the corner at the woman. "That," he whispered with great import, "is Miss Smith. Pray you never meet her in a dark room on a Saturday night."

"She looks like a nice lady."

"Don't let her fool you. I'm fairly certain Daisy picked her up in the lowest pit of Hell. She doesn't eat, she doesn't sleep, she doesn't age. She just sits there all day, knitting. Knitting and judging. She never leaves that spot, and yet somehow she knows everyone on the ship's affairs and sweater size."

"She freaks you out because she makes the crew sweaters?"

"If only that were the extent of her crimes. No, Martin. Miss Smith, as you say, 'freaks me out' because once, when Melody and I had only recently become acquainted, I snuck out of the Bachelor's Quarters after Seven Bells on the First Watch. Let us simply say that I did not make it to our rendezvous. Melody and I have been married for five years now, and I still can't walk down this hallway beside her without being overcome by shame and terror."

"So Miss Smith is like a hall monitor? Stopping the boys from seeing the girls and all?"

"Hall Monitors only punish the body. Miss Smith's jurisdiction is the soul." He shuddered one last time and then pulled himself to the heights of self-confidence that only a second-in-command can truly reach. "You've been warned. When you're in your quarters for the night, stay there. Now, on we go to the Captain's Quarters. Only the Steward and myself are currently able to enter without knocking. . . ."

MARTIN COULD NOT remember the last time he had been this tired. His body was still sore from the fall, and now his mind was full to bursting with new and possibly fictitious information. When Basil finally pronounced his training "complete enough" and dismissed him, Martin wanted nothing more than to find an empty bed in the Bachelor's Quarters and pass out in it. This was not to be for two reasons. First, his berth was one of twenty canvas hammocks rather than a bed of any sort to which he had been accustomed. Second, he was met at the door by a large, dark, angry man.

"So you're the new guy?" The man crossed his arms and stared down at Martin as if he were a particularly tasty before-bedtime snack. "You've got a lot of nerve."

Several times today, Martin thought he would be perfectly happy to discover this world was not the result of a serious brain injury. This was not one of those times.

"Do I?" he squeaked.

Fifteen others stood behind the large man and crossed their arms as well. "Our Captain's a lady. You'd best remember that if you know what's good for you."

Martin sputtered and tried to explain that he had not been on the planet long enough to form intentions, and even if he did he was in love with Hailey, but the men started laughing.

"Just messing with you, you old dog," the large man said as he gave Martin a hearty slap on the back. "Tony Angelo,

Communications Officer. At your service." Tony showed Martin a free hammock and introduced him to four engineers, three medical officers, two cooks, and six hands, all of whose names Martin promptly forgot. He was promised that later he would also meet Steuart Cook, the ship's Cook and Daisy's Steward. He figured he could retain that one.

"What've they got you doing?" an engineer asked. Martin told him. The engineer shook his hand. "Better you than me," he said. The rest of the men agreed.

"Personally," Tony admitted as Martin attempted to subdue his hammock into sufficient submission to allow him inside, "I'm always glad to welcome another man on the ship, whatever his job. Comm Channel chatter wouldn't be half as big of a problem if it weren't for all the women gossiping incessantly. Did you really sit in the window seat with the Captain?"

Martin admitted that he did, but he did not understand why such a simple action merited Comm Channel chatter. "Does Daisy not get out much?"

"She owns an airship," one of the hands remarked. "She gets out all the time."

"But no," Tony clarified, "she doesn't usually let any man within a two-foot radius of her. Well, except Basil."

A couple snickers went through the Bachelor's Quarters, suggesting that Mr. Underwood did not count in the male-proximity-to-Daisy competition.

"Remember the captain of the *Tatenen*? I wonder how his arm's doing."

"Probably better than his leg."

Guffaws followed this remark. Several stories of men who had made the mistake of attempting to woo Daisy McNamara were related, each topping the other in degree of suffering inflicted upon the hero. Martin would not have believed they were talking about the same woman who had so tenderly placed a pillow under his head only hours before had his back not still ached from when she had flipped him.

Were his visions of Daisy not already conflicting enough, Steuart Cook arrived with a tray of milk and cookies. Cheers went up from the men as the nightly ration was dispensed.

"Welcome to the A.S. *Nephthys*," Cook said with pride, handing Martin a chocolate chip cookie only just under the size of his head. "Our captain's a girl."

AFTER A FITFUL night's sleep in a hammock surrounded by large, smelly men, Martin Hathaway had hoped he would awaken in a sterile hospital room with Hailey sitting dutifully by. It was not to be. Rather, Martin was up at Two Bells on the Morning Watch and scrambled to get everything in order before Daisy arrived at Three. A whistle blew announcing the approach of the Captain, and Martin raced from the kitchen to Basil's side at the aft starboard stair. That everyone else was also frantically running to their places did not encourage him, but he was happy to discover he made it all the way without spilling a drop of coffee. If nothing else, he was sure this was a sign of a good day.

"Captain coming aboard!" Basil called as Daisy mounted the rope ladder. He stood at attention, and Martin tried to as well. It was a tricky maneuver to pull off while holding a cup, saucer, and a clipboard. By the time Daisy's head appeared at the stair, Martin had given up trying to look professional in favor of looking cheerful.

"Good morning, Basil," Daisy greeted the First Officer with a nod. "I trust we are shipshape and ready to sail?"

"Affirmative, Captain. All hands at their places and awaiting your address."

"Excellent."

Daisy turned to start down the hall. Basil gave Martin a nudge, and he stepped forward.

"I've got your coffee, Captain." Martin's hand was shaking, causing the porcelain cup to rattle in the saucer.

"Oh, thank you, Martin." Daisy's hand was steady as she took the cup and resumed walking. Basil and Martin fell in behind her. The former filled her in on the atmospheric conditions while the latter wondered how someone with such short legs could move so quickly.

Daisy took a sip of the coffee. She looked over her shoulder and said, "Martin, this is delicious."

"It's because I make it with love." Martin slapped his free hand over his mouth, realizing the absurdity of his automatic response at this particular moment. His career was saved, however, as Daisy had not listened to him. Basil, on the other hand, had heard and smirked.

Ever efficient, Daisy inquired, "How many hands, Basil?"

"Forty-three this flight, Captain."

She frowned. "That's an odd number."

"It can't be helped. You recruited an odd fellow."

They entered the Control Room. Basil called, "Captain on Deck!" and four people snapped to attention. Daisy nodded at each in turn, descended the stairs, and took her chair. Basil stood behind her on her right and Martin tentatively remained at her left.

"Mr. Angelo," she called to Tony, "is the main Comm Channel clear?"

"Clear as the solstice sky, Captain."

"Excellent." She set her cup and saucer down on the right arm of her chair and opened a panel on the left. A voice pipe popped up into which Daisy spoke clearly and confidently. "Attention, men and women of the A.S. *Nephthys*. No doubt many of you have heard of the strange visitors who found their way into the Valley yesterday. You may be confused, and you may be frightened. This is natural, and no one should feel ashamed. The Valley is our home. It has been threatened. Together we must protect it. Today we sail for Fitzgerald House, seeking not safe haven, but information. Information we will use to defeat this new enemy, as we have defeated all enemies before it!"

Cheers could be heard throughout the ship. For the first time since her arrival, Daisy managed a slight smile. She returned the voice pipe to its place, rose to address the Navigator, and walked straight into Martin.

"What are you doing by my chair?!" she demanded.

Martin clutched his clipboard to his chest. "Basil told me to stand here."

Her eyes narrowed. "Is that one of my hair clips attached to a piece of wood?"

"Yes. Basil said you didn't like this one."

"And that makes it fair game for arts and crafts?"

"Yes. No. I mean . . . I needed a clipboard to hold your official schedule and notes and things and, apparently, they don't exist here . . . so I invented it."

"To hold my what?"

"Your official schedule and things like that." Martin turned the board to show her. "See, right here I've got 'Three Bells, Morning Watch: Arrival and Coffee. Four Bells, Morning Watch: Sailing.' It's blank after that, but anything you want to schedule I'll write it on the clipboard and then it's official."

Daisy did not break her scrutinizing gaze on Martin as she cried, "Mr. Underwood! Did you give Martin a job?"

"Yes, Captain, I did."

"What job?"

"He's your Personal Assistant."

"Basil! You've pulled some stunts before, but this is ridiculous!" She turned to berate her First Officer, but her anger was cut off when she noticed his profile. "What's wrong with your eye?"

Basil cleared his throat. "Your Personal Assistant and I had a difference of opinion during his interview. Don't worry, he is NOT a violent revolutionary."

Daisy looked back at Martin. "Did you hit Basil?"

"Yes." Martin looked at the floor.

A shocked silence filled the room. Tony could hardly believe he had not yet heard about this over the Comm Channels.

Slowly, the corners of Daisy's mouth turned up. She clasped her hands behind her back and winked at Martin. "Mr. Angelo, is Miss Heart ready in the Engine Rooms?"

"Standing by for command to fly, Captain."

"Mr. Westfield," she called to the Navigator, "is your course set?"

"Aye, Captain. We should reach Fitzgerald House in time for lunch tomorrow."

"Excellent." She turned to the Helmsman and called, "Mrs. Westfield, take us to the skies."

"Aye, aye, Captain."

"Mr. Underwood, you have control. I'll be above." She side stepped Martin and made her way to the stairs. "Mr. Hathaway, I believe you have never been on an airship before."

"Um . . . no, Captain."

Daisy exited the Control Room and turned to the port. Basil sat in her chair, and Martin leaned against it, greatly relieved. His rest was short lived, as Daisy stuck her head back in the door and said, "Keep up, Martin."

BY TAKING THE PORT stairs two at a time, Martin was able to reach the top immediately after Daisy. "So," he said for lack of a better idea, "Mr. and Mrs. Westfield? Does that mean your Navigator and your Helmsman are married?"

"Yes. One year in . . ." Daisy calculated momentarily, ". . . three days."

"What's that like? Are they always arguing about stopping and asking for directions?"

"Directions are Mr. Westfield's job. But it is much nicer now than when they were not married. They flirted incessantly, and Jake once sent us five hundred miles off course because Emma mentioned wanting to see the Cape of Bellisimondo. It was sweet, but very annoying."

"What did you do?"

Daisy smiled. "I sent him to the Brig for three days and presided over their wedding on the fourth. This way, Martin." She stepped out onto the Bow Observation Deck.

Martin followed her into the sunshine. The air was warm and clear, and he breathed it in deeply. He was about to comment on how amazing it all was when the ship gave a lurch and he toppled to the side.

Daisy caught his arm. "They're releasing the tethers. Better hold on until you get your air-legs."

He tucked the clipboard under his arm and clutched the rail along the starboard side. Below, he could see the Ground Crew waving at them as the massive ropes were pulled onto the ship. Daisy returned their wave, and Martin smiled.

"Jocelyn should be starting the engines right about . . . now."

As she called it, Martin heard a hum emanating from the back of the ship. Though the engines were larger than any he had ever seen, the noise was not deafening. Rather, he would discover after a week on board that he had difficulty sleeping without their soft purr.

Slowly, the ship moved forward. Martin initially tightened his grip but relaxed as he felt the breeze on his face. It was like driving with the top down on a Sunday afternoon, and there's nothing the least bit terrifying about that.

"This is the part where I should say, 'I forgot how wonderful this is,'" Daisy shouted to him over the gathering wind, "but I never do. I always know exactly how wonderful this is."

They began to climb. Higher and higher the ship rose. Martin watched the ground recede from them, the details of the Valley turning into plots of color. It was the most beautiful sight he had ever seen, until he turned his head.

Daisy was standing with her eyes closed and her face turned up to the sun. Her meticulously coiffed hair had fallen loose in places and was blowing about her face. She was smiling and laughing, not like a person who could break a man's arm, but like a little girl off on an adventure.

"Steady as she goes, Westfield," Basil told the Helmsman. "Another thousand feet and level her out."

"Aye, aye, Mr. Underwood."

The sound of Daisy's boots was heard descending the stairs. All heads in the Control Room turned, because the sound of the boots was also accompanied by the sound of laughter. Daisy appeared in the doorway repinning her windswept hair. Martin, not realizing she was going to stop, walked into her. She shot him a look of admonition, but her smile remained.

"Mr. Underwood," she called into the Control Room, "as soon as Jocelyn is free to leave the Engine Rooms, I want you and her to report to my quarters. We have a mission to plan."

"We'll be there in a quarter hour, Captain."

"Excellent." She resumed walking, presumably to climb the starboard stair. Martin, his hair also disheveled by the breeze, grinned and waved at Basil.

"Keep up, Martin!"

He ran off after the Captain.

Basil stared at the empty doorway, then picked up the cup Daisy had left on the arm of the chair. After examining its contents, he took a sip. Even cold, it was delicious.

"You know, Tony," he remarked, "I think love might be an actual ingredient."

Gibson awoke and rubbed his head. He knew he should feel lucky to awake at all, but he did not. His head ached, his arm felt like pins and needles from the way he had laid on it, and bits of straw from the floor kept clinging to him. After a fruitless attempt to brush himself clean, he gave up and looked about the stone chamber in which he found himself.

"You're alive then, Gibs?" came a familiar voice behind him. He turned to see Gilly sitting on a barrel and looking out the iron bars that composed the door to their cell. At least they were imprisoned together; that was something.

Gibson answered, "Barely. Where are we? This doesn't look like any prison in the Hall I've ever been tossed into."

"I don't know. I've never been anywhere like this either. Walls made of stone. No beds. No window. No guards."

"No guards? Well, that's good news."

"No guards. Just this guy."

Gibson looked out to where Gilly had been staring. A man sat in a chair, watching them.

"No guards? Are you blind? There's a Monitor right there."

"He's not a Monitor. I don't think he's even a man. He hasn't moved in thirty minutes. He doesn't blink, and he doesn't breathe. And if you ask him a question, all he'll say is—"

The man in the chair spoke. "You are a prisoner of Mendax. You will appear when summoned."

"That. That's all he says."

Gibson sat quietly for a moment before asking, "Have you heard of a Mendax?"

Gilly shook his head.

⚙ CHAPTER EIGHT ⚙

DURING HIS FIRST thirty minutes as Daisy's Personal Assistant, Martin Hathaway learned the job was going to require a great deal of walking briskly and speaking when spoken to. He could handle the first requirement, but some bargaining would need to be struck on the second if he were to achieve maximum job satisfaction.

"So, can I ask you something?" he said as he once again caught up with Daisy at the top of the stairs.

"You frequently do." Daisy turned aft and made her way to the Captain's Quarters. Most of the crew was at work below, but Miss Smith remained at her post.

"It's about our destination. You said we were going to Fitzgerald House. That's your middle name. Fitzgerald, I mean. Not Fitzgerald House."

Her reply was curt, but a careful observer could note—and report via the nearest Comm Channel—a slight upturn around the corners of her mouth. "Well remembered."

Martin tended to remember things that were shouted at him. It was a large factor in his having survived Mr. Krasinski's eighth-grade gym class. Daisy pointed out that, thus far, Martin had uttered statements rather than questions.

"I guess I was wondering," he said, "if it was a family house or something."

"I'm fairly certain that was also a statement, but I'll allow it. Yes, it is a family house or something. It's the seat of the Fitzgeralds, my mother's family. It's where I grew up."

"You didn't grow up in the Valley?"

Daisy paused and considered Martin's expression. "You know, if you are a spy, you ask a lot of common knowledge questions."

"Me!" Martin gestured to his person with his homemade clipboard. "A spy!"

"Perhaps." She resumed walking, her long skirt swishing rhythmically with every confident step. "Anyway, I was born in the Valley but . . . but when . . . Five hundred years ago, Xavier Fitzgerald the First . . ."

"Do all your stories begin like that?" he laughed. "Two thousand years before the fall! and all?"

She did not resume her tale. Without another word, she opened the door to the Captain's Quarters and strode over to her desk. Martin had loved this room when he saw it the night before, and he loved it even more now that the sun was shining brightly through the windows that composed the entire back wall. Maps and books were everywhere, but there was an order to the collection. A great red rug covered most of the floor, and Martin very much wanted to know what it felt like in bare feet.

He could not enjoy the room to its fullest, however, as he was acutely aware that Daisy had not found his observation on or imitation of her quirks as a narrator at all amusing.

"Oh, now I did it again," he said, hurrying to her side. "I'm really sorry. I do want to know about Fitzgerald the First and .

. . well . . . everything."

Daisy touched a panel on her desk and a purple voice pipe rose from it. Clear as a bell, they heard Tony's voice saying, "I'm telling you, the two of them were laughing like a couple of kids."

"Mr. Angelo," Daisy spoke forcefully and clearly into the pipe, "you wouldn't happen to be using the Comm Channels for unofficial communications, would you?"

A momentary silence was soon followed by, "No, Captain. There was a . . . a nitrous oxide leak in one of the med supply rooms, and I was just updating the CMO on the condition of the hands who discovered it."

"How unfortunate. When you've finished, please alert Miss Gibson that Mr. Hathaway will be reporting to her momentarily. She is to pull for him copies of *The History of the World Thus Far, The Legend of Reginald McNamara, Fitzgeralds: A World Apart,* and *Tales from the Fair Folk.* Do you need that repeated?"

"No, Miss."

"Excellent. Inform Miss Gibson that Mr. Hathaway is to remain in the Library until either Mr. Underwood or myself come for him."

"Aye, aye, Captain."

"Thank you, Mr. Angelo. Oh, and Tony, send word to Sick Bay that the Captain is very sorry for the mishap that befell our hands and will visit them at Eight Bells."

Another short pause followed. Meekly, Tony acknowledged, "Aye, aye."

Daisy pushed the voice pipe back in its place. She took a seat behind her desk and looked up at Martin, who was rocking back and forth on his heels. "Well, Martin? I assume Basil showed you the location of the Library?"

"Um . . . yes. But . . . um . . . but don't you need me here for your mission planning meeting? You know, in case anything official gets decided?"

"Martin, how wise of a captain would I be to allow a potential spy into a planning meeting because my First Officer is annoyed I won't give him a day off?"

"Not very."

"No, not very. Therefore, until your allegiance is confirmed, you can consider any planning meetings to be your personal study time."

He bit his lip and looked at the ground. Uttering a weak, "Aye, aye," Martin slowly made his way to the door.

Daisy sighed. Having a crew could be exhausting sometimes.

"Martin," she called after him, "leave your clipboard. If something official gets decided, Basil can write it down."

He smiled. "I've already noted your Eight Bells appointment in the Sick Bay. Don't forget."

MARTIN'S DISAPPOINTMENT at being excluded from the mission planning was quickly replaced by his excitement at finally getting to see inside one of the many rooms he and Basil had zipped past the day before. He hurried to the Library and discovered it to be simultaneously exactly and nothing like he had expected.

The other spaces in which he had found himself had rather given the impression that Daisy favored dark woods and rich tones in her decorating, but the Library was as bright and colorful as any preschool that prides itself on exploratory learning. White floor-to-ceiling bookshelves lined every wall with several

curiously angled staircases attached to aid in reaching the vol-
umes. Martin thought a map might be necessary simply to find
a book on the third shelf. He was also fairly certain a room of
this size should not fit on the lower deck of a boat, but he did
not worry overly much about it.

"Are you Mr. Hathaway?" a pretty young girl shouted down
to him from the top of one of the staircases.

"Yes," he called up to her. "Martin's fine, though. Just Martin."

She giggled and said, "Have a seat anywhere, Martin. I've
got the last two titles the Captain requested to pull and I'll be
right with you."

Martin took a seat on a yellow sofa near one of the round
windows. The girl hurried down the stairs, smiling brightly and
clutching four large books.

"You must really like working in the Library," Martin observed.

"It has its moments. My dad's a Patrol, and he said, 'Annabell, if you only listen to one thing I say, you take a desk job.'
Jessica thinks it's boring, but she doesn't know anything, does
she?"

"Um . . . no, I guess not." He gestured to the books in her
arms. "Are those for me?"

"Oh, yes. Silly me." She giggled again and handed them
to Martin, who thanked her. "I'd forget my head if it weren't
screwed on. That's what Jessica says."

"Well," Martin reasoned for the sake of conversation, "she
doesn't know anything."

The young girl's smile widened. "No. No, she doesn't."

Annabell clasped her hands together and continued to smile

at Martin. Martin drummed his fingers on the top of the stack of books and smiled at Annabell.

"So . . . I should probably start reading these," he said eventually. "Captain's orders."

"Oh, of course. Don't mind me." She gestured to a great oak desk near the door. "I'll be right over there if you need anything."

Martin set the books next to him on the sofa and picked up the first one. *The History of the World Thus Far* was a square book with a raised, gold-embossed globe on the cover. Martin noted that the globe looked exactly and nothing like Earth. He opened the book and discovered the cover page bore the word "Daisy" printed in a large, childish script and decorated with several crudely drawn flowers. Tracing the letters with his index finger, Martin smiled. He opened to the first chapter and read:

You are a very lucky child. You are lucky, because you were born on the planet Arnica. Arnica is the third planet from Simsia, our sun. This means it is not too hot and not too cold, but just right for living things like you and me.

Martin flipped through the rest of the book to see if at any point it became less patronizing. It did not, so he set it aside in favor of *Fitzgeralds: A World Apart*. While switching books, he looked up and noticed that three women had taken seats in the library as well. They must have been enjoying their books very much, since they were grinning while they read. Martin turned to the first chapter of his own.

Five hundred years ago, Xavier Fitzgerald the First

Of course, Martin thought. She's memorized the whole damn book.

Five hundred years ago, Xavier Fitzgerald the First was the most respected craftsman in the Kingdom of Monopholis. His work was so renowned even the Dwarf King Gerd, Son of Gudbrandr, sought his opinion on matters of design and construction. In return for his great service in the building of the Dwarven hall Borghild, King Gerd granted Xavier lands in the Duidaean Mountains for as long as his house remained upon Arnica.

Martin read this paragraph several times and shook his head. Maybe it was a good thing he had not been assigned the role of Apprentice Historian.

Two more women had entered the Library, searching for books in the stacks on either side of where Martin sat. He traded *Fitzgeralds: A World Apart* for *Tales from the Fair Folk*, reasoning that fiction might make more sense than history. Just in case, he examined the table of contents rather than run the risk of reading something silly.

Tales from the Fair Folk
Compiled by Aster McNamara
Illustrated by Lydia McNamara

"Oh my God," Martin exclaimed aloud, "I've fallen into *The Lord of the Rings.*"

"What's that, Martin?" Annabell called from over at the desk. She had been scowling ever since Jessica and two other women had wandered into the room, but her face lit up at Martin's voice.

"Oh, sorry," he replied. "I shouldn't be talking in the Library. It's really a popular place, isn't it?"

"Not really," Annabell glared at Jessica.

One of the women perusing the shelf on his right asked, "What are you reading, Marty?"

Martin gave a start and stared at her. No one had called him Marty since Great Aunt Caroline died. He was also quite sure he had not authorized any nicknames in this universe.

"Mr. Hathaway is reading the books the Captain ordered for him," Annabell said severely. "He's working, just like I am."

"Alright, what are you working on, Marty?"

Everyone in the room was looking at him. "Well," he stammered, "I'm not really sure. I asked Daisy a question about Fitzgerald House, and she sent me here."

"Oh, you don't have to read those, then." The woman came over and sat on the other side of the sofa. Martin sat up a little straighter. "I can tell you all about Fitzgerald House."

"And the Captain," one of the seated women said, moving her chair closer.

"And everything." All pretenses of reading had been abandoned. Only Annabell remained at her post, though she had given up her catalogue work in favor of conversation.

"Ok," Martin said nervously. "Tell me about Fitzgerald House."

"It's where the Captain grew up," the woman on the sofa informed him.

"Yes. I gathered that much. But . . . um . . . why?"

Annabell sighed. "This story's so romantic."

"If by romantic you mean depressing," Jessica interjected.

"It's sad, but it's the good sort of sad. It makes you happy people can feel sad."

"Can I hear it?" Martin asked before anyone could comment on the silliness of that statement.

"Well, Aster and Lydia—" Annabell began.

Someone interrupted, "They're the Captain's parents."

"Yes, thanks, Sophie. Aster and Lydia were really in love, which was weird but so beautiful because he was a McNamara and she was a Fitzgerald, and those two families didn't mix, what with one in the Valley and one in the mountains and all. But Aster and Lydia lived in the Valley and were really happy until one day when the Captain was three and they left to travel to . . . oh, shoot, I forgot where they were going."

One ventured, "I think it was a fair or something."

"No," another insisted, "it was a wedding."

"Probably doesn't matter," Martin reasoned, "because it sounds like they didn't make it."

Annabell smiled. "You're right. They got attacked by bandits or something, and that's a real 'or something' because the Captain doesn't remember who it was so nobody knows. Whoever it was, Aster fought them off so Lydia could escape with the Captain. But when they got back to the Valley, the Protection was gone, so Lydia knew Aster had been killed. She took the Captain to Fitzgerald House so they'd be safe from Anatamenwar, and then she gave into grief and never spoke again."

Martin looked out the window at the bright blue sky and crisp white clouds. He was a bit ashamed of himself and did not want anyone in the Library to notice. Daisy had been trying to tell him about the death of her father the only way she knew how, and he had not let her.

His reflections had just raised the question as to what Annabell had meant by the Protection was gone when the Captain herself entered the Library followed closely by Basil. The women surrounding Martin all jumped to attention.

"At ease," Daisy said at the same moment Martin realized he should not be. The women sat back down, but they did not relax. Daisy greeted each woman by name and remarked on how nice it must be for them to have free time in the middle of their flight.

Basil whispered to Daisy, "I told you reading would count as something noble." Handing Martin back his clipboard, he said, "Well, come on, man. We're off to the Sick Bay to see what Tony's cooked up to not fool the Captain. This should be quite entertaining. Bring your books."

The two exited the Library. Martin was close on their heels, but paused at the desk and said, "Should I check these out or sign anything for them?"

"Oh, shoot," Annabell searched about the desk for her ledger, "I should have issued you a card and marked which books were pulled. How do you spell your name?"

Daisy's voice rang through the hall, "Keep up, Martin!"

Annabell gestured to the door. "You better hurry. Don't lose the books or it's five days in the Brig."

THAT NIGHT, Martin Hathaway lay awake in his hammock, staring up at the ceiling long after milk and cookies had been dis-
tributed and the lights had been extinguished. It was not the
snoring or like sounds that compose the ambiance of a male
dormitory that kept him awake, but rather a disquiet he had
carried with him to bed. Before turning in that night, he had
managed to read three of the stories in *Tales from the Fair Folk*,
reasoning since the book had been the work of her parents, it
was likely the one Daisy knew best.

He had learned that, over a thousand years ago, Reginald
McNamara had wooed and won the Elven princess Galedlothia, and he was given power over the Lost Valley as a wedding
present. This power apparently renewed in each first-born Mc-
Namara, but only if they claimed it on their twentieth birthday. Not much reading between the lines was needed to also
derive that the Fair Folk really didn't like the Dwarves, and
much of the conflict between later generations of McNamaras
and Fitzgeralds stemmed from which race had bequeathed their
lands.

These stories were fine in their own way and not unlike many
Martin had enjoyed in younger days before he had more important things to read like blogs and top ten lists. What bothered
him, however, was the distinct impression that Daisy did not
think they were stories. That was ridiculous, of course. There
were no Elven princesses or generations-old family feuds, not in
the real world. Martin missed the surety of the real world and
believed homesickness was keeping him up. He was also afraid

that if he fell asleep, he might awaken.

He thought some air could help him clear his head. He rolled out of his hammock and crept toward the door, careful not to rouse anyone. Basil's warning to stay in quarters rang through his mind, but he reasoned that he was going out to be alone, not to see someone. Miss Smith should not have a problem with that. She was likely another figment of his imagination, anyway, so he could handle her.

He tiptoed down the hall to the Bow Observation Deck without incident. Chuckling to himself about Basil's irrational fear of an old lady, he stepped out onto the deck to discover Miss Smith was already sitting there, knitting.

"Good evening, Martin Hathaway," she said. Her voice was soft to the point it was practically ephemeral. Though momentarily startled, Martin walked forward to hear her better. "It's a lovely night, is it not?"

"You know my name," was all he could think to respond.

The wizened old woman smiled and reached for something under her chair. "I also know this happens to be just your size."

She handed Martin a sweater. Puzzled, he thanked her and tucked it under his arm.

"Why don't you try it on? Then we can get rid of your other. Synthetics have no place on the *Nephthys*."

Martin complied but insisted, "My other one's not synthetic. It's 100% organic and postconsumer based. Hailey made sure herself."

"Of course she did, dear." Miss Smith took his discarded sweater and lightly tossed it overboard.

"Hey!"

"I wouldn't worry about it. Look how nicely your new one

fits. I knew the blue would bring out your eyes."

Martin had to concede Miss Smith's sweater fit better than any article of clothing he had ever purchased. The deep blue of the yarn reminded him of the clear night sky under which they were sailing, and touching the small, round insignia embroidered upon the shoulder filled him with a strange sense of belonging he had never quite felt back on Earth. He also thought it best not to complain too much about his lost sweater, lest Miss Smith also decide to take issue with the composition of his pants.

"Now, Martin Hathaway," she put down her knitting and folded her hands, "you may ask me a question."

Perhaps it was the stories he had read that evening, but a voice within his head told Martin he was in one of those situations where your question should be considered carefully, and he better not screw this up. He thought for a while.

"Am I dreaming?" he finally asked.

Miss Smith nodded her small gray head. "It's possible. But on Arnica we have a saying: When one has dreams, it's best to follow them."

Martin laughed. He did not do so derisively. Rather, he laughed for the best reason of all: he was happy.

"Why is Basil afraid of you?"

"Mr. Underwood is a very clever man. Clever people are often afraid of questions to which they do not already know the answer."

He sat on the deck next to her chair and was silent for a while. He found that he was not thinking of Basil's anxieties, but of the woman in the window seat watching the river.

"Is Daisy afraid?"

"Daisy McNamara carries a way of life on her shoulders. She is about to be humbled in a manner she has never known. She will need you when that time comes and before."

"Me? What can I do?"

The old woman smiled and looked down at him. "If I knew that, then I would be Martin Hathaway. Now, if you can excuse me, Mr. Angelo believes he will be meeting Miss Heart in the Starboard Engine Room in ten minutes. I have to go let him know he was misinformed."

⚙ CHAPTER NINE ⚙

DAISY'S QUARTERS WERE comprised of two rooms. The hall door opened into her study, but on the port wall three steps led up to a round red door. Behind this was her cabin, and no member of the crew, not even Basil, had been inside.

Based on Basil's accounts of Daisy's habits, Martin had expected her to still be in her cabin when he entered the study just before Four Bells the next morning. He was surprised to discover Daisy to be awake, fully dressed, and hard at work with charts and papers on her desk.

"Good morning, Martin," she said without looking up. "Nice sweater."

He set the silver coffee service he had been carrying down on a side table and poured her a cup. "Thanks. I'm supposed to tell you there was a bit of a mishap in the kitchen this morning, so Steuart's going to be late with your breakfast."

Daisy pushed aside her work and accepted the cup he offered. She made a mental note that his hand was much steadier today.

"A mishap?" she asked.

"Well . . ." Martin rubbed the back of his neck. "Thing is, when I went in to make your coffee, he threw a spatula at me and wanted to know why he was good enough to make all the rest of your food but couldn't be trusted with coffee. I told him you just liked mine better, and he went out to the Bow Observation Deck yelling that if this was what the world had come to, he didn't want to be a part of it anymore."

"I take it you fixed things."

"Sort of. I tried to talk him down and about all the things he had to live for, but then Basil showed up, drug him back to the kitchen, and told him to stop being a caterwauling culinarian."

"Oh good." Daisy smiled. "All better then."

She took a sip of her coffee and then asked Martin if he had eaten anything yet. He had not, as his breakfast time had been used up preventing a suicide. Daisy said she would make a call to have food for him sent up with her own, but before she was able, the door flew open.

Basil stood in the hall and cried, "Ship's Eye spotted a rukh at our eleven o'clock and coming in fast!"

"Not again!" Daisy sprang to her feet, grabbed a brass handle that hung from the ceiling, and pulled down another voice pipe. "ALL HANDS TO DEFENSE POSITIONS! ALL HANDS TO DEFENSE POSITIONS! ANYONE IN POSSESSION OF A LARGE EGG REPORT TO C DECK!"

"It's not me this time," Basil insisted as they ran out the door. "I haven't been near a nest in months!"

Martin was close on their heels by the time they reached the ladder to C Deck. Daisy jumped off it and grabbed his arm. "Not you. You're not on the Defense Team. Go wait . . ." She cursed, realizing all the safe places to stow a potential spy during an attack were on A Deck and time was of the essence. Racing back down the hall, she flung Martin into her cabin and locked him inside.

"Sit on the floor and touch nothing!" she yelled through the door before sprinting away.

WHEN DAISY REACHED C Deck, Basil had already organized the hands around the electrostatic guns. "Hold fire until she's firm in your sights!" he bellowed. "We want to roast this turkey, not fry her feathers!"

Daisy grabbed a rope hanging down from the great red balloon and pulled herself up. Three hands were waiting for her at the top, carefully balancing their weight and armed to the teeth. She stood in their midst and drew her blaster.

"We are to protect the balloon at all costs." She was cool and firm. "If it goes, so does everyone on the ship."

"Aye, Captain!" the hands shouted.

An enormous white bird appeared off the port bow. Its talons, large enough to lift an elephant and send it crashing to its death, gleamed in the morning light. Daisy adjusted the magnitude on her blaster and fired a warning shot between its eyes.

The massive bird screeched. Martin felt the ship rock slightly in the wake of the sound. When he was young, he had watched *Sinbad the Sailor* movies with his grandfather. It could not be the same beast attacking the ship now, though. That was impossible. Rukhs were myths, just like elves and dwarves. Unable to resist, he got up off the floor and went over to the windows along the back wall to catch a glimpse of a real, live rukh.

"FIRE!" Basil commanded the first of the guns. An electrostatic pulse hit the rukh, sweeping down from its head to its tail. The bird shook itself, screeched anew, and swooped over the ship.

"RECHARGE! RECHARGE! FIRE!"

"Captain, they had direct hit!" one of the hands cried. "Why didn't it take it out?"

"I don't know, Andrews! Hold your ground, and do your job. Our worry is the balloon, not the guns."

"Captain, I don't think it wants the balloon."

Andrews was right. The rukh circled the ship once, took two direct electrostatic hits, and hovered just outside Daisy's cabin.

The author is unaware if any readers have had the experience of one's wish coming true, but she can assure you from personal experience that it is one of the most terrifying events known to man. Martin Hathaway, who had not seconds before been standing before a wall of windows hoping beyond hope that he might see a real, live rukh up close, now found himself wishing just as vehemently that some nice, qualified Earth doctor would wake him with assurances that the sharpness of this vision was a perfectly normal side effect of being in a coma. As the rukh grew closer and the likelihood of medical intervention grew remoter, Martin took a tentative step away, just in case.

The bird's face filled the window. It smashed the glass to pieces with a single jab of its beak. Martin staggered backward. Thrusting its head inside the room, the rukh snapped at him. It caught Daisy's four-poster bed and split it in two.

Martin ran into Daisy's closet. The rukh's sharp beak tore open the door, but the bird was too large to get any closer. Looking desperately about for a weapon, Martin grabbed a parasol from a vase containing several delicately designed examples. He smacked the rukh with all his strength. The parasol broke, flew upward, and hit Martin in the head.

Out of better options, Martin was suddenly seized by a bold and stupid idea. Rather than continue dodging the rukh's beak, he jumped on top of it and ran over the bird's head. He had some notion of scrambling out the broken window and pulling himself up to C Deck, but the bird withdrew its head from the room too quickly for Martin to keep his footing. He clutched at a brass band the rukh wore on the top of its head for some insane but propitious reason and hung on for dear life.

"HOLD YOUR FIRE!" Basil cried upon spying Martin dangling from the rukh. "The pulse will kill him for sure!"

Martin was not the only person on the A.S. *Nephthys* capable of quickly forming bold and stupid plans. Andrews saw it on Daisy's face and cried out, "Wait, Captain!" but she did not.

Running as fast as one can wearing boots on top of a balloon, Daisy leapt off the ship, somersaulted through the air, and landed astride the rukh's back.

"Martin! Grab my hand!" she shouted. He did not need to be told twice. Grabbing Daisy's hand with one of his own and clinging to the band with his other, he managed to hoist himself back up onto the rukh. The bird flew about sporadically, trying to throw off its two uninvited passengers. Martin climbed behind Daisy and held onto her waist.

"What is this thing?" Daisy asked, pointing to the brass band.

"No idea. It's got lights and knobs; try smashing them!"

First, Daisy tried firing a shot directly into the rukh's neck and then at the brass band. The bird continued to buck and screech. Frantically, she thrust at the lights and knobs with the butt of her blaster. Martin leaned forward and tried pressing things as well. His hand found a small key on the side of the band. He pulled it out.

An eerie silence fell over them. The crew watched in horror as the rukh froze, hung in the air for a second, and the plummeted to the ground, still bearing Martin and Daisy on its back.

"Daisy!" Martin yelled. "You can make the next plan!"

"Lean forward, keep your head down, and hold on!" was the best she had to offer.

"You really should issue your crew parachutes, you know!"

"They're in Port Storage!"

"A lot of good that does us!"

The ground crew closer. It was time for last words. Martin came up with, "Thanks for dying with me," and Daisy chose, "Don't mention it."

Daisy buried her head in the rukh's soft feathers and hoped for the best. Martin rested his on Daisy's shoulder and had enough time before impact to note that she did, in fact, smell like springtime.

The rukh crashed into a clearing in a forest. It skidded along the ground, tearing a great divot into the earth. Finally, it slowed to a rest on the edge of a wide lake.

Martin blinked his eyes and slowly sat up. "We're not dead!" he cried.

Humans have evolved two responses to having experienced times of great stress: sobbing and laughter. These Martin and Daisy demonstrated simultaneously upon discovering they had survived the drop unscathed. They laughed until there were stitches in their sides. Daisy collapsed with her head on his chest, their bodies shaking and tears streaming down their faces.

When his laughter subsided, Martin wiped his eyes and looked down at Daisy's face. She was staring up as if seeing him for the first time. Something about riding a mythological beast not to your doom emboldens a man; Martin slid his arm around Daisy's waist. He cupped her chin in his other hand, closed his eyes, and pressed his lips against the cold muzzle of her blaster.

BASIL RACED INTO the Control Room, leaping down the stairs to the Lower Observation Deck. Jake and Tony were already there, noses pressed to the glass.

"Do you see them?" Basil demanded, a frantic note creeping into the end of his sentence.

"I can't see anything but forest," Jake answered.

"We're too high," Tony argued. "We'll never see them from here."

"Emma, turn us around! They fell from the stern."

Slowly, the ship circled the area. Forty-two people held their breath and peered out every available window.

"There!" Basil pointed. "It looks like a road leading to the lake. That must be the trail the rukh left! Westfield, bring us down!"

Emma shook her head. "The trees are too close together, Mr. Underwood. I can go lower, but we can't land."

"What about ladder's length?"

"I wouldn't want to risk it. We might get stuck on the branches."

"Can you get us close enough to use the cargo sling?"

"Aye, I can do that."

Basil charged off to the Starboard Storage. "Angelo, Jameson, to me!" he called as he went. "There may be lifting to do. Melody, get your bag!"

The four entered the storage room and climbed into a large leather sling attached by a chain to a pulley system. Andrews was on-hand to open the cargo door beneath and lower them down.

"Good luck," he shouted as they slowly descended, "and bring them back!"

Basil hung from the sling by one arm and scanned the area. He found the remains of the rukh lying by the lake, but he could see no sign of Daisy or Martin.

"Damn this sling!" he cursed. "Could it be any slower?"

"It's for cargo, darling," Melody sang at his side. "Cargo doesn't lose its patience."

Basil was going to point out that cargo does not lose its captain, either, when he saw Martin hobbling toward them, dragging one leg. Basil jumped from the sling and hit the ground running.

"Basil!" Martin cried. "It's Daisy—"

"Where is she?!"

His answer came with the sound of blaster fire. Martin fell to the ground.

Daisy emerged from behind a tree, roaring, "I'LL ASK AGAIN: WHO ARE YOU?"

Basil breathed a huge sigh. He turned to the three in the sling and waved his hands above his head.

"They're perfectly fine!" he called.

"I'm not!" Martin protested.

Daisy stood over Martin's fallen body. "Here's how this is

going to work," she growled. "I've stunned both your legs. Now I'm going to stun both your arms. Then, while you lie here, a helpless talking head, I am going to break every bone in your body one by one until you tell me WHO YOU ARE AND WHO YOU WORK FOR."

Calmly, Basil strode over, picked Daisy up by her waist, and carried her away from Martin.

"Daisy," he tutted, "allow me to answer for him. That is Martin Hathaway, he works for you, and we are all very sorry he was not more prompt with your coffee this morning."

"He's not," she insisted, kicking at Basil. "He's a spy. The rukh didn't attack the ship, it attacked Martin. And it was wearing some controlling device he knew how to disable. He must have got whatever it was that he came for, and he called the rukh to pick him up so he could get away and we would all think he was dead. He tried to kill me when I came to save him, and when that didn't work he tried to kill us both. That failed, too, so he tried to . . . he tried to confuse me."

Basil set Daisy down but kept a firm grip on her shoulders. "That's one theory of events, Daisy. Here's another. Martin is not only the unluckiest man in his universe, he is the unluckiest man in any universe. Now, which theory do you think will hold up best to Oswald's Razor? The simple, obvious one or your convoluted, rage-fueled one?"

Daisy sputtered for a while and then hung her head.

"Basil," she asked quietly, "do you think I'm losing it?"

"No. It is possible that Martin has some strange vendetta against your furniture choices, and you may have been unwise letting glass feature quite so prominently in your design schemes. But I do not think you, Daisy McNamara, are 'losing it.' Something weirder than usual is going on, but that's why we're on this mission. We're going to Fitzgerald House and we'll find out what it is and we will fix it."

Daisy punched him on the arm in lieu of thanks, and the pair meandered back to where they had left Martin. Melody was tending to him, though with little physically wrong beyond legs he could not feel, there was not much she could do other than offer him a lollipop.

"Martin," Daisy asked as they drew nearer, "are you okay?"

He propped himself up on his elbows and replied, "Yeah. Yeah, I think so."

"Good. Sorry for stunning both your legs and threatening to break all your bones."

Tony and Jameson stared at each other in disbelief, as they did not dare stare at the Captain. Jameson had once before heard the Captain utter the words *sorry* and *for* in that order, but as the uttering in question had concluded with the phrase *your pitiful miscarriage of an existence*, he was naturally all astonishment at their use in this case. Tony Angelo had never heard Daisy put those two words together, and he could not wait to get back aboard the ship and into the Enlisted Lounge.

Martin, unaware of his privileged state, merely shrugged his shoulders and replied, "It's okay. Sorry for almost killing you and . . . being . . . really . . . happy . . . we weren't dead."

Melody and Basil took their turn at stares of disbelief, though Basil's may have been better classified as subdued bemusement. Both Underwoods had a very clear idea of just what action Martin might have taken to express being . . . really . . . happy given his recent conquering of the window seat. They were in for a healthy, relationship-affirming round of giggling and speculation later, to be sure.

Regaining her regal bearing, Daisy cleared her throat and delivered her orders. "You three get Martin back on board and find him something to eat. Then, lower the sling again and we'll join you. Basil, come with me."

DAISY LED BASIL over to the fallen rukh. Examining the brass band, Basil thought the two of them might be able to lift it off the bird together and bring it back to the ship for further study. As they were about to try, however, the rukh opened its eyes. They ran for cover as the huge bird rose. It shook itself, sending the band sailing into the lake. It spread its wings and took to the skies.

⚙ CHAPTER TEN ⚙

MARTIN'S MUCH-BELATED BREAKFAST was interrupted six times by gaggles of well-wishers dropping by Sick Bay to marvel that he had, in fact, survived. When one is impressed by the act of sitting in a window seat, riding a rukh is positively giddying. Throw in not having every bone in his body broken by the Captain and it was almost too much to believe. Melody was forced to hang a sign on the door insinuating the containment of a highly infectious disease so he could finish his eggs in peace.

"I have to tell you," Melody said as she boiled water over what looked and functioned very much like a Bunsen burner, "while I'm happy you're here, I think I'll be even happier when you've been here long enough that your injuries won't be interesting anymore. I don't like having the Sick Bay door closed if I can help it. Basil and Daisy are always charging by, yelling about monsters and treasure and whose fault it was they were almost killed. It's very amusing."

"That doesn't make you a bit jealous?" Martin asked.

"Does what make me jealous?"

"You know. Basil and Daisy. Running around almost getting killed together all day."

"Oh, heavens, no. It makes both of them so happy. And why

would I want to be almost killed? No, I'd much rather stitch them back together and hear about their adventures than have an adventure and require stitching back together."

The effects of the blaster were slowly wearing off Martin's legs, leaving the exact pins-and-needles sensation as if he had been on an extremely long car trip riding in the trunk. Martin felt Melody might be the smartest of all the crew of the A.S. *Nephthys* he had met to date.

A whistle sounded signifying a call over the Comm Channel. Melody answered and informed whoever was on the other end that Martin's arms were not stunned and thus did not require help feeding himself. She placed the mute seal over the sound of Tony's cursing the misuse of the Channels and brought Martin a cup of tea.

"So you think all that's because I'm the new guy?" He gestured to the Comm Channel with his teacup.

"Oh, yes. That's the way it goes around here. We're such a small little family, you see. Every new face is exciting. Though you might be a bit more exciting than usual, what with coming from another world and all." Melody walked aft to a wall of cabinets and began resetting the jars that had been knocked about during the rukh attack. "I remember when Daisy first took Basil on; it was a positive giggle fest in the Women's Quarters for four days."

"What happened on the fifth day?"

"I married him."

Martin was astonished and did not make any effort to disguise the fact. "You married him after four days? You must have known him before Daisy took him on, right?"

"Oh, no."

"No?! Do you all move that fast around here?"

"We're all very quick on our feet, yes. But our courtship was rather rapid. You see, we had made a date to go for a walk the third night. Jocelyn Heart would never admit it now, but she was absolutely green with envy. Though she needn't have been, because he stood me up. I was very annoyed about it, but on my way back to quarters one of the First Watch stopped me and said I was needed in Sick Bay. Wouldn't you know it, but there he was, all huddled in the corner and shaking like he had seen a ghost. I treated him for shock and he proposed then and there. I told him I thought it was a bit too early to know if we had feelings for each other, but he said, 'I'm a very lovely person. You could do worse.' And he was right."

Martin sipped his tea. He could hear Basil's voice saying the words she had quoted, but he still could not fathom Melody accepting him.

"I guess it all worked out, though," he concluded.

"Oh, yes. Basil's always right about important things. That's why Daisy trusts him."

"Why doesn't she trust his theory about me? She thinks I'm a spy."

"Well, Basil's sometimes off on the details, I'll admit. It's physically possible you threw yourself into the skylight from the roof and pretended not to understand anything. It would have been a very clever trick, though. Basil would have to shake your hand before you were tortured and imprisoned."

He chose to ignore the latter half of Melody's last sentence and instead inquired, "Daisy doesn't trust people very easily, does she?"

"No. She does not. But she can't, really, being the Captain

and the Keeper. And then, of course, there's always—"

The Comm Channel whistle sounded again. This time the communication was Official.

"Captain's orders," Tony said in his Official Communication voice. "If Mr. Hathaway is capable of walking, he is to report to the Control Room. If not, Mr. Underwood is going to come and carry him."

While the latter option would have been the more entertaining, Martin knew it was less likely to help him in developing any sort of a rapport with Basil. Gingerly, he slid off the sick bed and hobbled toward the door. He waved goodbye to Melody on his way out and thus concluded what was the first of their many teatime conversations concerning Basil and Daisy.

"Up and about, then?" Daisy said as Martin appeared at the first of the three levels of the Control Room. "Excellent. Hurry down; we're preparing to land."

Martin was not sure what preparing to land had to do with him, but he attempted to hurry nonetheless. Not all the nerve connections in his legs were back online yet, and on the transition between the third and fourth step he lost contact with his right knee. This sent him tumbling down the stairs to the second level, arriving quite embarrassed at Daisy's feet.

"That was prompt." Daisy suppressed a smile. "Basil, you should follow orders so well."

Basil was busy at her right scribbling into a notebook and sighed without looking up. "I'm afraid I shall disappoint, Captain."

Daisy assisted Martin in rising much in the same manner

as she had the day they met. Also like that fateful day, Martin Hathaway was red in the face.

"I never fell this much at home," he mumbled.

Daisy ceased suppressing her smile. "Just the once, then?"

It was difficult for anyone close to Daisy McNamara to remain in a bad mood while she was in a good one. For Martin, it was impossible. He chuckled. "Once was more than enough."

"Captain," Tony interjected, "with respect, Ground Control sent a message wondering if we requested landing clearance on a whim or if we actually intend to visit Fitzgerald House sometime today."

"Oh, like Ground Control has anything better to do." Daisy guided a protesting Martin toward the stairs to the Lower Observation Deck. "And how does one transmit sarcasm via semaphore, anyway?"

"It's a lost art, Miss."

Daisy gave Basil leave to initiate landing procedures. Martin had assumed he would be assigned a task, but instead she led him up to the wall of windows where nose prints were still visible from the crew's search hours before.

"Can you stand all right?" she asked over the sound of Basil bellowing orders. "Or shall I send for a chair?"

"No, standing's fine. What are we doing?"

She pointed to the window. "That is Mount Hulda, the highest point in the Duidaean Mountains. We are about to fly around it, and then you will see your first glimpse of Fitzgerald House."

A fourth nose print joined the other three when Martin watched in amazement as they rounded the mountain. It was an imposing peak of gray stone, covered in snow and rising into

the clouds. How anything could live up here he could not fathom. Suddenly, nestled between the Duidaean peaks, Fitzgerald
House came into view.

Martin Hathaway felt, and rightly so, that he had been mis-
led by the term house. Before him now was nothing short of
a castle, perhaps even a fortress. Martin counted seven black,
spiraling towers before exclaiming, "Oh my god. Which room
is Dracula's?"

"I beg your pardon?" Daisy was not sure, but she felt she
might have been insulted. Martin's reaction to her childhood
home was not as enjoyable as the one to the Valley.

"Oh, nothing. It's just . . . it's amazing and all, but you didn't
really grow up there did you? I mean, all the rock and the snow
and the big black spikes . . . how could . . ." Martin paused and
looked at Daisy. He bit his lip. He knew he was about to say
something cheesy, but he could not stop himself. "How could a
Daisy grow where it's always winter?"

One corner of Daisy's mouth smiled. She was about to remark that it had not been easy, but just then Basil had joined
them on the Lower Observation Deck and exclaimed, "A direct
pun on your name, Captain! Shall I haul him off to the Brig
now or after we tie down?"

"Neither." She turned away and stared directly out the window. "I'll allow it this time, in exchange for having stunned his
left leg."

"Apparently, you had the right one coming, Martin," Basil
said in his ear.

The ship circled Fitzgerald House in ever decreasing circles
as it approached for a landing. Eventually, they hovered above a
snow-covered courtyard and began a direct, vertical descent. It

was then that Martin noticed the Ground Control crew for the first time.

"Wait!" He jumped back from the window, pointed, and pressed his face against it again. "Those are . . . no. Those aren't Dwarves, are they? Real, actual, high-ho it's off to work I go Dwarves?!"

Daisy sighed. "Basil, give Martin the Cultural Sensitivity Training."

"With pleasure. Martin, face me please."

Martin turned, and Basil slapped him.

"That's the Gender and Workplace Policy Training, Basil," Daisy admonished.

"My mistake, Captain. No harm getting that one out of the way as well, though." He gestured to the window. "Those, Martin, are Duidaean Dwarves. They are a noble people that branched off from a common ancestor to humanity several million years ago. They have a lovely and vital culture all their own and have contributed greatly to the fields of craftsmanship, construction, and drinking songs. When meeting one, do not stare or ask if he is real. Do not assume that the dwarf to which you are speaking is male. Do not refer to any as 'Shorty,' 'Beardy,' or anything other than his actual name. Do not agree to a checkers game unless you are willing to have your head chopped off when you lose. Do not drink more of their beer than you can handle, which for you would be any. Do not sign contracts without fully reading the Terms and Conditions. Anything else, Daisy?"

"Just don't," she said, turning to head back up the stairs. "Mr. Angelo, you have control. Mr. Underwood, Mr. Hathaway, Dr. Underwood, Miss Heart, and I are disembarking for

Fitzgerald House. When accommodations are offered to the rest of the crew, you are authorized to accept."

Basil had dutifully followed her up the stairs, but Martin remained at the window not staring at the Dwarves.

"Keep up, Martin," she called from the second level. She picked up a coat that had been laid across the Captain's chair and tossed it down to him. "Basil's graciously lending you one of his least necessary coats. Bundle up."

Martin pulled on the coat as he hurried up the stairs. It was warm, but itchy. It smelled of cigars, rum, and something else Martin could not quite make out.

"That coat," Basil informed him as they started down the hall, "I stole from the Pirate King of Baristrata. Try not to spill any wine or fall into any other universes while wearing it." He then lowered his voice and kept a wary eye on Daisy's back. "And . . . if you happen to find any . . . unusual substances in the pockets, they belonged to him. There's no reason to worry Daisy about them." Just before they reached Sick Bay, he added, "Or Melody. Especially Melody."

That explained the third scent.

Melody, wrapped snuggly in her winter lab coat, fell into place with the other three as they passed Sick Bay. Upon reaching the stern, the party was joined by another woman. Something about her looked strange to Martin. Her complexion was much darker than his other companions, but Martin did not think that was what made her seem different.

"Jocelyn Heart, Chief of Engineering," she said, offering Martin a firm, strong handshake. "You're our Fallen Star, I presume."

Now he knew what was odd about Jocelyn. She sported purple overalls.

"You're wearing pants!" Martin exclaimed.

"Daisy, I think you may have been correct this morning," Basil commented. "Clearly, Martin is a master spy. Are there no secrets safe from his penetrating eye?"

"That was a very clever rhyme, darling," Melody interjected, "but maybe Martin's never seen a woman in pants."

"Oh, but he has."

"If you all are done with your chat," Daisy barked, "I would like to call upon Fitzgerald House before midnight. Fall in and move out." As the party descended from the ship one by one, she drew Martin aside and said, "Now, listen. My uncle . . . he doesn't live in a mountain-top fortress for nothing. He's a bit of a recluse. He tolerates those three well enough because they're all experts in fields he enjoys. The rest of the crew will be spending the visit out of sight in the Servants' Hall. It's best if you try to say as little as possible until he decides he likes you, or you'll be sent there as well."

"Will you be joining us, Daisy?" Basil called from the ground. "It is your ancestral home, after all."

"Remember," she said, taking her turn on the rope ladder, "keep up and just don't."

THOUGH BANNED FROM speaking and lingering, Daisy had not given Martin any interdict on looking around. Upon setting both his feet in the paved courtyard, he spun slowly, hardly believing that he stood inside a castle large enough to encircle an airship with room to spare. Everywhere he looked, he saw either windows or stairs. Daisy need not have warned him to keep up;

there was no question that Fitzgerald House was not somewhere he would like to be lost. Having met a rukh and seen a team of Dwarves all within the last six hours, Martin would not be surprised to discover when left on his own that Dracula really did have a room here.

One of the Dwarves marched importantly and, Martin thought, a tad angrily up to Daisy. Had Martin bothered to finish *Fitzgeralds: A World Apart*, he would have known that the Dwarf in question had every right to be more than a tad angry. He was none other than Eitri, son of Agmundr, Skati of the Shipwright's Guild. The soft, dark, billowing curls of his beard alone would have been enough to identify him for anyone who had read at least to Volume Three.

The reader may very well ask what a world-renowned shipwright, let alone a guild's worth of them, is doing at the top of the highest peak in the Duidaean Mountains, especially when one takes into consideration what a novel, modern invention an airship is. You forget, of course, that a mountain extends down as well as up, and for generations the Duidaean Dwarves were as well-known at the foot of the mountain for their skills as craftsmen and toymakers as they were for service and lore at its top. Eitri and his guild had literally moved up in the world upon being summoned to bring Lord Fitzgerald's airship design to life in time for his niece's eighteenth birthday. It was the greatest of honors for a Duidaean Dwarf to be employed by the Fitzgeralds, for they, more than any other family on Arnica, truly understood and respected Dwarf kind. That is not to say, however, that they did not occasionally vex each other terribly.

"By Gudrun's Book!" the dwarf bellowed and waved his arms at the *Nephthys*. "What have you done to my ship?!"

Daisy smiled and curtseyed. "Eitri, old friend. Your beard flows as the very rivers."

"Don't 'your beard flows' me, Freya. A quarter of the upper stern is missing! Do you have any idea how long that's going to take for my team to repair?"

"Hours?" Daisy smiled innocently.

Eitri folded his arms and uttered a hearty, rolling laugh.

"Twenty-four of them, at least. I assume you'll want the molding restored."

"Of course. A thousand thanks, Eitri. May your descendants number as the jewels under the mountain."

"Go on with you," he gestured toward a large ebony door before them. "Lord Fitzgerald is expecting your party in the Fifth Blue Room."

The Fifth Blue Room was located somewhere down six hallways, up four flights of stairs, through seven more doors, and finally accessed by pulling a copy of *Fitzgeralds: A World Apart* off a bookcase. Martin gave up trying to remember where he was after the third hallway and was very happy for the straightforward tininess of the *Nephthys*.

Lord Fitzgerald was waiting for them in an armchair beside a grand stone fireplace. At first glance, Martin had almost mistaken him for another Dwarf; his legs only barely reached the marble floor. He wore glasses so thick his eyes appeared double their actual size.

"Hello, Petunia," he said as they passed through the bookcase. "How's your idiot father?"

Having known Daisy's sad history since yesterday, Martin felt an overwhelming urge to say something valiant in her defense. He was only able to stand with mouth agape, however, as Daisy wrapped her arms around her uncle's shoulders and placed a kiss on the top of his bald head.

"Still dead, Uncle Fitz," she said with only a hint of resentment. "But I'm sure he appreciates your concern."

"He should. Well then, Violet? Have you misplaced your valley?"

"No, the Valley's still there. My friends and I have come for a visit." She waved for Basil to step forward. "You remember Mr. Underwood. He helped you isolate Element 104."

"And what an explosion it was!" Lord Fitzgerald chuckled and shook Basil's hand. "Welcome, Mr. Underwood. I hardly recognized you with your eyebrows."

Melody and Jocelyn were likewise reintroduced to their host. After reminiscing over the trebuchet he and Jocelyn had built out of spaghetti noodles, Lord Fitzgerald pointed to Martin.

"And this fellow, Buttercup? I don't recall his face."

This was the moment. Daisy stood behind Martin and held his shoulder in clear indication of his acceptableness in the current wing of the house.

"This," she said solemnly, "is a present."

Martin exclaimed, "A what?!"

⚙ CHAPTER ELEVEN ⚙

"Rose, you've outdone yourself," Lord Fitzgerald chuckled as he peered into the brass microscope. "Mr. Hathaway is a much better gift than that tie with those little sparrows you brought on your last visit."

"They were Thunderbirds," Daisy muttered, "and it was embroidered by the Lady of Istrilgar herself."

She sat on the examination table beside Martin, periodically jabbing him with her elbow when he dozed off. They had been in Lord Fitzgerald's laboratory for hours. Martin had no idea what time it was, but he was exhausted. He had just finished recounting the history of the Earth as he knew it into a dictaphone while Daisy's uncle took blood samples from his arm and scanned his body with a handheld device that emanated a blue glow. After a Dwarf had brought their third tray of refreshments, Jocelyn had excused herself for bed, but the Underwoods were wide awake. They were busy making calculations and sketches, pouring liquids back and forth between various beakers, and evaluating the series of lights and clicks given off by machinery throughout the lab. There was no question that Science was being done, but to what end Martin was far too tired to care.

"He's right." Melody handed Daisy one of the notebooks in which she had been recording data. "Martin, your DNA is absolutely fascinating."

Martin yawned. "You guys know about DNA but not clipboards?"

"How to efficiently hold bits of paper was a tad low on the scientific priority list," Basil commented while examining 70 mL of liquefied Martin.

"But look at this!" Melody pointed to a series of chromosomes she had sketched. "Martin has exactly twenty-three pairs of chromosomes with a 0.1 percent nucleotide diversity from Basil's."

Daisy nodded. "So he's human."

"Of course I'm human!" Martin examined the sketches. "Is that what we've been up all night for? I could have told you how many chromosomes I had."

"That's very good, Martin. However, that's not the fascinating part. You and Basil have a 0.1 percent nucleotide diversity, but your fixation distance is one!" Melody was beaming. She looked between Daisy and Martin, astounded that they took the news unmoved.

"And that means?" Daisy asked.

Basil informed them it meant that the very roots of his family tree kept a respectable distance from Martin's.

"There's more," Lord Fitzgerald added. "Martin doesn't fit in a single haplogroup. His Y-chromosome has never been shared with any ancestor of Man, Dwarf, or Elf yet known to Science."

Daisy handed the notebook back to Melody and sighed. "Then the genetics support the alternate universe theory."

"Of course they do," Basil snorted. "Surely there was never

any question on that front. No, what we really need to ascertain now is whether or not that means he's sterile."

Before Martin had time to utter, "Wait. What?" Daisy cried, "Basil, why is that even a line of inquiry?"

"Why should we inquire if the unluckiest man in any universe is able to reproduce? Frankly, Daisy, I'm appalled by your lack of foresight."

"If he truly is the unluckiest man in any universe," she said, hopping down from the examination table, "then that should never be an issue. But seriously, Uncle Fitz, can we say for certain that Martin's DNA didn't come from this world? Is it possible Anatamenwar altered it so he could circumvent the Valley?"

Lord Fitzgerald smirked. "Having trouble with your Valley, Daffodil?"

"Could they do it or not?"

"No. Such technology is beyond me, let alone the dunces in Anatamenwar. Besides, isn't your Valley governed by the organic? Your friend still has plenty of carbon in him."

"So you agree that it's theoretically possible for a rift in Space-Time to have opened and closed in the exact seconds necessary for Martin and only Martin to fall through?"

"Theoretically, Lily, anything is possible. What you want to know is if it is both practical and probable. Of that, I am not certain, but I agree with Mr. Underwood that it is the likeliest explanation of all the evidence. The Fair Folk are said to be able to move between worlds, you know."

"Yes. But we just proved Martin has no trace of Elven blood. How can he move between worlds?"

Lord Fitzgerald pondered this. "There is some legend," he said slowly, "of a member of another race passing between worlds. If your mother was willing she could tell us. She was always better with stories than I."

"Basil, do you know the legend?"

He pressed his fingers together and reflected. "I know I do. It was a cautionary tale, and a particularly bleak one at that. I think it was a Dwarf—"

"Svadilfari," Martin interjected. "Svadilfari, the Ill-Fated Dwarf."

Everyone turned to stare at Martin. Basil appeared dumbfounded.

"What? You guys don't know that one? He built this machine out of iron to transport himself like the Elves could, but he used it too many times and he got his limbs all ripped apart and sent to different worlds. Terrible story for kids."

Martin grinned, quite proud of himself. Feeding and training an Apprentice Historian would have been cost-effective after all.

Daisy was the first to comprehend the import of Martin's moment of brilliance. "A machine could have opened the portal?" She pulled Martin's cell phone out of her pocket and handed it to her uncle. "Could this be it?"

"Hey!" Martin jumped off the table and ran over. "That's mine! When did you get it?"

"Remember when you fell down the stairs today? Then."

"Oh, okay. Wait . . . no, I don't remember dropping my phone . . ."

Daisy smiled.

Martin threw his hands in the air. "You pickpocketed me! Again!"

"It's not like you missed it. You haven't mentioned it once."

"That's not the point!"

"What, pray tell, is the point?" Lord Fitzgerald asked, holding the device aloft. "It's a very lovely bit of craftsmanship, but I can't see any function to it."

"The battery's dead," Martin replied. "I left my charger in the last universe."

Lord Fitzgerald inquired as to the phone's fuel source, rummaged around in a drawer, pulled out a metal box, and tinkered with it. As he worked, Martin launched into a surprisingly forceful homily on the sanctity of personal property and space. Basil stopped his investigation to watch and surreptitiously switched on the dictaphone.

"And another thing—" Martin ranted.

Lord Fitzgerald interrupted, "Voila! That should do the trick, Tulip."

Everyone looked at the desk where he had been working. Martin's cell phone sat atop the metal box, fully illuminated.

Martin sputtered, pointing at his phone, "How did you—"

"Simplicity itself. I merely reconfigured this blaster charger to fit your device. Let's see what it does—"

"NO!" Martin leapt forward and snatched up the box and phone. "I've had enough. I've been poked, prodded, scanned, questioned, and robbed. You all can sit around here and discuss my physiology as much as you like, but I am going to bed."

Daisy reached for his arm. "Martin, don't get upset."

"GET upset? What do you think I am now?!"

Lord Fitzgerald agreed with him. "Chrysanthemum, your friend appears to be growing feisty. Better let him rest."

Martin wheeled around and shouted at Lord Fitzgerald, "DAISY! Her name is Daisy. Not Begonia, not Apple Blossom, and not Lavender. It's Daisy. I don't care what crazy relationship you two have; she deserves the common decency of using her real name. Now, good night!" With that, he stormed out the door.

The occupants of the laboratory hardly had time to recover from the shock of Martin's exit when he reentered.

"Umm . . ." he asked, "can anybody show me where my room is?"

Sunlight shining in his eyes awoke Martin the next morning. He yawned, stretched his arms above his head, and settled back down amongst the soft pillows. Daisy's coffee could wait. If she had any sense, she was also wrapped up and cozy in her own bed.

The door flew open.

"Martin! What on Arnica are you doing? I've been waiting for you to get up for three hours! Let's go, man! Places to visit! Things to do!"

He dove under his covers. "Daisy! Get someone else to make coffee!"

"Coffee? Don't be ridiculous; I've had six cups while waiting for you to grace us with your presence in the Breakfast Parlor." She crossed the room, set a tray down on the side table, and shook the huddled lump that was Martin. "Up and at 'em, Morning Star. Look, I've brought you pancakes."

Martin poked his head out of the covers. "Thank you. Now get out. I'll report when I'm finished."

"Are you still being a grumpy boots about the pickpocketing?"

"No, I'm a 'grumpy boots' about an uninvited person in my bedroom."

Daisy laughed and sat on the bed next to him. "You forget. This is my room. They all are. I don't recall this place being christened Hathaway House."

"Why don't you go bother someone in another room, then? You could wake up Basil and Melody. That's a two-for-one."

"Melody's in the West Tower entertaining my mother. Basil and Jocelyn are working on a project with my uncle. Thank you, by the way. Uncle Fitz . . . well, he never liked my father. He liked him even less for dying. Thought it was a sign of weakness. He built the *Nephthys* with the idea that I would base operations from here. He never really forgave me when he found out my first mission was to visit my father's Valley. He hasn't called me 'Daisy' since I reclaimed it."

"No problem. Can I eat my pancakes in peace as a reward?"

"No. You should have thought of that before you slept 'til nine. Sit up, have your breakfast, and I'll brief you on today's developments."

Reluctantly, Martin propped himself up on his pillows. More readily, he took a cup of coffee off the tray and eyed the pancakes. *There are worse bosses*, he decided.

Daisy sat at the foot of the bed, her legs swinging over the side like a child on her first train ride. Her eyes were on her boots as they repeatedly peeked out and then disappeared behind the folds of her skirt, but her address was professional and efficient. "Eitri says the repairs on the *Nephthys* are coming along, but he estimates they won't be finished until this evening. We could sail then, but I don't like to risk nightfall in the mountains, so we'll sail at first light tomorrow."

Martin started in on the pancakes. "Is there cinnamon in these? They're delicious."

"Thanks. Now, everyone has their assignments already, and you needn't worry about them. You and I are going to Borghild as soon as you're finished."

"Wait. You made these? Not a team of Dwarves pledged to do your family's bidding from time immemorial?"

"I got bored. Everyone was busy. Are you listening or not?"

Mouth full of pancakes, Martin affirmed, "Sailing tomorrow. Borghild today. Why are we going to Borghild?"

"To find out if the Scop knows anything about Svadilfari. Anything historic, that is."

"Right. How far is Borghild?"

"We're sitting on top of it right now."

"Of course we are. So do we get there via some secret door in the basement?"

"Did you only read the story about Svadilfari? Because *Fitzgeralds: A World Apart* clearly states . . ." Daisy whipped her head to the side with the intent of casting an intimidating glare at Martin. Instead, her brow furrowed. She looked down at his chest and back up at his face.

"What?" he asked, pancake crumbs splattering on the blanket.

"Martin, why aren't you wearing a shirt?"

"I was sleeping!"

"Oh." Daisy turned her head to the side, quizzically. "Do people do that when they sleep?"

"I do. At least, I do when I am in a private room with a door that shuts. By the way, I'm pretty sure it was locked."

"And . . . um . . . are you also . . ."

Martin nodded.

"Alright, then." Daisy hopped off the bed and made her way to the door. "Report to the Courtyard in twenty minutes. And dress in layers. It's freezing out there."

Thirty minutes later, having lost his way twice, Martin stepped out into the snow-covered courtyard. Daisy was busy at the stern of the ship discussing repairs with Eitri, snowflakes caught in her hair. Martin waved to her and was filled with nostalgia for Christmas. He wished he had a present with which to surprise her. He wanted to take her ice-skating and return to a roaring fire in front of the insanely large tree he imagined one could fit inside Fitzgerald House. Briefly, he considered chucking a snowball at Daisy, but then he remembered that he liked the way his arm was attached to his body.

"The sleeper wakes!" Daisy said as she walked past him. "Keep up, then. We haven't got all day."

Martin trotted behind her across the courtyard. "We do, actually. You don't have any other plans until we sail."

"Well, we won't have all day if you keep wasting bits of it, will we?"

They stopped on the other side of the courtyard at an iron door that stood twice Martin's height. The image of a great tree adorned the bulk of it; at the ends of its branches were runes carefully shaped to resemble leaves. Martin ran his hand over the intricate work.

"This is the Fitzgeralds' private entrance to Borghild," Daisy explained. "Each of the leaves represents a member of the family. This one's mine." She touched a small leaf at the bottom of the tree, revealing a keyhole. She pulled an iron key from one of her pockets, placed it inside, and the door creaked open.

"Did Xavier have to use a ladder to open his leaf?" Martin asked.

Daisy ignored the remark, though she had wondered the same thing when she was young.

They stepped inside the mountain. The door clanged shut behind them. All was black.

"Umm . . . Daisy?"

"Wait for it."

Abruptly, two torches on either side of them burst into flame. Then two torches ahead followed suit, and the pattern continued, illuminating a seemingly endless staircase. Above their heads was revealed a ceiling of pure crystal, which caught the light and sent it sparkling down on the adventurers.

"That. Was. Amazing!" Martin cried.

"Was it?" Daisy began descending the stairs.

"Oh, come on. Automatic torches? That has to be cool in any universe."

"I always hated the waiting. When I was little I would have nightmares the lights wouldn't come on and I had to stand in the dark, unable to open the door to go back."

Martin had to concede that would dampen some of the excitement. He also learned that the thrill of entering a Dwarven city for the first time was likewise brought down by the sheer number of stairs one was required to descend in order to get anywhere. He felt like they had been walking downward for days. He had stopped asking where all the side tunnels they passed went in favor of using that air to keep breathing. Finally, the row of torches came to an end outside a golden door. This had to be it.

Daisy took a torch off the wall and turned down another staircase.

"You've got to be kidding!" Martin exclaimed and pointed to the gold door. "Why is this not our destination? The torches think it is!"

"That's the Great Hall of Borghild, where the King holds his court. But we're not going to see the King; we're going to see the Scop. Scops are lore masters. She's the one who will know if Svadilfari was ever real."

"You don't think we could stop and say 'hey' at least? The King might know stuff."

Daisy advised Martin to take a torch as well. "Dwarves," she explained, "have excellent abilities to see in the dark, so the residential tunnels are pretty sparsely lit."

"How much farther does the Scop live?"

"The very heart of the mountain. That's where its secrets are."

"Right. No point in keeping secrets at the top where anyone can reach them." Martin grumbled and picked up a torch. He was revived by this act, however, as carrying a torch made him feel more like a proper explorer. He whistled the theme to *Indiana Jones* as they continued down the increasingly winding stair, both happy and sad that Daisy did not understand.

Eventually, Daisy turned and entered a side tunnel. She was still able to walk upright, but Martin had to stoop to walk through it without scraping his head on the crystal. Small doors dotted the walls. They walked past eleven of them before coming to a halt at a door at the end of the tunnel.

Daisy knocked. The door opened, revealing an ancient

Dwarf in a tattered dress.

"Greetings, Gudrun." Daisy bowed low. "Freya Bergdis has come to seek your wisdom."

"Bergdis, you look more like your mother every day. Welcome." Gudrun took Daisy's torch, handed it to Martin, and the two women went inside. The door shut. Martin was alone.

"I'll just wait here then," Martin shouted at the door. He sat down on the cold stone floor. *Daisy's a piece of work*, he thought, *dragging me down here just because she's afraid of the dark.*

Martin . . .

Someone was calling his name.

Martin . . .

He knew that voice.

Martin . . .

"Hailey?" he called.

"You're certain?" Daisy asked again.

"Certain as death on a sunny day. Elvish lies, the lot of it." Gudrun had become angry when asked if there was any truth to the tale of Svadilfari. Had she not loved Freya Bergdis's mother and grandmother, she would have turned her from the house on the spot. "Why would Dwarves envy the Fair Folk? The world is for shaping, not escaping!"

Daisy made her apologies and got up to leave.

"No luck, Martin," she said, stepping into the tunnel. She looked around. "Martin?"

Gudrun stuck her head out the door. "Have you lost your porter, Bergdis?"

"Look!" Daisy picked up two discarded torches. "How could

he . . ."

Gudrun stroked her hoary beard and turned back inside her dwelling. Shortly after the banging and clanging that indicated frantic rummaging ceased, she reappeared in the tunnel carrying an iron stake.

"Better take this, love."

⚙ CHAPTER TWELVE ⚙

MARTIN . . . I'M WAITING FOR YOU.

Slowly, Martin Hathaway followed the voice down several narrow tunnels. He turned corners, climbed over barriers, and walked far from any inhabited region of the mountain. It was much too dark for him to see where he was going, but Martin did not know that. He could see a light glowing ahead. This had to be where she was waiting. Sliding past a large rock, he stepped out into a cavern. It had not been carved by any Dwarven hand; stalactites formed slowly over thousands of years hung above his head. Martin hardly noticed. She stood by a pool in the midst of the cave. She was waiting for him.

"Hailey?"

Hailey held out her arms. She wore a long, flowing green dress, and her hair brushed about her face as if caught in a breeze. The light Martin had followed was the glow of her alabaster skin.

"Oh, Hailey," Martin sighed, "I am dreaming."

Come, Martin. I'm waiting for you.

He walked toward her, open armed. "I'm so sorry, Hailey. I'm sorry I got drunk and I'm sorry I'm in a coma and I'm sorry I can't come home."

Come home, Martin.

"I want to. Help me, Hailey."

Hailey embraced him. She caressed the back of his neck, just like she never did at home. Her body swayed as if they were dancing.

Martin, I can help you. Help you come home. I'm waiting.

"Please, Hailey," he looked into the glow where her eyes should be. "Take me home."

Hailey raised her hand. Her fingernails were long and blood red. She curled her hand like a claw and reached for his throat.

An arm wrapped around Martin's neck. A blinding light flashed before his eyes. Hailey and Martin screamed.

"You cannot have him, She-Devil!" Daisy cried, jabbing her torch at the creature's face. The creature released him, retreating from the light of the fire. Daisy tried to drag Martin along with her, but he grabbed her arm and flipped her over his back.

Leave her, Martin. Come home. Come home to me.

He started to walk back toward Hailey. Daisy kicked his legs out from under him, and he slammed onto the floor of the cavern.

Daisy sprang to her feet and ran at the creature, sweeping the torch in an arc.

"He is protected!" she growled. "Go back to your sisters, hag."

The creature sprang at her. Sharp nails dug into Daisy's wrists. The torch fell. Daisy gripped the iron stake with both hands. She thrust it into the creature's chest. Blood gushed out, splattering her face. The creature screeched. Martin held his head and wailed. Daisy drove the stake in farther, pushing the creature down onto the ground.

"I am Daisy Fitzgerald McNamara, and I release you to the darkness."

The creature fell lifeless. Daisy let go of the stake, stood up, and pulled a handkerchief from her pocket.

"Men," she grumbled as she bound the wounds on her wrists. "I knew I should have gone with the all-girl crew."

Martin stood up and stumbled toward her. It was difficult to see in the light given off by the fallen torch, but he knew without a doubt that whatever Daisy had killed was not Hailey.

"What was that?!" he asked, fumbling through Basil's coat pockets for something to help clean Daisy's face. "It was in my head."

"That was a baobhan sith. They latch on to lost travelers. Lost male travelers, specifically. This one must have found a way into the mountain to hide from the sun. It had to call you out here, because the Dwarf city is full of iron. Baobhan sith can't go near the stuff."

"What . . . what was it going to do?" Martin was not sure he really wanted to know.

"It was going to cut your throat with its nails and drain all your blood."

"Like a vampire?"

"Nothing like a vampire. Like a baobhan sith."

Martin could not find a cloth. He licked his thumb and wiped the blood from around her eyes. "You saved my life. Again. How can I ever thank you?"

"You can start," Daisy said, brushing his hand away, "by never doing that again."

"Right. Sorry." Martin shoved his hands in his pockets.

Martin . . .

"Daisy . . . please tell me that's an echo. A really, really delayed echo."

Martin . . .

He looked at her, wild-eyed. "You can hear them, too, right?!"

Martin . . . we're waiting.

Daisy cursed, scooped up the torch, and grabbed Martin's hand.

"Excellent. You found a coven."

BASIL STOOD UP and massaged the small of his back. He was stiff from having been bent over the intricate machinery for hours. Pushing his magnifying goggles on top of his head, he rubbed his tired eyes.

There was a knock on the workshop door. Melody poked her head into the room.

"Sorry to bother you all," she said in her singsongy voice, "but I was wondering if you were going to take a break for lunch or if I should tell Brokk to bring you a tray?"

Jocelyn was all for a break. Lord Fitzgerald opted for the tray. They looked at Basil.

"A break for what?" he asked as if dazed.

"Lunch." Jocelyn informed him that it was well past midday.

"Mid-day!" Basil walked over to the window to confirm this news. "Do you realize what this means? I've been working all morning!"

"Wasn't that the plan, darling?" Melody asked.

"Of course it was the plan. But I haven't been interrupted

once to go fetch a hat or investigate a strange sound that inevitably turns out to be some hideous beast bent on my personal destruction."

"Wasn't that also the plan?"

"Yes, but . . ." his voice trailed off.

Melody smiled and joined her husband at the window. Sliding her arm through his, she asked, "Darling, do you miss the Captain?"

"What? Don't be absurd. It's just . . ." Basil stared at the iron door to Borghild through the frost-covered glass. "I've raised her since she was twenty, haven't I? I've a right to worry."

Laughing and patting his arm, Melody said, "Don't worry, darling. I'm sure the two of them are having a nice, quiet little adventure."

"It's going to be alright, Martin!" Daisy cried as she dragged him out of the cavern. She found running through the dim recesses of the mountain much more difficult when maintaining a firm hold on a person whose subconscious wanted to go the other direction. Martin found running through the dim recesses of the mountain difficult as a rule.

"Basil and I ran from a baobhan sith before. Just keep hold of my hand and remember I'm here. I'm here, and I'm real. Think about me, Martin. Think about me being here and real and they can't touch you."

"Ok, Daisy," Martin said. He stopped running and pointed behind them. "But why do you want me to go back to the cavern?"

"What?!" This was not going to be like that time with Basil.

"Oh, god. Martin, stop thinking about me!"

Martin started to walk away. Daisy managed to hold him in place by digging her heels into the ground, but she could not keep this up. She would need both hands soon. They were not safe here. The coven was coming.

"I'm trying to keep up, Daisy," Martin said to the voices in his head.

She looked around frantically for a weapon. Nothing remotely helpful against a single baobhan sith was in sight, but she did see a tunnel to their right with a ceiling just high enough for Martin to pass through. With all her strength, she pulled him to it, only to discover that the tunnel came to a dead-end in a small alcove.

It was too late now. She shoved him inside and turned to face the entrance. Five hideous white figures appeared in the opening. Green fabric hung about their emaciated frames. Their mouths opened, wide and toothless.

Martin tried to walk out to them. Daisy kicked him and flung the torch at the baobhan sith in one fluid motion. The baobhan sith retreated from the flame with a collective hiss, but they quickly rallied and continued their advance. Daisy had enough time before their return to draw and aim her blaster.

"You shall not touch him, you filth!" she cried and shot the roof of the tunnel. The rocks rumbled and fell, cutting Daisy and Martin off from the baobhan sith, the light, and the world.

"An all-girl crew," she repeated, fumbling in the darkness with the settings on her blaster. "We could have worn matching hats. It would have been epic."

"Umm . . . Daisy?" Martin called, his consciousness restored.

"Wait for it."

Suddenly, the alcove was filled with the soft glow of a blue light radiating from the blaster. Daisy set it down between them and took a seat on the floor.

"Your blaster doubles as a flashlight?"

"I modified all the kill settings that way. Better use of the power."

"Why were we carrying torches then?"

"You can't shoot things if you're in flashlight mode." Daisy shrugged. "Also, it feels more like a proper adventure if you're carrying a torch."

Martin snorted. "A proper adventure." He hauled himself up to a sitting position, acutely aware that during his rescue Daisy had managed to pummel the previously unbruised places on his body. As these were few, such an achievement was worthy of note. "Looks like a proper adventure also requires saving me from certain doom."

"Maybe not this time. It's possible I pulled you from a quick, excruciatingly painful death to a slow, agonizing one."

Perhaps it was the singularly calm manner in which Daisy stated their predicament, but Martin found it hard to imagine she did not have everything perfectly under control.

He asked, "What's the plan, then?"

"We sit here until someone notices we're missing, discovers this pile of rocks, and decides moving them might be worth a go."

"Should we yell for help or something?"

Daisy shook her head. "Wouldn't do us any good unless someone were right outside, which shouldn't be for awhile. Actually, to conserve oxygen it's best if we don't talk at all."

"Right." Martin tried to stretch his legs but could not find a way to do so without entering Daisy's side of the alcove. Deciding an invasion of that nature was best postponed until absolutely necessary, he pulled his knees to his chest and rested his chin atop. Daisy closed her eyes and leaned back against the rock wall. She sat perfectly motionless, so much so that Martin began to wonder if she was breathing. He had seen movies where the hero was able to hold his breath and alter his pulse to enter a dormant state when in grave danger. Maybe this was what Daisy was doing. He opened his mouth to ask her and quickly shut it again, realizing that doing so would defeat the purpose. He drummed his fingers against his legs. He started to whistle, also realized that went contrary to the objective of oxygen conservation, and tapped the rhythm with his feet instead.

Daisy sighed.

"Martin, why don't you tell me about your home?"

"What?" He popped his head up. "Well, okay . . . I mean . . . if you're sure you want to hear about it. Could take awhile."

"Now." Daisy smiled. "We have all day."

Following the sage advice of Maria Von Trapp, Martin started at the very beginning. He told Daisy the story of his parents meeting in coffee shop when their orders were mixed up. He told her about growing up and going through school two years behind a sister who could do no wrong and a year ahead of a cousin who could do nothing else. He told her about bad dates and heartbreaks, the year he worked as a shovel bum for an archeological dig, and the antics of his favorite students. He told her how completely blindsided he had been when his parents filed for divorce. He told her about the cool place around the corner from his apartment that made the best cupcakes he had ever had and how adorable his nephew was.

Through it all, Daisy remained silent. Martin began to wonder if he was simply babbling to an uninterested audience. After describing the horror that was last Thanksgiving with Mom's new boyfriend, Martin ceased his narration.

"Do you miss it?" she asked.

"What? Well, yeah. Yeah, of course I miss it. I know it's kinda boring, what with nobody getting attacked by mythological creatures every twenty-four hours, but it's home, you know?"

"I think it sounds wonderful."

"Really?"

"I never had a perfect older sister or a ne'er-do-well cousin. I can't remember my parents' voices. Everything I know about my relatives I read in a book. When I was eighteen, I decided to build a family, and by twenty I had."

Martin stared at Daisy through the blaster light. He wanted to take her hand, but he opted for what he knew to be a surer way of cheering her.

"Why'd you pick up Basil, then? You already had a crotchety, reclusive-genius uncle."

She laughed and opened her eyes for the first time since the waiting began.

"You know where I found Basil? In my kitchen. I came down the stairs one morning and he was making himself breakfast. He tried to stab me with my own butter knife. I shot him. When he came to, I had just about finished his waffles. We've been friends ever since."

Martin decided to test his luck. "How long before you decided he wasn't a spy?"

"Things were . . . different then." Daisy tilted her head toward Martin. "So, you've told me about Michelle, Lucy, and your sister's roommate. What about Hailey?"

Martin reddened. She had been listening.

"Hailey . . . well, she's special. She's the best thing that ever happened to me." Gesturing to the pile of rocks blocking their path to civilization, he added, "Not that getting buried alive hasn't been fun and all."

Daisy nodded. "But you don't love her."

"Excuse me?!"

"I'm sorry, Martin. This is your fourth day away and, quite frankly, you seem perfectly happy. Basil would be a nightmare if he'd not seen Melody. And the one time we were away from her that long, he never tried to kiss me."

"We weren't dead! It was a big moment!"

Daisy shook her head. "My parents—"

"Ok, look. Your parents' story isn't love so much as excessive-soul-mate-codependency. That's one couple in a century sort of stuff. Real-life love is more about commitment and compromise."

Inhaling deeply and mentally, counting to ten before speaking, Daisy repeated, "My parents used to dance. Do you dance at Eagle's Peak?"

"Oh. Well . . ." Martin was going to explain that he was not much of a dancer, as Hailey would only tolerate his presence on the floor after her third drink. He realized in the nick of time that this was a new universe, and Daisy did not need to know everything. "Yes. I love dancing. Sometimes I dance in the kitchen just for the heck of it."

"By yourself?"

"Of course. See, where I come from, dancing is an individual, freestyle sort of thing." Martin Hathaway was suddenly seized by a wonderful idea. "I can show you," he said, pulling his phone out of his pocket.

"Do you have pictures of dancing?" Daisy asked and scooted closer.

"Even better. I have music."

In his own universe, Martin had always found the act of choosing what to play for another person a bit tricky, as the goal on such occasions is more to impress the listener with one's taste than it is to actually play something enjoyable. Selecting a song for Daisy had the additional difficulty of Martin's complete un-awareness of any type of music she might like outside the vague impression he had that whatever she enjoyed probably involved harpsichords and lutes. As he had no chamber music in his col-lection, Martin decided a person could not go wrong with the Beatles. In a flight of poetic whimsy, he pulled up and played the soundtrack to *Help!*

Daisy jumped when the music started, which was to be ex-pected. Setting his phone on a natural ledge in the rock, Martin stood up and gestured for her to do so as well.

"Now, the key to Earth dancing," he explained with all se-riousness, "is to look as silly as possible. If you're even a little self-conscious, you aren't doing it right."

Martin Hathaway bent his knees and twisted his torso. He flailed his arms as much as the confined space and proximity to Daisy would allow. At first, Daisy thought he was teasing her. This was not what she had meant by "dancing." However, this also was not what she would have meant by "music." Tenta-tively, she bent her elbows and waved her hands.

"That's it!" Martin cried. "Now your knees, too!"

Soon Martin and Daisy were giggling and spinning about

the alcove. It was by far the merriest cave-in since the Great Rock-Slide of Duridsmach.

Four minutes and fifty-six seconds later, the beat changed. Daisy glided effortlessly into the new song, but Martin stopped and leaned against the cave wall. When he caught her eye, he extended his hand.

She took it, stepping over to his side of the alcove.

"This," she said softly, her other hand on Martin's shoulder, "is how I remember my parents."

Martin nodded and bit his lip. He was not about to ruin this moment.

Daisy noticed. "Is something wrong?"

"No. Not wrong. It's just . . . well, you really are supposed to let me lead."

She laughed. Relaxing, she laid her bloodstained head on his chest.

"Sometimes," she whispered, "I thought I might have made this up."

Martin held her a little tighter, wishing her demons were as easy to drive away as his had been today.

Abruptly, an electronic cadence replaced their music. Daisy lifted her head and wrinkled her nose.

"I don't like this song."

Martin stared at his phone.

"That's not a song," he said, bewildered. "It's my ringtone."

☼ CHAPTER THIRTEEN ☼

MARTIN CREPT TOWARD his phone as if it were a particularly sensitive land mine. He did not know much more than the average consumer about cellular phone technology, but he was sure that he should not be getting reception here below the heart of the mountain.

He picked it up and examined the screen. The display indicated the call to be coming from the number "2." Out of the instinctive curiosity that caused the first man to wonder what would happen if he were to bang these rocks together, Martin answered the phone.

"Hello?"

"WE DID IT!" Basil's voice thundered through the line. Martin held the phone away from his ear, but he could still make out cheering in the background. "Twenty-seven prototypes and we did it! Jocelyn, I'm so happy I could shake your hand!"

"Who is this?"

"Martin, you giant labradoodle! Don't ruin a Great Moment in Science with your characteristic confusion! Say something that can be written down for the history books."

"No . . . but . . . you can't. How?"

"Listen, my loquacious lad. It took all morning and most of the afternoon, but we've reverse engineered your phone. By the way, did you know it has more functions than the showing of dirty pictures and the not-calling of your friends?"

Martin found his voice. "You can't reverse engineer cell phone technology. There are like twelve other things you have to invent first. And you never even saw the inside of my phone."

"Of course we can! We did just what you said: bits of metal with electricity running through them. I will concede that we were unable to reproduce the streamline design of your unit, but I'm sure you'll find ours has a bit more pizzazz."

"You need satellite dishes and towers! Even then you can't call the inside of a mountain!"

"Fine. You're right, Martin. We didn't reverse engineer a phone and we aren't capable of talking to you. Can you put the Captain on now, please?"

"No, wait. Does this mean I can call my friends?"

"In another universe?! I'm a scientist, Martin, not a wizard. Now put the Captain on."

"Are there wizards?"

"Maybe if I shout loud enough Daisy will hear me. CAP-TAIN, PLEASE KNOCK MARTIN UNCONSCIOUS. ALSO, HOW WAS YOUR DAY?"

Martin rubbed his ear and handed the phone to Daisy. "It's for you."

Daisy stood tall and poised. She held the phone and said, "Captain speaking."

"Daisy! We did it!"

She squealed in a manner that reminded Martin very much of the girls in his freshman World History courses on the days he showed films.

"I know! I'm so proud of you all! Is it what I thought?"

"Negative, Captain. There doesn't appear to be any program for opening a portal between worlds, circumventing the protection, or summoning mind-controlled rukhs. There is a way we can aid some strange, flightless birds in their war against even stranger bodiless pigs, but I've yet to ascertain what's in it for us if we do so. Anyway, we can officially state that Martin is exactly who he and I have been saying he is."

"Good news, Martin," Daisy said, covering the microphone with her hand. "You're not a spy."

Martin gave her a thumbs-up and sat back down. He did not want to know how Daisy knew to cover the mouthpiece of a phone.

"Well, tell everyone what a good job they've done. Oh, and Basil, we're in a bit of a spot down here."

"Let me guess. You took Martin, Destroyer of Worlds, into the mountain and he caused a cave-in, exactly like a certain dashing First Officer told you he would when you described your misguided plan to him at breakfast this morning."

"For the record, I caused the cave-in."

"Oh?"

"Yes. On a quasi-related note, there may or may not be a coven of baobhan sith lurking down here, so wear something iron around your neck and make sure all hands you bring with are female."

"Ah. You know, Captain, I'm not sure I'm aware of what the proper plural of baobhan sith is. We've never had to talk about more than one before we got a Martin. Remind me to thank him for bringing this linguistic curiosity to my attention after I rescue you both from your own folly."

"Very amusing, Basil. If you're done gloating, I'll try to describe where I think we are."

"No need, Daisy. I made a few modifications of my own to the basic technology. I can trace your device's location to within three feet."

"Excellent. See you soon. Remember the iron. And the girls."

"Affirmative. Basil out."

Daisy switched off the screen and placed the phone in her pocket.

"Hey!" Martin called from the floor. "That's still mine!"

"I'm commandeering it. Captain's prerogative."

"No, Daisy. We went over and over this. You can't commandeer my things."

"Alright. Remember when you asked how you could ever thank me for saving your life? Thrice now, I might add. Here's how: you can give me your phone."

Martin hung his head and waved his hand to indicate defeat.

"Oh, cheer up, Martin," Daisy said, taking a seat beside him. "Your phone saved our lives. And just think what this means for the crew! We can make a phone for the patrols. We'll always know their location within three feet, and they can report back instantly! Why, if we had these earlier, we would already know what Gilly and Gibson discovered!"

"Who?"

"Alright, Gibs," Gilly said, unconcerned as to whether or not the guard heard their plans. "Are you ready? On three."

They had each broken a board off of the barrel in their cell.

These they wedged just below the hinges of the cell door in an effort to pop them loose using the right combination of leverage and force.

"One . . . two . . . three!"

The men strained. The boards cracked. Gilly and Gibson toppled backward onto the straw-covered floor. The iron door remained unmoved.

"That's the last of the barrel." Gibson cursed and threw his board onto a pile of broken wood in the corner. "I think it's time to admit we don't know what we're doing."

"I'm telling you, this is how Mr. Underwood got us out of the Tomb of the Falcon Queen. We just have to find the weak spot."

"Oh, we've found the weak spot . . ." Gibson began. He was silenced by the sudden movement of their previously unflappable guard.

The guard stood up and walked toward the cell door. "The one called Gilly has been summoned," he said. He placed his index finger into the lock and the door creaked open.

Gilly hit him over the head with the broken board. The cell filled with a clanging sound, and the guard visibly vibrated.

"You are the one called Gilly?" he said, unfazed. "You will follow me. Please leave your weapon behind. If you wish to be stunned, beaten, and dragged before Mendax, I can accommodate you, but it would be much simpler if you would follow me without further attempts at heroics."

Gilly handed the board to Gibson. "Keep at it, Gibs," he said as he followed the guard out of the dungeon. "If you break out, don't search for me. Run like hell for the Valley, and tell the Captain that Anatamenwar's created supermen."

"The Captain's coming for us!" Gibson shouted through the bars of the cell. "She won't forget us, Gilly! Don't you forget either!"

The guard led Gilly up a winding stone staircase. The walls were close enough that he wagered he was in a tower, though whether the tower was connected somehow to a larger structure or stood on its own he could not determine. At the top of the stairs was a heavy door with a brass knocker. This, the guard opened. Gilly stepped into the circular room and saw the sunlight for the first time in three days.

A man in a flowing black cape stood at the window, his back to the room.

"Well, Gilly?" he said. "Still blindly following the great Captain McNamara? Tell me, when does one get pension benefits? Before or after one becomes decrepit past the point of use? I suppose not even then, if our Miss Smith is any indication."

Gilly clasped his hands behind his back and thrust his chin forward. "Now, I don't know who you are or how you know me, but you'll get no word out of me against the Captain."

"I don't need your words, Gilly. I have my own. But are you sure I am not familiar to you? I think you once knew someone very like me. Very like, indeed. Perhaps it would be wise for you to closely look."

Slowly, the man turned. Gilly gasped.

"You?! But . . . it can't be. That's impossible!"

The man smiled, sinister and threatening. "It is improbable, Gilly, but hardly impossible. However, I'm not the man you knew. I am Mendax."

THE WIND HOWLED outside the Third Evening Room windows. Martin was thankful to be sitting beside the great fireplace with a mug of hot chocolate and would have felt this way even if he had not been only recently rescued from uncertain doom in the deep recesses of the mountain. Melody and Daisy were together on the sofa, the former tending to the wounds on the latter's wrists. Basil and Jocelyn lounged on opposite ends of a loveseat, each vying to outdo the other in conveying the tale of the invention of the cell phone. With the terror of the coven relegated to the far corner of his mind, the only thing preventing Martin from declaring himself to be present in the best of all possible worlds was the unsettling manner in which Lord Fitzgerald glared at him from the other armchair.

"Well, I'm very proud of you both," Daisy said before Basil and Jocelyn could come to blows, "and you, Uncle Fitz."

"Thank you, *Daisy*," Lord Fitzgerald replied. "It means a great deal to me, the man who taught you everything you know, that you can still be impressed by my efforts."

Daisy cast a reassuring smile Martin's way and continued, "I only wish our day had been as productive. We didn't learn anything from our trip to Borghild that we couldn't have discovered over a cup of tea in the Solarium."

"On the bright side," Jocelyn suggested, "it's possible your entombment raised our technology beyond that of Martin's world. Maybe the twentieth prototype would have been able to call Martin from across the house, but we didn't realize what we had achieved until we pushed it to reach inside the mountain."

"Yes, it's always reassuring to learn one's failures bring out the best in others." Basil smirked. "Just think, Daisy, before today we had no idea how many rocks I could lift while wearing an iron collar and still have energy to climb several hundred flights of stairs."

"And I'm sure you'll sleep like a baby tonight because of it."

Melody packed up her medical bag and settled back. "Yes, you all had a very big day. I did as well, in my own way. I told Lydia all about what's happened since we visited last. She was particularly interested when I mentioned Martin's connection with Svadilfari, the Ill-Fated Dwarf."

"You're a saint." Daisy sighed. "I don't know how you can spend all day talking to someone only getting facial expressions as a response. I sit with her for ten minutes and I want to scream."

Martin chuckled. "That doesn't sound so bad. Try telling someone your life story while wondering if she's asleep."

The corners of her mouth turned up ever so slightly, Daisy rejoined, "I'm not your mother."

As if on cue, the door to the Third Evening Room opened and Lydia McNamara entered. Martin thought Gudrun's assessment of Daisy's appearance was accurate as far as her stature was concerned. Short, slender, and striking, Lydia inspired in most a desire to protect and care for her, yet somehow it was also clear that she was capable of great feats of self-reliance. Martin struggled, however, to see a resemblance in the faces of mother and daughter. Perhaps it was the difference in years and activity, but to him Daisy seemed softer and ruddier than Lydia. Such an impression was likely aided by the fact that Lydia McNamara reminded him of Dickens's Miss Havisham.

Lydia glided over to the sofa and took a seat between Melody and Daisy. She had carried a large book, which Martin was sure had to contain incantations for summoning familiars. Daisy took it and thanked her.

"I'm sure you remember my friends," Daisy said, "except for the one by the fire. Martin, this is my mother, Lydia. Mother, meet Martin Hathaway of Eagle's Peak."

Martin waved. Lydia turned and smiled at him.

"Hello, Martin," she said softly.

Every head oscillated between staring at Lydia and at Martin. Martin was not sure if he had worked a miracle or committed the crime of the century.

Daisy leapt off the couch, clutching the book to her chest.

"HELLO, MARTIN?!"

Lydia reached for her, but Daisy backed away.

"HELLO, MARTIN?! Twenty-two years, and it's 'Hello, Martin'?! Just like that? HELLO, MARTIN!" Daisy covered her mouth, shook her head, and ran from the room.

"Daisy, wait!" Martin sprang from his chair. Pausing only to set his mug on the side table, he took off after her. Basil was on hand to intervene. He caught Martin by the collar of his sweater and pulled him back into the room.

"Do you have a death wish, man?" he demanded. "Do you have any idea the kind of injury she could cause with a tome of that size? If you want to survive your post, you need to learn to discern when it is time to comfort and when it is best to cower. I'm not always going to be here to prevent her from breaking every bone in your body."

He nodded to Melody, who calmly rose and followed the Captain.

Lord Fitzgerald had gone over to the couch to comfort his sister who was crying soundlessly. Martin paced in front of the fire. He held several conversations with Daisy in his head, but as all of them at some point led to his saying, "Sorry your mom spoke for the first time in twenty-two years," they were dismissed as unsatisfactory. Basil sat in the chair Lord Fitzgerald had vacated, his fingers pressed together and his eye on the door. Jocelyn studied the architecture outside the window and calculated the probability of her being able to climb to the Servants' Hall to tell Tony about this and return unnoticed.

Having convinced Lydia that she had exerted herself entirely too much today, Lord Fitzgerald helped her to rise and led her toward the door. She stopped before entering the hall, dropped her brother's arm, and returned to Martin.

"It's not your fault," she said weakly. As she spoke she moved closer and closer to him, until Martin found himself with his back firmly against the mantelpiece praying that his corduroys would not alight. Lydia had waited years for this; she was not about to cease talking merely because her audience was terrified.

"She's too much of a McNamara, and she always has been. But you and I, we understand each other."

Lydia could not have been more mistaken if she had insisted she remembered Martin from elementary school, but he nodded nonetheless.

"When she tells you to go, stay with her. Stay by her side or you will regret it forever."

Now Martin Hathaway understood Lydia McNamara. He embraced her. Lydia smiled, patted his cheek, and followed her brother out of the room. Martin held his breath until they were out of sight and then collapsed into the armchair. Basil drew a small notebook out of his breast pocket and scribbled inside it.

Jocelyn pulled herself back in from the window and asked,

"What was that all about? You aren't actually with the Captain, are you, Martin?"

"What? Oh, no. I don't know what that was." He stared into the fire and reflected, "Moms just love me, I guess. When I met Hailey's mother, she kept feeding me pie all night. Don't get me wrong, it was great pie, but after the fourth piece I never wanted to eat again."

Jocelyn looked at Basil and mouthed, "Who's Hailey?"

Basil raised his eyebrows, waved his hands in the shape of an hourglass, and resumed his writing. Jocelyn nodded knowingly and slid back out the window.

⚙ CHAPTER FOURTEEN ⚙

THE NEXT MORNING, Martin Hathaway was the first of the guests to arrive in the Breakfast Parlor. Lydia and her brother were already seated at opposite ends of the long table, each reading and ignoring his presence. It occurred to him that perhaps he had caught a lucky break in having slept late yesterday. Had he met Daisy's mother at breakfast rather than at the end of the evening, it was likely the cave-in would have been a much less merry event.

The three other principal characters arrived and were served, but still there was no sign of Daisy. Martin wanted to take her a tray, but both Basil and Melody waxed emphatically on the importance of laying low until no longer a target of Daisy's wrath.

Just when Martin had given up on waiting for Daisy and accepted a plate of food for himself, she entered. She greeted no one and kept her face from Martin. Setting the book her mother had given her the night before on the table, she opened it and pointed to one of the pages.

"This was his source for *Tales from the Fair Folk*," she said to Lydia. "And this must be a drawing of Svadilfari's machine."

Martin leaned over to get a look at the page. Basil kicked him under the table and shook his head. Following his example,

Martin focused on his plate.

"But the writing is in Ancient Elvish," Daisy continued, "and Uncle Fitz and I can only read Modern. You can read it, of course. I don't suppose you want to explain it to your new best friend?"

Lydia looked at her daughter wearily.

"Right." Daisy closed the book and turned to Basil. "When you've finished, ready the crew. I want to be in the Blessed Isle by dusk tomorrow."

Basil grinned. "The Blessed Isle? Come now, Daisy, it's not yet . . ."

"Not today, Basil."

The First Officer resumed the study of his breakfast, though his good humor was evident. Daisy crossed the Breakfast Parlor and dropped the book in Martin's lap as she passed him, muttering, "Take charge of this." She poured herself a cup of coffee from the service on the side table. Her back to the others, she took a sip.

"Basil," she asked, "did he make this?"

"I'm sorry, Daisy," Basil set down his fork, "but when we confirmed his allegiance beyond a shadow of a doubt yesterday, I assumed my watch had come to an end. Would you like me to resume round-the-clock surveillance on your Assistant's movements?"

She turned and regarded Martin. "Well?" she said, taking another sip.

Martin cast a sidelong glance at Basil and ventured, "I . . . um . . . got lost on my way to the Breakfast Parlor and found the kitchen and thought as long as I was there I'd be . . . helpful."

Daisy crossed the room again, paused before Martin, and

picked up his plate.

"I'll be in the Solarium," she announced as she exited. "Alert me when we're ready to sail."

Martin watched her leave. Placing the book on the table where his plate had been, he squeaked, "The Captain commandeered my breakfast."

"Thank god!" Jocelyn cried. "Saved you a trip to the Brig. Or the Sick Bay."

"Possibly both." Basil no longer made any pretense of holding back his glee. "Buck up, soldier, you're in for a treat. We're going to visit King Super-Good-Looking."

"THING IS, MARTIN," Basil explained as they marched through the Servants' Hall, "I'm sure your very special time with us and residence in the hotbed of fiction that is the Bachelor's Quarters has rather given the impression that our Captain's entire emotional output consists of blind rage and disarming placidity."

Basil paused his speech to bark orders at any crew members they passed, usually adding the admonition that they were not on a pleasure cruise, at a day spa, or on an extended holiday. Martin would then smile and wave. In general, the crew thought this pairing a welcome addition to the management.

After suggesting that Jameson prepare for an early checkout, Basil continued, "But that's not quite the case. Though she hates it, Daisy is more than capable of experiencing and expressing the full spectrum of human emotion, including pure, unbridled adoration. The object of her ambitious yet girlish dreams is none other than King Dathúil."

"Wait," Martin interrupted, "I know that name. It was in the tale of Galedlothia and Reginald. Galedlothia's brother, I think he was. Gave Reginald the Valley. Is this Dathúil a descendant or something?"

Basil chuckled. "Well done, Martin. But no, he is not a descendant or something; he is the original Dathúil himself."

"No, he can't be. That would make him over a thousand years old. And related to Daisy."

"Guilty on both charges! I suppose I should give you Cultural Sensitivity Training: Fair Folk Edition, but they're a much more forgiving race than the Dwarves. Well, not forgiving, per se. More long-suffering. They expect humans to commit the regular faux pas like the idiot relative you have to invite to the wedding even though you know he will take full advantage of the open bar. But I digress. Point is, Elves—don't call them that, it makes them angry—Elves live so ridiculously long we aren't sure if they can die on their own, and yet they always maintain a youthful glow."

Martin shifted the weight of Daisy's book from one arm to the other and muttered, "My god. I did fall into *Lord of the Rings.*"

"What's that?"

"Nothing. We have legends of Elves in my world. I was just remembering one."

"Ah. If you could save your remembering until I'm finished with exposition, I'd be much obliged. Shake a leg there, Westfield! This isn't a couples' retreat! Now, where was I? Oh yes, Dathúil is a member of Daisy's family tree. I presume you bring this point up to express disgust that she also believes him to be steamier than the Starboard Engine Room in midsummer. Rest assured, after a thousand years the gene pool is so polluted there's hardly any Elf left in the McNamaras. Actually, were you to trace ancestry back that far I'm sure you'd find we're all mixed up in this together. Except you, of course! Our little genetic anomaly!"

Basil chuckled to himself over this while Martin pondered why Basil would assume that he would find a trip to Daisy's boyfriend's realm a treat.

"Anyway," Basil resumed after having chased Annabell and a gaggle of girls out of the Servants' Library, "as I was saying before you cross-checked my tale with literature, Daisy has, but more importantly will not admit to, a crush on the aforementioned Dathúil. Every year, usually around the winter solstice, she discovers some puzzle that cannot possibly be solved without the help of the Fair Folk, and hey-ho-off-we-go to Tír na nÓg, or The Blessed Isle in Common Tongue. I look forward to the visit with relish, and not just to see Daisy pretend she has not given up all capacity for rational thought."

Martin did not particularly care if Basil elaborated on his reasons for enjoying himself at Daisy's smitten expense or remained silent until the end of all days, but he could tell from Basil's tone that the First Officer required a response at this point in his soliloquy. Politely, with only a touch of peevishness, Martin supplied the necessary, "Oh no?"

"No." Basil winked and continued on his merry way. "You see, my boy, the Fair Folk in general and King Super-Good-Looking in particular have the best wine cellars in the world. I always manage to make off with a barrel of the King's private stock. But this year should be even better, since you'll be joining us."

Martin looked up, his spirits momentarily revived. "Really?"

"Yes. You can carry a second barrel."

"Oh. Right. But . . . isn't that stealing?"

"I believe we've already been over the moral ambiguity of our profession, Martin. If it is any consolation, the Fair Folk don't actually have a concept of personal property. The taking of the wine is really more of a battle of wits between King Super-Good-Looking and myself, which, naturally, I always win."

"And . . . um . . ." Martin rubbed the back of his neck with his free hand, his usual sign of embarrassment. "Why exactly do you call him King Super-Good-Looking?"

Basil rolled his eyes and tutted, "Martin, I really feel like that one is self-explanatory. Now, the crew's been spurred into action. Will you be fetching Daisy or shall I?"

BRAVELY OPTING TO fetch Daisy himself and then remembering that he had no clue where she was in relation to where he was, Martin followed Basil to the Solarium. They found Daisy sitting in a wicker chair surrounded by exotic plants. She gave a start when they approached, and Martin wondered if she might not have dozed off in the warmth of the sunlight. The Captain was herself in no time, however, and expressed her desire to be in the skies. As the trio marched off to the ship, she ordered Martin to take the book to her quarters upon boarding and begin an inventory of her personal effects. Once he was finished, he was to check his inventory with the one Basil had done last month to see if anything was missing after the rukh attack. He was assured his presence would not be missed on the flight deck.

Martin complied and only slightly resented the busywork. When he heard the purr of the engines and felt the ship loose its moorings, he took a seat in Daisy's chair and watched out the wall of windows as Fitzgerald House disappeared from view. Sighing to himself before resuming his task, Martin wondered when Daisy would cease being angry with him.

His answer came at Six Bells on the Middle Watch. Shaken awake in his hammock in the Bachelor's Quarters, Martin blinked and rubbed his eyes. Jameson's grizzled visage filled his field of vision.

"Captain requests coffee," Jameson whispered so as not to disturb the others. "Said to wake you and not Cook."

Though he grumbled his way through the brewing process, by the time Martin made it back up to B Deck with the silver coffee service, he was as wide awake and chipper as one not assigned to the Middle Watch could be at Six Bells. He opened the door after knocking and set his burden down on a side table. Daisy, fully dressed, leaned against her desk and stared out the window into the clear night sky.

"Good almost-morning, Captain," Martin said as he fixed her cup. "Did you have a nightmare?"

"Hmm? Oh, no. Just the one." Daisy did not turn from the window, and Martin thought it a tad rude to have woken him up if she was still bent on ignoring him. As he approached with her cup, however, she broke from her reflections and said, "I was too hasty. I should have waited for Gilly and Gibson to report back before making for Fitzgerald House. I can't figure out the Who or Why, and without those answers the How is meaningless."

Martin started to say something about how that entire sentence sounded meaningless, but halfway through he understood.

"Wait," he said, "you're worrying about the Monitors in the Valley."

"Of course."

"Daisy . . . when you said there would be no sleep for you until you knew how the Monitors got into the Valley, you didn't mean that literally, did you?"

"Of course. Why would I have said it if I didn't mean it?"

"That was five days ago! No wonder you're bipolar! You have to sleep!"

"Thank you for your concern, Martin, but if I wanted an opinion on my mental health, I would have called Melody. I called you because I want you to hand me that cup of coffee."

Martin jumped away and hid the coffee behind his back.

"No," he said firmly, "you can't have this. You need to go to bed. I'll bring more in the actual morning."

Daisy protested that this was not in the least amusing and tried grabbing for the cup. Martin held it over his head, taunting her diminutive stature. She rolled her eyes and drew her blaster.

"That's fine, Daisy," Martin said. "Go ahead and stun me. Then when I come crashing down to the floor, you'll be the only one conscious to clean up the spilled coffee."

Captain Daisy McNamara kept a copy of Fionn mac Cumhaill's *Science of Warfare and Other Human Relations* by her bed. She knew when it was time to change tactics.

"Martin," she said sweetly, walking forward. She slid her arms around his neck and wrapped a delicate finger around one of his curls. Pressing softly against him, she turned her head up toward his. Her eyes were large, bright, and innocent. "Please, Martin?"

With superhuman effort, Martin shook his head.

The light left her eyes. In one swift motion she kicked his legs and caught the cup as he plummeted past.

"I win!" she said to the Martin at her feet, still using her sweet voice.

He picked himself up and said, "Daisy, you have really got to learn to take advice."

"If I wanted advice, I'd have called one of my advisors." She walked back to the place at the desk where she had previously stood and resumed her post, satisfactorily sipping her coffee.

"You know what? Fine." Martin went to the silver service. Rather than picking it up and stomping out of the room as was more than his right, he poured a cup for himself and joined Daisy at the desk.

This was not an opposition covered in *Warfare and Other Human Relations*. Daisy gaped at him and demanded what he thought he was doing.

"I'm assisting."

"Very funny, Martin. You've done your job and then some. You're dismissed."

"No, no. You could have woken the Steward up if you just wanted coffee. You woke your assistant instead, which means you must need assistance. So, Monitors in the Valley?"

She considered him for a few seconds and then replied, "Monitors in the Valley. I think I've worked out how they got in. Now, this is only something that Basil, Jocelyn, the patrol, and anyone the patrol blabbed to knows: the Monitors were ticking."

"Ticking?"

"Exactly. I don't think they were real men. I think they were clockwork."

Martin conceded that as real men did not tick and clocks were known to, Daisy's conjecture sounded reasonable.

"It makes sense," she continued, "because a clockwork man isn't a living thing, he's made of metal and springs, so the Valley wouldn't even know he was there. But, if they are clockwork, then they represent leaps forward in the technology. Uncle Fitz made a clockwork man before, but he was a toy, not a sentient being who could respond to unscripted speech like these did. So the question is, who made them?"

"Anatamenwar doesn't have that level of technology?"

"They might. But the ability to create talking, thinking clockwork isn't the only factor in determining who. Whoever made them also understands the nature of the Protection."

"Then we can strike me off the list."

Daisy laughed. She set her cup aside and turned to face Martin.

"I'm going to tell one of my stories," she warned, "but listen, because this is important to the problem. A thousand years ago, King Dathúil gave Reginald McNamara the Lost Valley in order to keep his sister, Reggie's bride, safe from warriors, which was a much bigger concern back then than it is now. What you have to understand is that Elves have this connection to the world that humans simply don't. They can actually talk to living things like trees, which is utterly bizarre to watch and makes you wonder how they could ever build homes or eat anything. So when I say he gave the Valley to Reg, what I mean is that he sat down and had a chat with it and asked it if it would be super nice and take care of us for the rest of forever.

"When I turned twenty, I had to stand on the bank of the

river and declare that I was a first-born McNamara and that I claimed the promise to my people. The river rose up and grabbed me, it pulled me in and I had to relax and convince myself I wasn't going to drown. When it spit me back out, the Protection was renewed. The Valley knows me. It knows how I think, what my dreams are, and the type of people I prefer. The land itself judges people when they come near and decides whether or not I would like them. If I would, it lets them pass. If I wouldn't, the land sends them on their way without giving any indication that they were ever anywhere interesting."

Martin was not sure he was buying this, but he was intrigued. "So . . . it's like magic?"

Daisy's eyes lit up. "Is there magic in your world?"

"What? No. Just stories about it."

"Well, there's no magic here either," she sighed. "Just people who are connected to the world and everyone else. But this is the important part—"

"Oh, good."

"—people can't find the Valley if I don't want them to. They just can't. It's not like the Blessed Isle, where you can go there if you have a guide who knows the way. You can walk right up to the river with me, but if I don't like you, I'll keep going and you'll wander around and maybe in a day or two wonder where I went. You can't plot the missing area on a map, because you won't know it's missing. Do you understand what that means?"

Martin thought about this. He shook his head.

"Whoever made the clockwork men knew where to send them. He knows where the Valley is."

She waited for Martin to take up where she left off. Martin waited for her to continue.

"He has to be one of us!" she cried.

"He couldn't have just sent his guys out to search and gotten lucky?"

"No. They knew where they were going. No question. The patrol would have seen them wandering around first. That's why we have a patrol."

Martin crossed his arms. "That is a problem, then."

"Yes. My life really would have been much simpler if you were a genetically engineered super-spy, which is saying something."

The allusion to Daisy's former assessment of his origin naturally brought to mind memories of the day she had chased him around the forest demanding the name of his employer.

"I don't think I know your crew well enough to weigh in on who might be a traitor," he said, reaching into his pocket, "but if you're worried about someone who can make clockwork, I do have this. Maybe it could help." He produced the key he had pulled from the band on the rukh. "Clocks use keys to turn their springs, right? And there's a word on it."

He handed the key to Daisy, who held it by the lamp.

"Mendax," she read. "I don't know that word. Does it mean anything to you?"

"Yes, but my word's not helpful. It's from an ancient Earth poem. It means untruthful. There was a guy in my world who leaked people's secrets, and he used that name as a cover."

"Martin," Daisy said slowly, "how could a situation in your universe that exactly mirrors this situation of mine be not helpful?"

"Well . . . it's Latin. No one knows Latin in this universe, so how could it mean the same thing? It's like Q.E.D. all over again. I only kept the key in the first place as a kind of a souvenir of our trip to Death's Door."

She turned the key over in her hand. "You said 'Mendax' was from an ancient poem?"

"Yeah, by a guy named Horace."

In the dim light Martin did not notice, but Daisy smiled. She handed him back the key.

"You're probably right," she said. "About the coincidence. And the sleep. It's making me paranoid; soon I'll think everyone's a traitor. When the coffee wears off, I'm taking a nap."

"You can go to bed now." Martin grinned. "I made you decaf."

"I beg your pardon?"

"Daisy, it's three in the morning. Even if you hadn't been up for five days, you need to go to sleep. Also: I win."

She put her hands on her hips, but when she spoke she did not seem angry.

"You know I can have you sent to the Brig for this."

"Good. Maybe I can get some sleep there. Off you go, then. I'll wait here 'til you go in your cabin. Sweet dreams."

"You too." Daisy climbed the stairs to her bedroom. Holding the door open, she said, "Martin, in the morning, inform the Steward that if he ever stocks decaffeinated coffee again, he will rue the day."

Martin mimed writing on an invisible clipboard. "Rue. The. Day. Got it."

THERE WAS ONE more act necessary before he could go to bed: Martin had to return the silver service to the kitchen. He decided he could clean it later, and after placing it on its customary shelf, he opened the kitchen door to return to the hall. A figure exited the Enlisted Lounge. Martin held the door so that it was only open a crack and peered into the hall. Astonished, he watched as Basil walked aft and mounted the stairs.

Why would Basil be out this late? he wondered. Or early. Either way. This is Miss Smith's time. Maybe Basil was not as frightened of the old woman as he had led Martin to believe.

When he was sure Basil had reached B Deck and would not be returning, Martin crept across the hall and into the Enlisted Lounge. The lights were off, and there was not a soul to be seen. This made sense, given the hour. What did not make sense was why Basil would be there.

Feeling a little like James Bond, Martin opened the door to the First Officer's Lounge. Nothing sinister attacked or ensnared him.

"You're getting as paranoid as she is," he said to himself. Then he saw it.

On Basil's chair was the book. The book containing the picture of the machine that could open portals to another universe. The book Martin had definitely left in a locked drawer in Daisy's quarters.

⚙ CHAPTER FIFTEEN ⚙

Martin Hathaway's first instinct was to inform Daisy of his suspicions. Halfway up the aft port stairs, however, he thought better of it. Daisy trusted Basil, more so than anyone else on the ship, possibly even more so than anyone else in her life. Not only that, but she also trusted him without ordering his DNA analyzed or any of his effects reconstructed. No matter how he presented his discovery, Daisy was not about to take Martin's word over Basil's. He also realized that he did not have much to accuse Basil of in the first place. For all he knew, Daisy could have given Basil the book while Martin was off-duty. Daisy knew him better than Martin did; surely she was smart enough to put the man capable of reverse engineering a cell phone on the list of clockwork-men-creator suspects without Martin's input.

Returning to the Bachelor's Quarters to think over the problem, he passed Miss Smith at her post in the rotunda. She looked up from her knitting to smile at him. He waved, and then he had an epiphany.

She is about to be humbled in a manner she has never known. She will need you when that time comes and before.

What could possibly be more humbling than discovering the

man she trusted implicitly for five years was plotting against her the whole time? This was it. This was the reason he was here. Martin Hathaway had fallen through Space and Time to protect Daisy McNamara. All he had to do was outsmart the cleverest man he had ever met.

Martin knew he was going to need proof of Basil's guilt. Indisputable proof. Indisputable proof, a blaster, and a rope.

Clearly, to collect what he needed, a degree of subtlety and tact would also be necessary. Martin's first chance to employ both came the next morning at breakfast.

He entered the Galley, picked up his ration, and took his usual chair at the officer's table. Martin was not, technically speaking, an officer, but as the Captain's right-hand man and the *Nephthys*'s newest celebrity, no one gave the technicality any thought. Like most mornings, Martin bestowed upon the table a cheery greeting, which was met with grunts and nods.

"Buzz around the Comm Channels says someone got summoned to Captain's Quarters in the middle of the night." Tony Angelo shook an oatmeal-covered spoon at Martin. "Wouldn't know anything about that, would you, Mr. Hathaway?"

"Captain had a nightmare." Martin shrugged.

Jake Westfield snickered. "If Daisy hadn't saved me single-handedly from a troop of Monitors, sometimes I'd swear we were following a giant two-year-old."

"I suppose you would be an expert on the infantile, Westfield," Basil grumbled. He slapped a hand on Martin's back. "Should have warned you, my boy. As everything we currently see and touch is rightfully hers, the Captain has a warped conception of her due. You'd be wise to negotiate a contract before Daisy starts developing habits. Set your hours now, or you'll wind up without days off later."

"Thanks," Martin replied, casting a sidelong glance at Basil. "Where's . . . um . . . where's Melody this morning?"

"She's the Officer on Watch. Switched shifts with Jocelyn so we could have some time together this afternoon before we reach Tír na nÓg. I have to keep telling myself how sweet that is of her so that I don't dwell on the fact that she woke me at Eight Bells on the Middle Watch getting ready."

"Aww," Jocelyn mocked, "is little Basil-wasil sweepy-weepy?"

"Little Basil-wasil need not dignify you with a reply. But I will have you know I had very little sleep as it was. I would recommend holding off any pushing of my buttons this particular morning."

Martin saw his chance to gather information on the sly.

"You had a late night, then?" he asked, stirring his cereal.

"Very."

"But . . . um . . . Melody . . . she was with you the whole time, I suppose?"

Tony froze with his spoon halfway to his mouth. Jocelyn choked on her orange juice, and both Westfields tried very hard not to giggle.

"Martin." Basil picked up his knife and twirled it between his fingers. "Do I need to create a Cultural Sensitivity Training: Human Edition?"

"What?"

"I am unfamiliar with what constitutes fodder for breakfast table conversation at Eagle's Peak, but I can assure you that on Arnica the nocturnal whereabouts of other people's wives is decidedly taboo, especially when coupled with a discussion of deviations from their sleeping patterns."

"Right. Noted." Martin apologized, but he was not actually sorry. Verbal dexterity aside, Basil had not confirmed that Melody was with him all night. Martin figured he must be counting on his indignation to supply the place of an alibi.

THAT AFTERNOON FOUND Martin in the Control Room training Tony on the use of a cellular phone. Both men were impressed by the handiwork and astonished by its functionality. The team at Fitzgerald House had even managed to reproduce the ability to send text messages. Martin found it difficult, however, to impart to Tony the usefulness of this feature.

"But why," the Communications Officer repeated, "would I want to send a message to someone when I could hear their voice?"

Martin reasoned, "Well, maybe you don't want to hear their voice."

"Why? Don't I like them?"

"Sure. But if you don't want everyone around you to hear the conversation as well, then you could send a text and only you and the recipient will know whatever it is you're talking about."

Tony did not think much of this idea at all. "It's just asking for unofficial communications," he warned the Captain.

"Don't worry, Mr. Angelo." Daisy smiled from the Captain's chair. "Thus far I have no plans for issuing phones to the entire crew. We'll test them on an as-needed basis for patrols and expeditions like today's."

"As you please, Miss," Tony sighed, "but it'll never replace the Comm Channels."

Emma Westfield called over from the helm, "Oh, heavens,

no. The last thing we need is another piece of equipment to carry around all day."

"No, really," Martin protested, "they're very useful. People carry them all the time where I'm from. Even children."

"Even children!" The Communications Officer was aghast. "Your world must be one constant stream of noise! No wonder you invented texting."

"I'm sure we've a lot to learn from Martin's world," Daisy said in her Q.E.D. tone, "as he surely has from ours. Now, Mr. Angelo, I want you to report at Five Bells on the Last Dog Watch every day that we're in the Blessed Isle. Since that is the only Arnican phone in existence, I also trust you will not let it out of your sight."

Tony assured her that her trust in him was justified. Martin wished they all could say the same.

"Yes . . . thank you, Martin," Daisy said, concerned by his cryptic quip. "Now, run along and fetch my father's book from my quarters. We should be in sight of the Blessed Isle within the hour. That is correct, Mr. Westfield?"

"Aye, Miss. We'll have you there well in time for dinner."

"Excellent. And Martin, if you see Basil on the way, inform him of our location."

He exited the Control Room and debated which way to turn. If he did not know that Basil had stolen the book, then he should head directly to Daisy's quarters, but he did know. Basil did not know that he knew, of course, but he would know if Martin succeeded in fetching the book.

"Mr. Hathaway," Daisy called from the Control Room, "are you lost?"

"What? No, just . . . thinking."

"Hmm. Think you could think while you walk?"

"Aye, Captain." Martin took the starboard stairs. He had determined to carry on as if he knew nothing, even if that meant the theft be exposed earlier than he would have liked. He was mulling over possible ways to tell Daisy the book was missing when he reached the top of the stairs and saw a light flashing from the Bow Observation Platform. Creeping forward, Martin peered outside just as Basil turned from the rail and slipped a mirror into his pocket.

He gave a start when he saw Martin's head peering from the doorway and said, "Oh, hello there. I would have thought you'd still be crowing over the wonders of the cellular phone with Tony."

"We've just finished." Martin smiled and did his best to look as vacuous as possible. The dimmer Basil thought him to be, the more likely he was to make a mistake. "Where's Melody? I thought you two had the afternoon together."

"We did. And we do. I was just . . ." Basil eyed Martin. "Well, I might as well tell you. I had to step out and signal to the Isle that we were approaching. I know you have a penchant for dropping in unannounced, but the Fair Folk tend to frown upon such breaches in civility."

"You were signaling to the Elves? But Daisy says we're an hour away. How can they see your message?"

"Oh, they can see it. When it comes to the Fair Folk, anything we can do, they can do better. Except guard wine. We've got them beat on that front."

"Right. But . . . um . . . I thought signaling was Tony's job."

"It is." Basil looked about the hallway and lowered his voice. "Thing is, Martin, Tony's Elvish is atrocious, and the damn snobs at the Isle's watchtower refuse to admit they know Common Tongue. Thus, whenever we make this particular journey, Daisy always distracts Angelo and I handle the announcing of our intent to visit. Now, there's no reason to mention this to Tony or anyone else and risk harming his surprisingly delicate ego, is there?"

"No," Martin grinned, "no reason at all. I better get going. I have to fetch that book Lydia gave Daisy."

"Ah. I say, it just so happens that I'm on my way to my own cabin to bid a final adieu to Melody. Why don't I fetch it and save you the trip?"

"Oh, that's awfully nice of you."

"Think nothing of it. I haven't fetched anything in five days; I almost miss it."

"Thanks, Basil." Martin started down the stairs, then snapped his fingers and said, "I almost forgot to tell you where it is. I left it in the bottom right drawer of Daisy's desk. It's locked, so you'll need my key."

"Of course." Basil laughed. "I keep forgetting you're the man with the clipboard now."

"That's right," Martin said a touch more sternly than he had intended, "I am."

IT IS DIFFICULT to remain bitter and jaded when one is aware that the world is a beautiful and mysterious place, and Martin Hathaway nearly forgot his purpose on Arnica when he saw the shores of the Blessed Isle through the windows of the Lower Observation Deck. The island was immense, stretching far enough into the horizon that Martin wondered if it truly was an island and not a peninsula of some heretofore unmentioned continent. White sands and rocky cliffs marked the shoreline, while atop the latter green trees rose up into the clouds. As long as a place like Tír na nÓg existed, Martin was certain everything would work out for Good in the end.

Daisy seemed to concur. Standing next to Martin and pointing out places of interest as they sailed past, her voice had taken on a breathless quality. At first, Martin thought he would like to hear her talk in such a tone forever, but he began to wish she would not go into quite so much detail when mentioning how King Dathúil's heroics and taste in architecture had shaped the land.

". . . and then he shouted to the Goblin Lord, 'Stand if ye are able!' and he sliced him in half with his sword *Biorach*, given to him in the ancient days by—"

"Now, Captain," Basil called from the upper Control Deck, "you forgot the part where King Dathúil swings across the great hall via the chandelier. That's my favorite."

"Thank you, Mr. Underwood." Daisy backed her story up to fill in the missing anecdote.

"Yes, thank you, Mr. Underwood," Martin called over his shoulder.

"Just want you to have the full Tír na nÓg experience, Mr. Hathaway."

The *Nephthys* pulled alongside a dock built into the side of a high cliff. Martin, Basil, and Daisy made their way to stern and disembarked. Their feet firmly on Blessed soil, they turned and watched as the ship sailed away. Martin held the Elven book and his clipboard in one arm so he could wave to the ship with the other. Suddenly, he realized an inherent problem with the scene in which he participated.

"Wait. They're leaving us here?" Martin asked with a slight panic.

Daisy began walking briskly down the stone path that led away from the dock and into a forest. "The dock is for drop-offs only. The ship is to sail to the far side of the isle and await our return. Now, keep up, Martin. I can't vouch for you if you aren't with me."

"Too much iron holding the ship together," Basil whispered when Martin caught up. "Fair Folk despise the stuff."

"What, like the baobhan sith? But I thought the Fair Folk were . . . well, good."

Basil smirked. "It's odd, isn't it, how very alike Good and Evil appear when one looks closely?"

When the trio had reached the heart of the forest, they came upon two tall, terribly intimidating-looking guards. Daisy made a formal courtesy, then stated her full title and the purpose of their visit.

"You may pass with our blessing, Neòinean," the guard on the right responded, "but for your companions can you vouch-safe?"

"I swear by the setting sun and the rising moon, none in my company harbor any ill-will in their hearts."

Martin snorted. All heads turned toward him.

"Sorry!" he squeaked. "Allergies. No ill-will here."

The guard shook his head, but he allowed them to pass.

They stepped through an archway made by two ancient, in-tertwining trees. Beyond this, Martin saw what he supposed to be a city. It looked as if every building had grown fully formed from the trees themselves, so impeccably designed were their facades. By now Martin had perfected his art of spinning on one foot and jogging to catch up with his companions, and he relied on all his skill to take in the wonder surrounding them.

Daisy paused in the center of the city. Basil and Martin fell into place behind her. Martin was about to ask what they were waiting for when a horn sounded in the distance, announcing *his* arrival.

There was good reason the early peoples of Arnica referred to these immortals as The Fair Folk before adopting the less appreciated colloquial term Elves. Picture, if you are not doing so already, the most attractive person who has ever caused you to forget your own name and taste in movies. Hold that image in your mind, but now make the individual taller, fitter, and back-lit by summer moonlight. Were this vision to have pointed ears and impossibly perfect hair, it would come close to the likeness of the average Arnican Elf.

King Dathúil, of course, was anything but average.

Regally, he descended a staircase directly in front of the party from the *Nephthys*. Though flanked on either side by a bevy of beautiful beings, even Martin had to admit that he was super-good-looking.

Martin cursed under his breath.

Whether or not Basil had heard him, Martin could not be sure, but practically at the same moment Basil leaned toward him and whispered gleefully, "Showtime!"

"Ah! Dear Neòinean," Dathúil said in a voice entirely too masculine for Martin's liking, "you look more like your father every day."

Daisy smiled slightly before assuming an air of quiet dignity and replied, "I thank you for the compliment and your hospitality, King of the High-Hall."

"The Keeper of the Lost Valley is always a welcome . . ." the King began, taking Daisy's hand. He stopped abruptly, having caught sight of Martin. Pushing her aside with less ceremony, he asked, "Daisy, who is your friend?"

Stunned, Daisy decided the best course of action was to continue in the ceremonial manner in which they had previously been engaged.

"This is Martin Hathaway of Eagle's Peak," she announced, "Explorer of Worlds, Rider of the Rukh, and . . . Inventor . . . of the . . . Clipboard."

"And Foe of Mahogany!" Basil added in similar seriousness. Daisy glared at him, but the King did not notice.

Dathúil walked majestically toward Martin, who tried to stand as straight and tall as physically possible. Lightly touching his hand to Martin's cheek, the King cried, "He. Is. Adorable!"

No one knew quite how to respond, least of all Martin. Paying none of them any heed, Dathúil continued, "And so much sweeter than that nasty little man you usually bring with you. You know, the one who makes off with all my best wine."

"I'm still here, actually." Basil waved from behind the Captain.

"Oh. Yes, hello . . . *Aisléir*." Dathúil whispered to an Elf who stood directly behind him, "Double the guard on the King's cellars!"

"Like that will stop me." Basil chuckled.

Dathúil took the book and clipboard from Martin and thrust them at Daisy. Slipping his arm through Martin's, he led the bewildered man up the stair. "Come, Martin Hathaway of Eagle's Peak. Tonight, you shall be the guest of honor at the Hall of

Feasting, and there you will tell me of your journeys through worlds and invention of the clipboard."

The King and his entourage ascended the stair, leaving Daisy open-mouthed in the center of the city. Basil wrapped his arm around her shoulders.

"Daisy," he declared, "this is the best trip ever!"

⚙ CHAPTER SIXTEEN ⚙

As THE GUEST of honor in the Great Hall of Feasting, Martin sat at a raised table on the right hand of the king. Basil and Daisy were seated several feet away at the far left. Martin often glanced their way for reassurance, but Daisy kept her face resolutely turned toward Basil. From him, at least, Martin was given some indication that he was not embarrassing the human race, though the mirth in Basil's eye tended to undercut his nods of encouragement.

Given the choice, Martin Hathaway would greatly have preferred being an undistinguished guest to his current role. He was nervous about saying too little or too much, appearing insufferably vain or endearingly modest, and over- or under-indulging in food and drink. The final fear governed his actions the most, particularly after he took his first sip of the King's private wine. He did not blame Basil for coveting it in the least. To keep from losing his head, Martin employed the time-honored party practice of holding onto one's drink at all times and sipping from it rarely.

One of his fears proved groundless, as King Dathúil seemed predisposed to find everything Martin Hathaway said and did to be unquestionably charming. Having only been on Arnica for six days, Martin's slightly embellished tales of heroics were run through quickly, and the King soon called for a recitation of poetry. Martin was delighted by the stories of warriors and lovers spun by the Fair Folk. He considered making a break for the door, however, when it became clear that he was expected to respond in kind. Sputtering and protesting against the King's entreaties for him to share the poetry of Eagle's Peak, Martin glanced down the table and caught Daisy's eye for the first time that evening. She raised her goblet in salute and inclined her head, clearly interested in what his next move was to be.

He said a silent prayer of thanks for Ms. McGurdey's eleventh-grade English class. If Daisy wanted a bard, she was going to get one. Mustering all his courage and sucking in his gut, Martin rose and addressed the Great Hall of Feasting:

That those whom you call'd fathers did beget you.
Be copy now to men of grosser blood,
And teach them how to war. And you, good yeoman,
Whose limbs were made in England, show us here
The mettle of your pasture; let us swear
That you are worth your breeding; which I doubt not;
For there is none of you so mean and base,
That hath not noble lustre in your eyes.
I see you stand like greyhounds in the slips,
Straining upon the start. The game's afoot:
Follow your spirit, and upon this charge
Cry 'God for Harry, England, and Saint George!'

The silence that followed Martin's recitation was palpable. He bit his lip and tried to make himself as small as physically possible. A single cheer broke out from the back of the hall, followed thereafter by an eruption of applause. Martin grinned, waved, and resumed his seat. He leaned forward to see Daisy's response, but his view was cut off by Dathúil, who was in raptures.

The night progressed in a similar fashion for hours. Martin began to grow tired as well as short on Shakespearean quotations and song lyrics. He looked about to see if Daisy or Basil could give him any indication of the current time or anticipated length of the feast only to discover that they had already vacated the hall. Concerned for Daisy's welfare and miffed that she was not for his, Martin decided it was time to bow out of the festivities. It took several exaggerated yawns and declarations of how exhausted he was before Dathúil took Martin's hint and ordered another Elf to show him to the Guest House.

"Sleep," Dathúil waxed rhapsodically, "that second curse of the mortals, younger brother to the first. How careless of me to forget his hold on your fragile life. I bid you goodnight, Martin Hathaway, and on the morrow we will walk together once more, as you might say, into the breach."

"Night!" Martin replied as he sidled off after his guide.

THE GUEST HOUSE was nestled amongst the top-most branches of a stately oak tree. Judging by its height and the length of time it took to climb the winding stairs to his destination, Martin was of the opinion that this particular tree must have been in existence since the dawn of existence. He was surprised to discover upon reaching the final platform that, while beautiful and masterfully crafted, the Guest House was not overly large. He wondered if they were all to be crammed into three little rooms or if the house was a space just for him. If that were true, he would need to search out Daisy's location before he turned in, to be sure she was safe.

As was often the case with Martin Hathaway, both his surmises were simultaneously correct and erroneous. He opened the Guest House door to reveal a single airy room with an ample sunken bed composing most of the floor. On this Basil and Daisy were sprawled, the former clutching a nearly empty bottle of wine.

Martin jumped to the side as a flash of blue light shot past and burned a mark on the door inches to the left of where his ear had been.

"See, Basil?" Daisy said, tossing her blaster across the bed. "I told you I could do it."

"An excellent shot, Captain, but I can't help but point out that he is still standing."

"What was that for?" Martin demanded.

Daisy staggered to her feet and meandered toward Martin. "I told Basil I could kill you from ten paces at a moment's notice. He says I've had too much wine." She backed Martin up against the wall and held her hand as if to point her blaster in his face, apparently unaware that she no longer carried one. "Well, Martin? What do you think?"

Martin held her at arm's length and said firmly, "I have no doubt you could kill me at the drop of a hat. I also think you may have drunk a little too much tonight."

"That's rich, Mr. Schmoozing-with-the-King-All-Night. You've drunk too much!"

"Me?! I haven't been drinking!"

Basil clapped a hand on each of their shoulders and declared, "We've all been drinking, which means this is the perfect time to unleash my fantastic plan!"

Tossing his head back and laughing maniacally, Basil went out the door.

"Come along, puppies!" he called from the platform. "Follow Uncle Basil!"

Daisy skipped after him, giggling as she went. Martin did not think Basil was incompetent enough to actually reveal himself as a traitor if he were truly intoxicated, but he followed along, just in case.

The trio crossed several bridges between trees before descending to the ground. Basil then led them over a grass-covered hill, admonishing them to keep quiet along the journey, despite the fact that, other than a few giggles from Daisy, none of the party had uttered a sound. On the far side of the hill, they came to a heavy wooden door. This Basil pulled open with great ceremony and not a little effort.

"Basil!" Daisy whispered. "You're lost! These aren't the King's Cellars. This is the Common Storeroom."

"I am not lost," Basil replied as they crept down makeshift stairs that had been cut into the dirt. "I have it on the authority of a singularly sweet kitchen maid that King Super-Good-Looking thinks to outwit me this year by shifting the location of his private reserves. He's doubled the guard on a lot of rot and hopes I shall take the bait!"

Martin was aghast. "A kitchen maid? Is this how you carry on when Melody's not here?"

"Remind me, Martin, to begin keeping a log of how many times you bring my wife up in conversation. It is my current hypothesis that the number is fast approaching one too many."

They reached the bottom of the stair. Basil threw his arm across Daisy, who threw hers across Martin, and the three did their best to become one with the wall behind them.

Peering around the corner, Basil said, "I can see five guards. Perfection. Everyone, shh! Shhh! Shhh!"

"You're the only one talking."

"Shh, Martin especially! Now, Daisy, are you ready?"

Daisy nodded and held her invisible blaster near her face.

"Martin, you adorable man, are you ready?"

"Ready for what? I don't know what the plan is!"

"Precisely!" With that, Basil grabbed Martin and flung him at the guards.

"Hey!" Martin cried as he went sailing into the dirt cellar. One of the guards caught him and demanded to know what this was all about.

"Umm, yes, hello," Martin stammered up at the guard's fair face. "I'm . . . well . . . the thing is . . ."

"You're Martin Hathaway of Eagle's Peak!" another guard exclaimed. "This is the man I was telling you about. The guest in the Great Hall of Feasting."

The first guard expressed his astonishment and admiration. A third inquired if the tale of his poetic prowess was true, and the fourth declared that he saw no reason why they shouldn't have a nice little feast themselves, seeing as how everyone else was partying while they were working. The fifth concurred and fetched a bottle of wine. Offering Martin the first slug, the guard admitted that he considered himself a bit of a fair poet and wondered if Martin would not mind giving his opinion on some of his work.

Martin sat down on a proffered wooden box and endeavored to make himself as agreeable as possible. Out of the corner of his eye, he caught sight of Basil and Daisy creeping past, and later they emerged rolling a barrel each down a side tunnel. Martin decided he would stay for fifteen minutes or until the bottle was empty, whichever occurred first.

FORTY MINUTES LATER, Martin stumbled up the stairs and back out into the cool night air. Shutting the door on the laughter of the guards, he looked around and realized his grave error. He had no idea where Daisy and Basil had gone. He conjectured they would have made for the ship with their ill-gotten gains, but knowing their destination got him no closer to locating it. Basil could have caused Daisy any number of harms while he had been cavorting, and Martin had no clue where to search for her if rescue was needed. Cursing his failed post and holding his head, Martin spun in place, desperate for the slightest sign of where to go.

Fortune smiled upon him, however, as he was not only given a slight sign but his very object herself. Daisy's auburn head appeared over the grass-covered hill. Martin ran to her, exclaiming his gratitude and relief.

"S'all right, Martin." Daisy laughed when he hugged her. "I wasn't going to leave you out here on your own. I know how you are with new places." She took his arm and led him back toward the Guest House.

"It's not me I was worried about," Martin explained as they stumbled along their way. "I don't think it was a good idea, running off alone with Basil like that."

"But I run off alone with Basil like that practically every day. Why shouldn't I now?"

"Well . . . you two've been drinking."

"So have we. Should I not be running off with you? Or is it ok since we're walking?"

Martin gave up. She would not understand him without more information, and he knew it was not time for that yet. "Well, I'm glad you're safe anyway."

They reached the Guest House without incident. Daisy opened the door, took a seat, and removed her boots. Martin was ready to collapse, but looking about, he was struck by two new problems. He decided to address the less awkward first.

"Where is Basil?"

"He went back to the ship. We called Tony. He met us in the woods, and the two of them rolled the barrels back."

"What?! He's not staying with us? What was all that about today then? The switching watch shifts and afternoons together if he's just going back to Melody tonight?!"

"Well, I'm not supposed to know he sneaks back to the ship whenever we're on missions. I do, of course. And I doubly do tonight since I saw him off, but I usually pretend I don't know. I told you that one time we were away four days that he was a nightmare. Never doing that again. Don't worry, he'll be back before you're up."

"Why don't we all sleep on the ship?"

"That would be rude to our hosts. And a lot of walking."

"But . . . Basil . . ." he sputtered.

"Martin, first you were upset that I was with Basil. Are you now upset that I am not?"

"Well . . . no. Maybe. It's just . . ."

Daisy smiled. "If your problem is because we have one sleeping area, I understand. I am not sure that the addition of Basil would have made it more comfortable, but here we are. I suppose you're welcome to sneak back and forth as well, but it's very late. And I don't think you'll make it, for that matter."

The sleeping arrangements were not why Martin thought Basil should not be on the ship unsupervised, but it was the second problem he had foreseen. He did not mind discussing it.

"Why the one room?" he asked. "Especially if they thought we were three people."

"Elves don't sleep," she explained as she unpinned her hair, sending soft curls tumbling down her back. "And they have a very communal sort of lifestyle. This is the only human bedroom they built. Basil and I inquired about separate rooms during our first visit, and we were told we should have made our requests for special accommodations known eight hundred years ago.

"But don't worry," she continued, "you're safe with me. At least, you're safe on the condition you don't give me any reason to grievously injure you. And sleeping like you did at my Uncle's house would qualify as more than enough reason."

Daisy crossed the room. Along the back wall hung a tapestry depicting the meeting of Reginald and Galedlothia. Next to this hung a gold cord. Daisy pulled it, and the ceiling over the sunken bed retracted.

"Anyway," she sighed, "you wouldn't want to miss this."

Daisy flopped onto the bed and looked up at the opening in the ceiling. Cautiously, Martin joined her. He was delighted that he did.

Nothing obstructed their view of the stars. No city lights, no cloud cover, no tree branches, and, obviously, no ceiling got in the way. The vast expanse of the universe lay out before them, and it was magnificent.

"I've never seen so many stars." Martin sighed. "Well, maybe when I was younger. My friend Dave and I went to this camp every year. We stayed in cabins, but once a week this awesome counselor would let us sleep outside by the campfire. He told us all the stories of the constellations. I remember them all; it was how I first got into History. My favorite one . . ."

Martin stopped talking and sat up. Daisy sensed a change in him.

"Is something wrong?" she asked.

"The stars!" Martin pointed out the hole in the ceiling. "The stars are wrong! I can't find any of the constellations. Not even the Big Dipper. Kids can find the Big Dipper!"

Daisy rose and took his hand. "Martin, this isn't your world. The stars are in different places. There may even be a different number of them."

This was true, but it was not reassuring. Martin fell on his back, a tear in his eye. Daisy laid her head on his chest and held him, hoping as humans do that everything can be made better with warmth.

"I guess," Martin said eventually, "it's just been kind of a game until now. Running around, getting attacked by things, fetching coffee. But it really is true. I'm not dreaming. I'm not at home. I'm nowhere I ever could have thought about being."

Daisy held him tighter. Softly, yet with all the assurance only an airship captain can offer, she promised, "I will get you home if it is in my power. If the machine is real, I will find it or Basil and Jocelyn will build it. But I will get you back home, Martin.

Back where the stars are right again."

They lay together in silence. Martin ran his hand through Daisy's hair as he stared up at the stars. They were not right, but they were still beautiful.

"Daisy?"

She did not answer. The wine and the hour must have finally taken their toll. Believing her to have fallen asleep, Martin took a risk and kissed her forehead.

"I'll miss you," he whispered.

MARTIN'S BREATHING FELL into a soft and regular pattern. Daisy opened her eyes. Carefully lifting his arm, she slid away from the sleeping Martin and climbed out of the bed. She walked out onto the platform and took a seat on a wicker lounge. She needed to think this through. It hardly seemed possible, but the situation had become more complicated.

⚙ CHAPTER SEVENTEEN ⚙

MARTIN AWOKE AND rubbed his eyes. Having consumed the equivalent of an entire bottle of the King's second-best wine with the cellar guards, he had expected to wake with at least a headache and more likely cursing the day he was born. However, as he stretched and got his bearings, Martin discovered that he felt more refreshed than he could remember having been in quite some time. He rolled over to remark on how wonderfully he had slept to Daisy, but it was not the Captain he found reposing beside him.

"Good Morning, Martin, you minx," was Basil's greeting. "Decided to join the world of the living again, I see."

Martin sprang upright, stumbled out of the bed, got his foot tangled in the sheets, and subsequently crashed onto the wood floor. Along his way, he demanded of Basil, "Where's Daisy? What have you done with her?"

"Good god, man. You are the only person I have ever met who can fall out of a sunken bed. I'd offer you some coffee, but I'm not certain your nerves are up for it."

"Are you going to tell me where she is?!"

"I have no idea where Daisy is. She said something about taking stock of her wasted hopes and dreams and wandered off after breakfast. I'm sure she's fine."

"What?!"

"I can see you are not yet sufficiently awake for a good-natured ribbing. Fair enough. The Captain's gone for a walk to"—Basil paused to draw a notebook out of his breast pocket and flip through its pages. Having found the one he sought, he continued—"quote, 'think things through' and 'seek the wisdom of the Isle.' She left orders for you, if you think you can handle them without crumbling into a ball of nervous goo."

Martin relaxed and inquired after his orders. It was explained that, as Martin was clearly the King's favorite, the task of asking Dathúil to translate the Ancient Elvish had fallen to him.

"And you can get right on that," Basil said, handing him a letter written in what Martin assumed was Elvish, "as you have be invited to a private breakfast with the King. Lucky sot. We were only delivered a tray of assorted muffins. They must have noticed the missing wine. Elves excel in passive-aggression."

Martin hesitated. "Just me?"

"Just you," Basil affirmed. "Well, I am assuming this letter is for you, as it is addressed to 'Aoibhinn.' Congratulations, by the way. You have your first hero name. Daisy has thirty-five, but she's been at this longer than you. I'm sure you'll catch up in no time."

"What . . . um . . . what does it mean? *Aoibhinn?*"

"It means we need to get you shaved and freshened up sometime before King Super-Good-Looking decides to serve lunch."

As one might imagine, the next few days were a near constant trial for our hero. Each day Martin Hathaway endeavored to interest King Dathúil in Daisy's book of ancient lore. With the skill of Scheherazade, each day Dathúil managed to put off

Martin's inquiries with promises for tomorrow. There always seemed to be far too many things to be done. There were walks to be taken, portraits to be painted, hunts to be ridden, and skills to be taught before Martin could participate in many of these extremely important activities. Each evening, of course, there were feasts to preside over and dances to lead. Martin returned to the Guest House each night thoroughly exhausted, mildly intoxicated, and absolutely defeated.

Each night, however, made the misadventures of the day more than worth the effort. After Basil crept away for the ship, Martin and Daisy would awake from their feigned sleep, pop open another bottle of wine, and pull back the ceiling. Daisy pointed out constellations and told Martin the stories each of the known cultures of Arnica had devised. In return, Martin related the tales of the stars from his own world. He made up a few of his own as well, knowing the sort of story that would put a smile on Daisy's face.

As it is for most mortals, the visit to the Blessed Isle was a wonderful and confusing time for Martin Hathaway. The dual nature of his experience is perhaps best summarized by the fact that each night he fell asleep beside Daisy McNamara and each morning he awoke to Basil Underwood.

ALAS, BUT ALL weird things must come to an end. On the afternoon of their fifth day in Tír na nÓg, Basil was walking through the King's Zen Garden carrying two goblets of wine when he noticed Daisy sitting upon a large, flat rock. King Dathúil had once explained at some length that the rock in question symbolized the Great Tree of Life, but Basil could not remember why.

As he pondered this horticultural conundrum, Daisy looked up from her musings and smiled weakly.

"That's just what I need," she said, gesturing to the second goblet. "Thank you, Basil."

Basil thought of three excuses to get him out of the garden plus two goblets and minus a chat about feelings, but the angst in Daisy's eye ruled his tongue. Taking a seat beside her on the Great Rock of Figurative Life, he handed Daisy the second goblet.

"How did you know I was out here?" she asked after a refreshing sip.

"I didn't. These Elven goblets only come in one size and the wine is quite delicious."

"Should have known. Thanks all the more for the sacrifice, then."

"My pleasure, Captain." Basil proceeded to draw intricate spiral patterns in the gravel with his toe, perfectly happy to wait for Daisy to bring up whatever ludicrous triviality was bothering her today. He had concluded that the spirals should symbolize the inherent struggle between Man and Art when Daisy launched into a tirade about the amount of time Martin had been spending with King Dathúil.

". . . And the really annoying part," Daisy made vehement gestures as she spoke, causing the waves of wine in her goblet to rise to what Basil thought to be alarming heights, "is that Martin doesn't do any of the things Dathúil likes to do. I had to teach him how to ride a horse and dance the Venegasia Revolute—"

"Not to correct you in the middle of your zeal, Daisy, but I seem to recall in some detail that I taught him the Revolute."

"Yes, thank you. Point is: you think it would be simple for him to say, 'Oh, shoot, I don't know the first thing about archery and will probably injure anyone who tries to teach me, so why don't we spend the afternoon reading this very interesting book instead?' But noooo, 'Dathúil and I are going shooting' and 'Dathúil and I are weaving tapestries' and 'Dathúil and I—'"

Basil held up his hand. "If I could interrupt you one more time, Daisy, would you mind clarifying something for me?"

"What?" the Captain snapped, not suffering interruption lightly.

"Are you jealous *of* or *for* Martin? Because I feel two very different conversations hinge on your preposition of choice."

"Don't be ridiculous. I'm neither jealous of nor for anyone."

"Ah. And we're sitting in the Zen Garden fuming about two men because . . . ?"

"Because of the Valley."

"The Valley." Basil pressed his fingers together and nodded, his expression conveying a calculated mixture of friendly support and complete disbelief.

"We're running out of time, Basil! We need at least two days to get back to the Valley before the 'Monitors' come and claim the 'Citizen.' And that's with perfect weather conditions and nothing attacking us, and how often do those happen together?"

"Not very, I'll concede." Basil set his empty goblet down and took Daisy's full one from her hand. Attempting a reassuring smile, he said, "I wouldn't worry too much about the further prolonging of our voyage, Captain. Do you know—not from experience, of course, but academically—how long the Elvish courtship period lasts? If you need a hint, you could ask the adorable man running toward us as we speak."

Daisy looked in the direction where Basil pointed. Sure enough, there came Martin running at top speed and flailing his arms to get their attention.

"Guys," he doubled over and panted for air upon reaching them, "we've got to go. Now."

"Five days precisely," Basil said with satisfaction. "And it appears Martin turned him down. Pity. I was looking forward to seeing you in a tiara, Aoibhinn."

"It's not funny. We've really got to go."

An arrow whizzed past Martin's head and stuck firmly into a non-symbolic tree. A barrage of shots then rained down upon them like a storm of freakishly large mosquitoes.

"Now!" Martin cried and took off for the woods. "Let's go! Keep up!"

Daisy and Basil had the instincts and reflexes of rabbits when it came to running from danger. In no time, they had caught up with and overtaken the fleeing Martin Hathaway. Martin did not resent being outrun by a girl; he had survived Mr. Krasinski's eighth-grade gym class with a progressive and sensitive nature. To be outrun by a girl wearing a full skirt and high-heeled boots in the woods, however, was a bit embarrassing. He reminded himself that Daisy had not been running for her life for the past ten minutes, and his self-esteem was moderately salvaged.

"Tony! Tony!" Daisy whipped Martin's cell phone from her pocket as they ran and dialed the *Nephthys*. "We're under fire! Get the ship in the air and lower the cargo sling! Don't bother with the dock; we're coming to you."

"Under fire!? What happened, Captain? It wasn't—"

"NOW, MR. ANGELO!"

"Aye, aye. Now it is. Now is good. I'm on it. Tony out."

Hundreds of Elves leapt through the treetops after the runners, pausing only seconds to take aim before firing and continuing pursuit. The trio ran serpentine to avoid arrows, ravines, and the occasional fallen tree.

"They must still like you, Martin," Basil called over his shoulder. "They're missing!"

An arrow zipped past Martin's left arm, tearing his sweater and leaving a shallow cut.

"This is missing?!" he cried.

"Oh, yes. We should all be dead by now. Elves, you see, have impeccable eyesight. They can even—"

"BASIL!" Daisy interrupted. "SHUT UP!"

Not one easily silenced by danger or the Captain, Basil merely switched subjects.

"Anyway, they're clearly not mad enough to want to kill us. Martin, are you sure you don't want to go back and reconcile? You'd look divine in a robe."

"NO, I don't want to reconcile!"

"I'm just wondering if you're really considering all your options. Did you see the King's library? You could crash into it anytime you wanted!"

"BASIL . . . " Daisy began, but suddenly she was struck by a horrifying thought. "Library! Martin, do you have the book?!"

"Look," Martin panted. "I was very firm about Dathúil reading the book today. He told me to bring it to his private chamber. Now we're running. Any more questions?!"

"You left it?! We have to go back!"

"NO, WE DON'T!"

"I have to take Martin's side on this one, Daisy," Basil shouted as an arrow grazed his knee. "I'm sure Super-Good-Looking will leave Martin's things in a box on the dock in a couple weeks. He never was particularly sentimental. Remember that watercolor you gave him?"

Daisy did not have time to renew her request for Basil's silence, as the *Nephthys* rose into sight. Martin had never been so relieved to see a red balloon in his life. The appearance of the ship was enough to give him a second wind, and he matched pace with his two companions. The wind was subsequently knocked out of him, however, when Martin realized two very important factors in the success of their escape.

"It's moving!" he cried. "And that's a cliff!"

"Spot on, Martin! Daisy, our little fugitive is going to need flanking!"

The *Nephthys*, in the previous five days of peace, had been anchored on the shores of a beach, and the crew had enjoyed their stay immensely. After Daisy's call there had been a panic in getting all the hands and beach equipment back on board, which meant the massive ship had only just begun its ascent to the skies. Martin did not know it at the time, but this was a lucky break, as the cargo sling to which he was about to leap was below him. Catching a moving object on your way down is much simpler than grabbing one on its way up, as anyone who has ever leapt off a cliff to escape heartbroken Elves can attest.

All Martin knew at the time, unfortunately, was that he was running headlong off a cliff with Basil and Daisy holding fast to his arms in case he changed his mind.

"Get ready to jump, Martin!" Daisy shouted on his right as

they neared the edge of the cliff. "On my mark—"

On his left, Martin could hear Basil's disparaging report, "Captain, I hate to bother you with Mathematics at a time like this—"

"One—"

"—but given our current horizontal distance and the inclination angle of the ship—"

"Two—"

"—to reach optimal trajectory we need to be running at a rate of—"

"Three! Jump!"

They jumped. The trio went sailing through the air, Daisy and Basil's free arms making wide and wild circles. Martin instinctively clung to them and shut his eyes. The Elven archers ceased their volley, intrigued as to whether or not the mortals would make their target.

Basil's math, once again, was correct. Their speed, direction, and force of their jump were not enough to send them safely into the cargo sling. Nonetheless, all factors were sufficient to send them near enough for Basil and Daisy to catch hold of it. Daisy gave out a sharp cry as Martin's weight pulled down on her arm, but she was able to hang on to him. Straining, Basil lifted Martin until he could grab a hold likewise and haul himself to safety.

As Andrews raised the cargo sling inside the bowels of the *Nephthys*, he could hear the laughter of three people who knew how wonderful it was to be alive.

Martin and Basil hopped out of the cargo sling onto the storage room's retractable floor. Heartily thanking Martin for the most fun he had ever had in the Blessed Isle, Basil strode toward Andrews to describe their most recent escape from the hands of Death. Martin turned to see if Daisy was still happy to be alive or if she had passed over to being angry at the loss of the book. As it happened, she was neither. She slid gingerly out of the sling, which was not like the graceful and energetic Captain McNamara that Martin knew. When she looked up at him, Martin saw that her eyes were wet, and not with tears of joy.

"Daisy, what's . . ." Martin began, but then he noticed the odd manner in which Daisy held her left arm. "Oh my God, I broke you!"

She tried to protest that everything was fine, but he did not hear her. Scooping Daisy up in his arms, Martin Hathaway dashed off for Sick Bay.

"If you'll pardon the liberty, Mr. Underwood," Andrews pointed toward the doorway recently vacated by Martin and Daisy, "it looks like someone's taking over your job. Injuring the Captain and fretting? Not much left for you to do, Sir."

Basil held his chin in a most dignified manner and tutted, "I have no idea to what you could possibly be referring. Any overlaps of labor between myself and Martin are purely the result of my excellent personnel training skills. Now, if you'll excuse me, I think I'll meander down to Sick Bay and verify that the Captain arrived with her remaining limbs in place."

"I'll ring Dr. Underwood and let her know to put the kettle on," Andrews called after Basil's rapidly retreating figure.

It was a very good thing that Melody was in the habit of keeping the Sick Bay door open, since Martin made no attempt to check his speed as he burst through the entrance.

He flung Daisy down onto an examination table and cried, "She's hurt! She's hurt! Arms don't look like that! Why does it look like that?!" and continued to do so as Melody rushed over to determine why Daisy's arm looked like that and how best to make it stop looking like that. She nodded to one of the medical staff, who waved his arms frantically in the air and jumped up and down.

"Mr. Hathaway! Mr. Hathaway!" he yelled.

Reluctantly, Martin acknowledged him. "WHAT?!"

"I'm a distraction!"

Martin heard a cracking sound of bone against bone; Daisy screamed.

"All better!" Melody sang. "You can look now, Martin."

It was all better. Daisy lay with her eyes closed, but the relief on her face was evident.

"Did you fix her, darling?" Basil inquired as he nonchalantly ceased running and helped himself to some tea from the kettle over what looked and functioned very much like a Bunsen burner. Melody replied in the affirmative and sent the other two medical staff to examine various injuries Basil and Martin had acquired during their flight from the Elves.

Martin brushed his attendee aside with the assertion that there was nothing wrong with him. Taking her right hand, he said, "God, Daisy, I am so sorry."

"It's ok, Martin." Daisy managed a smile. "This is why we have a Sick Bay."

Thirty-eight heads gathered outside the door. Melody suggested it might be best if the two medical staff go disperse the crowd and spread the word that the party from the Blessed Isle was all alive and well. Suggestions from Dr. Underwood carrying the same weight as direct orders, the two exited, pulling the Sick Bay door shut behind them.

"Mustn't be too hard on yourself, my boy," Basil said over the din of voices in the hall. "I once gave the Captain a concussion while playing chess with the Anatamenwarian Ambassador. Best to think of these things as occupational hazards."

Martin was still not at ease. "But I messed everything up. The whole mission failed because of me."

"Oh, Martin, don't be so maudlin," Basil admonished. "The whole mission was a joy because of you! And if you're upset about losing the book, there's no need. I took the liberty of copying the relevant bits before we left. Darling, you don't happen to have the larger notebook around here, do you?"

Melody did, and retrieved it from one of the glass cabinets. Martin noted that it was the same notebook in which Basil had recorded the substance of his job interview. Concern for Daisy gave way slightly to interest in how Basil was going to explain his procurement of the book.

"You copied it?" Daisy asked while Basil showed her the corresponding pages.

"Yes. As you had placed your new Assistant in charge of its keeping, I thought it prudent to make sure we had a backup in case of its loss. Someone has to think of these things."

Martin was flabbergasted. "You decided I was going to leave the book behind in the King's private chamber before we even landed?"

"Well, no. I did not anticipate the exact wonderfulness of your misplacing the book, only its inevitability."

"Now just a minute—"

Daisy interrupted, "It doesn't matter why he did it, Martin.

Nor does it matter that he did. You copied it in the Ancient Elvish, Basil. We still can't read it."

Busy immobilizing Daisy's relocated shoulder, Melody interjected, "Basil reads Ancient Elvish. Don't you, darling?"

"It is one of my many skills, yes."

As one, Daisy and Martin cried, "Wait. What?!"

"Why didn't I know this?" Daisy demanded.

"Well," Basil reasoned, sipping his tea, "the clichéd answer is that you never asked. But it's closer to the truth to say I never told you."

Daisy sat up, much to Melody's dismay. "Five years," she said. "Five years we've been running off to Tír na nÓg and not once did you bother to mention that the trip was unnecessary?"

"I'd hardly say 'unnecessary.' It always made you so happy, Captain. And need I cite the particular deliciousness of the wine?"

Daisy made an exasperated sigh and allowed Melody to guide her back down. The latter informed them that she was going to give the Captain a mild sedative, as keeping her still for the next few hours would likely prove a fruitless effort otherwise. She walked back to her workbench and readied a syringe.

"You better report, Basil, while I can still process it," Daisy said with resignation.

Setting aside his tea, clicking his heels, and clasping his hands behind his back, Basil delivered his report. According to the book, Svadilfari was an actual historical figure. The picture of his machine was, in fact, a crude blueprint sketched by his Elven biographer. From the specifications, Basil was able to learn that the machine operated by altering the frequency and patterns with which the various strings that make up elementary particles oscillate, thus changing the fabric of reality. By controlling oscillations, Svadilfari was able to create points where non-interacting dimensions met.

"And this means?" Daisy asked as Melody delivered the sedative.

"It means the machine could open a portal between Martin's world and ours, and anyone who was skilled enough in its use could specify when, where, and for what duration the portal opened."

"Someone like you?" Martin inquired, slyly.

"Yes. I flatter myself I could get the knack of running any piece of equipment within a few hours. There was, I should mention, another implication of the machine, which is likely why your Scop did not want to discuss the matter."

Basil informed them that, according to the tale, it was the Elves, and not Svadilfari's overuse of the machine, that brought about his demise. If used incorrectly or too frequently, the Fair Folk theorized that it was possible the strings could forever change their oscillations and impart the changes to others in a chain reaction that would result in the ripping apart the fabric of Space and Time and, thus, destroy the universe. Rather than run the risk, the Elves turned the machine on Svadilfari, using the strings that comprised his body to open a final portal.

"A MACHINE EXISTS THAT CAN DESTROY THE UNIVERSE AND YOU WERE GOING TO TELL US ABOUT IT WHEN?"

"Darling, are you sure you gave the Captain the proper dose? She doesn't appear particularly sedated to me." Basil deposited the notebook in a pocket inside his jacket. "Of course, I was going to tell you in due time, Daisy. But, as we were headed to the Isle anyway, it seemed to me that, if the universe were going to be destroyed, I damn well wanted some decent wine first."

Daisy could hardly argue with such sound logic. "Excellent work, Basil," she said, a faraway tone creeping into her voice. "You've got control. Relieve Tony and tell the Westfields to take us home."

She looked to Martin and squeezed his hand.

"Martin?"

"Yes, Daisy?"

"I just want you to know . . . you would have . . . looked lovely . . . in a . . . tiara."

"And . . . Captain out!" Basil laughed as Daisy succumbed to the effects of the sedative. He exited to head for the Control Room, but not before slipping the small notebook he carried in his breast pocket into Melody's hand.

Martin pretended to continue to fuss over Daisy so the couple would not realize that he had noticed their exchange. He had seen Basil write in that notebook at least once a day, usually after Daisy said or did something. Basil had even directly quoted the Captain from that notebook to Martin not days before. If he was chronicling Daisy's command, why would the CMO need the information? Melody had made it clear her role on the ship had nothing to do with the missions, and she liked it that way. For that matter, it also did not make sense to Martin why Melody would have the notebook in which Basil had recorded their interview and the contents of the Elvish book. It was possible that he had given it to her for safekeeping while they were on the Isle, but Basil did not strike Martin as the sort of person who trusted other people with his things, even if that person was his wife.

Martin was deep in thought when Melody addressed him.

"Would you like some tea, Martin? You've got at least two hours off, by my calculations."

He thanked her and happily accepted.

Melody smiled as she handed Martin his cup. "Isn't it funny how things come full circle?"

"What do you mean?"

"Oh, I was just thinking that the first time I saw you, you were lying down to recover from falling off a cliff, and Daisy was sitting beside you. Now you're sitting beside her in just the same way, only she jumped off a cliff and is actually injured. Maybe it's not exactly full circle, but I still think it's very sweet."

Martin grinned and was about to suggest they run a scan of her brain for old time's sake when he recalled a different scene from his first day in the Valley.

Standard protocol. You may have been carrying weapons or dispatches.

Dispatches! He thought. *That's how these people think! That's what's in the notebooks! Basil's recording Daisy's movements and using Melody to send out dispatches.*

He could hardly believe that someone as lovely as Melody was in on the betrayal as well. Perhaps she did not fully understand her husband's plan. Martin certainly did not. He decided then and there, however, that it did not matter. The universe was at stake, and he had come to be fond of this one. Basil would have to be dealt with, and Martin Hathaway could think of no better time to do so than while Daisy McNamara was unconscious.

⚙ CHAPTER EIGHTEEN ⚙

EVEN THOUGH he had abandoned his quest for indisputable proof, Martin Hathaway's plan still required a blaster and rope. The first he obtained from Daisy's belt while Melody had turned from him, chatting away and cleaning out the syringe and teacups. He slid the blaster in the back of his pants the way he had seen done in action movies. Fairly certain a blaster was noticeable even when concealed thusly, Martin bid adieu to Melody and exited Sick Bay with his back to the wall.

Martin located two coils of rope in Port Storage next to the parachutes and slung these over his shoulders. He devised several cover stories in case anyone in the hall wanted to know why he needed so much rope, but everyone he ran into merely smiled and greeted him with a polite, "Afternoon, Mr. Hathaway" or "Good to see you back on board, Martin," depending on their degree of acquaintance.

These people are all crazy, Martin thought to himself as he lugged the coils of rope into the Enlisted Lounge. Nothing the least bit strange about a man with a blaster in his pants carrying around a bunch of rope. No wonder Basil got away with spying for so long.

Shutting himself inside the First Officer's Lounge, Martin

hid the rope behind Basil's chair. He then crossed the room and squatted down, relying on several stacks of books as cover. He held Daisy's blaster at the ready. It was only a matter of time, now.

Nearly an hour later, his legs and back aching, Martin began to wonder if it might not have been a better plan to simply head to the Control Room and shoot Basil in front of everyone. The element of surprise would still be on his side, as he was fairly certain not even Basil would have seen a direct assault like that coming.

"Afternoon, Mr. Underwood," Martin heard a voice in the Enlisted Lounge saying. "Had a merry trip to the Isle, did you?"

"The merriest," Basil's baritone confirmed. This was it. Basil would not stay long for conversation in the other room. Martin's palms began to sweat, but he held firm to the blaster and his resolve.

The door handle turned, and Basil entered. Martin waited until he heard the sound of the door click closed, and then he rose. Basil flopped into his chair and lit a lamp. He picked up a book and settled in. Sensing something not quite right, Basil looked up.

Martin fired.

WHEN BASIL CAME to, his entire body tingled, and not in a manner that was in the least bit pleasant. His head lolled back against his chair. He blinked his eyes and tried to remember where he was and what he had been doing before this annoying interruption.

"Hello, Mr. Underwood."

Basil forced his head to look forward. There sat Martin Hathaway on a pile of his favorite books, holding a blaster.

"Now it's time that you and I had a talk, man to man," Martin said in an uncharacteristically intimidating tone.

Basil blinked again. He tried to move his arms, only to discover that he was firmly tied to his chair.

"Good God!" he exclaimed, the implications of the scene washing over him. "You really are a spy! Daisy's dramatic delusions were spot on for once!"

"Yes, now . . . wait. What?"

"I have to admit, Martin—if that is your real name—this is one clever trick. Bypassing the protection unnoticed, flinging yourself through the skylight, and carrying on as if you were a complete dunce for nearly two weeks. Remind me to shake your hand before you're tortured and imprisoned."

The interrogation was not going exactly as Martin had planned. Then again, Basil was very crafty. Martin Hathaway was not about to let him talk his way out of this.

"I'm not going to be tortured and imprisoned! You're the one who's going to be tortured and imprisoned!"

"Nooo . . . I'm going to be rescued and commended, as I caught the spy." Basil tried to slip his hands out of the knots but found they were quite possibly the best he had ever been restrained by. At least he was tied to his favorite chair instead of something uncomfortable, like Daisy. As he was a full foot taller than her, Basil imagined such a confinement would wreak havoc on his back.

"Granted," Basil continued, "I caught you in a roundabout way. But no matter. All I have to do is keep you talking until we're missed. So, Martin, tell me all about your evil plan."

"No. Stop it. I'm not the spy, and you know it."

"You're not a spy?"

"Of course not!"

"Hmm." Basil squirmed and wriggled, but he still could not loose the bonds. "This isn't about Melody, is it? I hate to be the one to break your fragile heart, Martin, but she gives lollipops to everyone. You aren't special."

"What? No, I don't care about the lollipops. Quit pretending like you don't know what's going on!"

"Ok. Not Melody. Are you sure? You do talk about her an awful lot."

"Not Melody!"

"Ah. Is this about the Captain, then? Because I can assure you I am no threat to you. I have never, not even in my darkest nightmares, thought about going there. In fact . . ."

Basil's face contorted in horror. He began to sweat, and Martin was afraid he might break loose utilizing some inhuman strength.

"OH GOD!" Basil cried. "IT'S IN MY HEAD! GET IT OUT! GET IT OUT!"

"Get what out?!"

"DAISY! DATING DAISY! OH GOD, WHY?!"

Martin sprang forward and shook Basil by the shoulders.

"Basil!" he shouted. "It's ok! You never dated Daisy!"

"ARE YOU SURE?!"

"Positive! You weren't single long enough!"

"Oh, thank god." Basil collapsed against the chair. "You, Martin, are a master of psychological torture. Are you sure you aren't a spy?"

"We both know I'm not."

"Hmm. Would you mind if I inquired as to what this is all about then? Because, quite frankly, I'm out of ideas. And while I'm sure you're enjoying your psychotic little game, I certainly am not."

Martin sat back on the stack of books. Basil grimaced.

"Daisy knows," Martin said.

"Knows?"

"She knows the person who built the clockwork men knows where the Valley is. But she doesn't know what you and I know, does she?"

Basil squinted at Martin, mentally graphing his previous sentences to make sense of them. Slowly, it dawned on him.

"Martin, you rabid Newfoundland! You think I'm a traitor!"

"I know you're the traitor."

"I knew it would be a mistake issuing you a blaster." Basil required only a moment to curse his unfailing rightness before realizing an important detail. "Wait a phoenix's flight, I didn't issue you a blaster!"

"You might have underestimated me, Basil, but I've been watching you. I saw you sending signals to someone using that mirror, and I'm not stupid enough to have swallowed your lies."

The First Officer groaned. "Oh for the love of . . . Martin, they weren't lies. Ask Daisy. Tony's Elvish really is quite atrocious."

"Fine. Cling to your little story. It doesn't matter. You're the only one on the ship capable of building the clockwork men."

"Well, thank you for your faith in me, Martin, but—"

"And you resent Daisy's command."

"Now, see here—"

"And you're the only one she trusts enough never to suspect

anything."

"Ok, that one's probably true—"

"And you knew I wasn't a spy. Why? Because you knew who the spy was!"

"Now you're just being silly!"

"And you stole the book!"

"I already explained that one!"

"Yes," Martin rose, triumphant. "But you don't know that I saw you. Why were you out so late, Basil? If you were innocently working, why not do so in your quarters, instead of running the risk of meeting Miss Smith?"

Basil sighed. "It's all very simple, Martin. Melody had switched to the Morning Watch and needed her sleep. It wouldn't be very gracious of me to keep a lamp burning in our cabin all night, would it? I came down here to work and went straight to bed when I had finished."

"Oh, of course. I'm sorry. I forgot what a caring and considerate husband you are."

"Now, see? That's what I was talking about. Are you sure this isn't some misguided way of coping with your feelings for my wife?"

"I don't have feelings for your wife!"

"Of course you don't, Martin. You just shot me and tied me to a chair because I stayed away from our cabin for six hours."

Martin had enough. He aimed the blaster at Basil's head.

"I shot you because you're trying to destroy Daisy. And I can prove it." He reached into Basil's jacket and pulled out the notebook. "You're carrying dispatches."

Basil turned white.

"Ah," he squeaked. "You . . . you don't want to read that."

"Oh, no? Why not?"

"Well . . . look, it's not what you think."

"I think it's exactly what I think. Why don't I read it right now and we'll find out whose hypothesis is correct. Science, Basil!"

Basil jumped frantically in the chair, desperate to get loose. "These are surprisingly well-done knots, Martin."

"Thank you. I went to camp."

"Look here, my boy," Basil gave in. "You caught me. I'm the traitor. Why don't you go see if Daisy's up and tell her? You can leave the dispatches here until you get back."

"Oh, right. You really must think I'm stupid, Basil."

Martin flipped open the notebook. The first passage he came to read thus:

Hello Darling,

You were right again: Daisy's decided to keep the fallen angel. Apparently, she thinks he's a spy. That's just like her. Never accept a simple answer when there's a dramatic one available. Anyway, I'm interviewing him as we speak, and he is just adorable. I've never met someone so easily rattled. I've insinuated he's a dangerous menace and he's practically gone purple tryi

The text fell off there and picked up again on the next page:

Darling, you will not believe this, but that giant cocker spaniel actually hit me!

Martin looked at Basil in disbelief. He flipped through the book until he saw a second handwriting. He read:

Hello Darling,

At work making the cutest little labels for the medicine jars when the Captain came on the Comms announcing we were under attack. I simply can't wait to hear about your battle, though I do wish the ship would not rock so. I just finished organizing the cabinets, and you know what a nuisance they can be.

Oh, Darling, just as the ship stopped rocking, I happened to look out the window and saw Martin and Daisy plummeting by on the back of a rukh. Somebody must have met Miss Smith, for he has the most adorable new sweater! I'll put a blue lollipop in my bag to match it, just in case they're still alive. There you go, charging by the door in a most dashing way. I better leave off now and get my things in order.

Yours always,
Melody

Martin closed the book and slid it back inside Basil's jacket pocket. He sat down, thinking this development over.

"I did try to warn you," Basil said, reddening slightly.

Martin took a moment to ponder his discovery. Biting his lip and rubbing the back of his neck with one hand, he inquired meekly, "You two write letters to each other all day?"

"Yes. As we exist in very different spheres of life on the *Nephthys*, I thought it the best way to keep abreast with the relevant in each other's lives. We have two notebooks, a large and a small, which we trade whenever we happen to see one another."

"That is so sweet I think I'm going to be sick."

"I know. Melody's a very lucky woman."

"Wait. Why would you copy the Ancient Elvish in a love-letter book?"

"Well, she's also a very clever woman. Your crush on her is well bestowed."

"I don't—"

"Shh, Martin. I understand. Anyway, I recorded the Elvish in our notebook so she and I could work out some of the finer nuances of translation together on our afternoon off."

"You and your wife spent an afternoon off translating Ancient Elvish," Martin restated for confirmation, as the list of things he could think to do with an afternoon off and a hypothetical wife did not include any similar activities for reference.

"Of course," Basil replied in his usual matter-of-fact manner. "Now, am I cleared of charges? Because I would very much like to not be tied to this chair anymore."

Martin was defeated. He got up to undo the knots, but paused and asked, "You . . . you aren't going to tell Daisy about this, are you?"

"Typically, this sort of gaffe is exactly the thing I would tell Daisy about," the First Officer snorted. "However, given that I was hoisted with this particular petard, I think the less said about this matter the better. Agreed?"

Martin Hathaway grasped his hand firmly and shook it to the degree that the rope allowed. "Agreed."

MARTIN WAS JUST about to undo the first knot that bound Basil's hand to the chair when they heard a sound that sent a chill to their bones.

"At ease, everyone." Daisy's voice came from the Enlisted Lounge. "Jameson, you say they've been in there how long?"

"Over an hour, Miss. Longer for Mr. Hathaway."

"Quick!" Basil whispered between gnashed teeth. "Intercept her!"

Martin leapt out of the First Officer's Lounge, pulling the door closed behind him and leaning against it. Had he not have been preoccupied with getting rid of the Captain, he might have noted that the Enlisted Lounge was the fullest it had been since his first day on the ship. As it was, all that concerned him was the no-nonsense expression Daisy currently bore.

"Hello, Daisy," he said in what he hoped was a perfectly casual manner, "how's the arm? That's a nice sling you've got there. Did . . . um . . . did Melody do the embroidery?"

"There's one of them," Daisy said to Jameson. "Step aside, Martin. I want to see Basil."

"He's . . . not here," Martin Hathaway had never been a skilled liar, but today he made his best effort. "Let's go look for him. We could try the Observation Deck."

"Martin, let me tell you about my afternoon. I took a drug-induced nap because someone ripped out my arm. When I woke up, Melody informed me that the same someone had made off with my blaster. While I'm processing this news, Tony stops by to see how I'm doing and ask if I've heard yet that Mr. Hathaway was seen wandering the hallway with a bunch of rope and a blaster sticking out of his pants. Then, Jameson here begs my pardon, but 'Mr. Hathaway and Mr. Underwood have been in the First Officer's Lounge for over an hour and now Mr. Underwood is screaming.' Half the crew thinks you killed him!

"Now, I may have one arm, NO BLASTER, and laudanum in my system, but I can still take you out." With her good hand, Daisy grabbed Martin's collar and pulled down until his face was even with hers. "And. You. Know it. I'll say this again: step aside. I want to see Basil."

Martin swallowed and yelled, "The jig's up, Basil. Sorry!"

"Good choice." Daisy let go of his collar. Martin held the door open for her and slid in after, shutting it on the curious crowd. At least he could try to keep the details of this mishap between the three of them.

"Hello, Captain." Basil smiled from his chair. "Excuse me for not rising in greeting. How's the arm? That looks like Melody's handiwork on your sling. I'd know those daisy chains anywhere."

Daisy stared at the bound man before her.

"Basil, report."

"Oh, well . . . Not much to report here. Though, I do have a recommendation." The First Officer leaned his head toward his Captain and whispered conspiratorially, "In the future, when you have doubts as to the loyalty of your crew, do not share them with your Assistant. He's a bit high strung."

Daisy turned to Martin, blinking rapidly.

"I told you I thought there was a traitor, and you went out and captured Basil?"

"Um . . . yes. But you have to understand: he was acting really suspicious!"

She fluttered her hand in front of her face.

Basil gasped. "Good god, Daisy! Are you crying? Martin, look what you've done!"

Martin attempted to apologize, but she waved him off. When she had recovered her wits, Daisy announced, "It might be the medication talking, but this is the sweetest thing anyone has ever done for me!"

Martin grinned. Basil bellowed, "IT HAD DAMN WELL

BETTER BE THE MEDICATION TALKING!"

"Oh, come on, Basil!" Daisy ran forward and wrapped her arm around the First Officer's neck. "He caught you! Anyone could have taken out Tony or Westfield, but he got you!"

"Daisy, don't encourage him. While his conquest may be impressive, he missed the fairly significant detail that I am NOT a traitor."

"No." Daisy stepped away from the chair and fumbled in her pocket for Martin's phone. "But you are pretty suspicious. You met your wife when you were trying to steal chloroform from Med Supply."

"It was for Science!"

"That doesn't make things not suspicious. Face it: if there were a traitor on board, Martin would have got him."

Unable to master snapping a photo with one hand, Daisy gave the phone to Martin, who proudly showed her that one could also set the picture to appear whenever #2 called her line.

"I should have been the traitor," Basil grumbled while Daisy squealed with delight.

"I am so happy!" she declared, slipping the phone back in her pocket. "Martin, I'm promoting you. Now you're Basil's assistant, too!"

Martin thanked her for the honor but modestly declined.

Basil hopped violently about in the chair. "Daisy Fitzgerald McNamara! If you do not untie me this instant, I will become the traitor so fast—"

"No, you won't, Basil! Don't worry; we'll be right back to let you out."

"Wait! Where are you going?"

"To get Melody!" Daisy skipped out of the room, calling as

215

she went, "Keep up, Martin!"

⚙ CHAPTER NINETEEN ⚙

"Basil, you aren't still angry that no one in the Enlisted Lounge warned you Martin was lying in wait in your closet, are you?" Daisy sighed and rubbed her temples. It was a cold, rainy morning three days after their escape from Tír na nÓg. Expecting to come in sight of the Lost Valley within the hour, she had called her officers together to plan tomorrow's defense.

"Oh no, Captain." Basil lounged with his feet on Daisy's desk, knowing that acts of defiance are always best when they are both subtle and unmistakable. "I merely think it's been a while since anyone's been on Triple Watch indefinitely. It would be a shame to let the hands off now simply because you wish them to be rested enough to counter animatronic invaders. It's not like they would be missed if it came to a fight, since their apparent response to danger is 'Let's wait and see how this plays out.'"

Tony interjected that the Comm Channel buzz had odds on the encounter going in Mr. Hathaway's favor at 2:1 against, which meant they all really were obligated to let the situation develop naturally.

Basil ignored his remark and continued, "By the way, I happened to notice that we've neglected to assign Martin to a watch shift. Might I suggest we begin with all of them? That way, we can learn which one he likes best."

Melody patted his knee. "Darling, you really should at least forgive Martin. He made you that lovely sorry-for-thinking-you-were-evil card and the smiley-face pancakes."

"You also hit me in front of everyone in the breakfast line when I gave them to you," Martin added from his seat in the corner where he was busy creating a second clipboard to replace the one lost in his flight from the Isle, "but I wouldn't let anyone take me to Sick Bay."

Basil mumbled something that Daisy thought sounded a great deal like, "The day you go back to Sick Bay is the day you die," but since he subsequently uncrossed his arms and nodded to Martin, she decided to let the matter slide.

"So we're all agreed, then," she said, "that watch on the *Nephthys* will be limited to Ship's Eye alone while we're in the Valley."

Affirmations were made, and the business moved on to discuss strategy. Jocelyn Heart had drawn up schematics for the clockwork men based on the Captain's account and conjecture. She unrolled these on the desk for everyone to examine while she gave her report.

"The best my team can figure," Jocelyn stated, "is that if the technology behind the 'Monitors' and the band on that rukh are the same, then the key that powers the 'Monitors' must be very small and placed somewhere on the back, otherwise the Captain would have noticed it. Any attack, then, would need to focus on getting behind the 'Monitor' in order to search for and remove the key. If it exists, that is."

"And you haven't had any success building one of our own?"

the Captain asked.

"Negative. At least, not with any degree of sentience. Martin's phone was child's play compared to the technology you witnessed. Ba—"

Jocelyn dropped her sentence and looked at the floor.

"Yes, Miss Heart? What did Basil suggest?"

With a shrug of her shoulders, Jocelyn continued, "Basil suggested we could try building one with a human brain. He said he had a list of people who weren't using theirs. But, if I may speak freely, Captain, I think he was kidding."

Basil replied dryly, "Ordinarily, I would say I never kid when it comes to Science, but as there are those of us who have become quite literal of late, I should point out that I was in jest about actually carrying out the experiment. Not on the likelihood that these machines are using a human brain, mind you."

Daisy sat back in her chair and considered this. "Shouldn't a human brain be subject to the Protection on the Valley?"

"Captain, there really are only so many theoretical axioms from which one can postulate before the entire proof becomes an exercise in fantasy. That being said, I believe the clockwork men are our best evidence for the existence of the soul and its location elsewhere than the brain. I've pondered the question many an hour and can see no other way they could respond to the subtle nuances of language with the given degree of success otherwise."

"Excellent."

Martin had been rather pleased with how well he had been following the conversation at the mission-planning meeting up until this point.

"Wait," he called from the corner. "Why is it 'excellent' that someone is putting human brains inside machines? That kinda seems like the opposite of excellent news."

Daisy smiled. "If we've learned anything in the last seventy-two hours, Martin, it is this: even the most superior human brain can be caught off-guard."

THE RAIN CONTINUED to pour as the A.S. *Nephthys* touched down in the Lost Valley. Martin Hathaway had been sent to fetch the Captain an umbrella, and as he held it for her he discovered that by taking a series of quick, short steps he was able to stay underneath and relatively dry as well. It should be noted for those readers who despise the eccentricities of the elite that Daisy had not requested Martin hold her umbrella and thought it very strange when he returned from fetching it with no indication that he intended to hand it to her, but since the task seemed to make him happy and she was short the use of one arm, she felt no great qualms with utilizing her Personal Assistant thus.

Daisy, Martin, and Basil disembarked and made for the main house. They were met along the way by a thin, young man who looked as if he had neither slept nor shaved in days.

"Mr. Jefferson," Daisy called to the man as he approached, "how are the girls?"

"Getting bigger every day, thank you, Captain," he replied before launching into a series of questions as to the success of the mission, the lateness of their return, and the extent of Daisy's injury. Hardly pausing for either a response or a breath, Jefferson pointed at Martin and said, "And who's this guy?"

"This is the man holding the Captain's umbrella," Basil

stated, water dripping off his long nose. "If you want more information I suggest you consult Mr. Angelo. Now, Jefferson, report. How goes the Valley? For God's sake I hope you at least got Daisy's skylight fixed before this deluge hit her library."

Jefferson trotted beside them as they continued on to the house and reported. Life in the valley had been quiet over the past two weeks, the gardens were all coming along nicely, Daisy's skylight had been repaired without mishap, and the Cartwrights had announced they were expecting again. Only one cloud seemed to hang over the otherwise sunny life of the Free People.

"It's Gilly and Gibson, Miss. They still haven't returned."

Daisy stopped walking, and Martin crashed into her.

"They haven't returned at all?" she asked.

"No, Miss. We were hoping you might bring news of them."

"Did you send out a search party?"

"Aye. We covered the forest as far as the gates of Antamenwar on all sides. Not a trace of them to be found. Their families are starting to get concerned."

"So am I." Daisy resumed walking and for a while no one spoke. As they came in sight of the house, she announced, "Excellent work, Jefferson. You should return home. Angelo should be around to all the cottages with tomorrow's plans presently."

Jefferson tipped his water-soaked hat and ran off. Entering the house and shaking out his greatcoat, Basil remarked, "We may now have the penultimate piece of the puzzle, Daisy. It sounds exactly like what I thought."

"It usually does, Basil. I'm still taking the precaution, nonetheless."

"As you wish. Though, I'll say it again: if we're fighting living inanimate objects, he might just be our man."

"Who . . . um . . . who might be our man?" Martin inquired tentatively despite being certain he knew the answer.

"The kitchen's the fourth door on the left," Daisy said as she crossed into her parlor. "Martin, why don't you fetch us something warm to drink while Basil builds a fire? And when Cook arrives, ask him to make sandwiches."

Martin left for the kitchen, but he did not head for the fourth door on the left. After his misinterpretation of Basil's actions, Martin Hathaway never wanted to act without all of the facts again. If Basil and Daisy were discussing him, he was going to know what it was all about. Turning right and crossing behind the stairs, he stood against the wall just outside the other parlor door and listened.

"So you think I'm being overly cautious, then?" he heard Daisy's voice asking.

Basil chuckled. "If anyone who jumps headlong off a perfectly good airship hoping to land on a rukh can be described as overly cautious, then, yes, I think you are. We've been over this, Daisy."

"Go over it again."

"We've been trying to solve two problems: the appearance of Martin and the nature of the 'Monitors.' The first we've likely explained with Svadilfari's machine and the latter with your conjectures about clockwork. Now, Oswald's Razor says that the simplest answer to any problem is statistically the most likely. It follows that our problems are not actually two, but one. Thus, whichever local boy made the clockwork men also summoned Martin. It is highly improbable that someone would go to the trouble of building a legendary machine simply to bring Martin down upon our heads, destructive as he may be. What is more likely is that our foe has located his lair elsewhere and is using Svadilfari's machine to transport his minions to and from the Valley. Our inability to find any trace of Gibson and Gilly supports this, assuming they were captured and spirited away."

"And Martin?"

"Svadilfari's machine is unstable. During the transportation, the strings composing the air above your skylight were inadvertently affected, and our hapless hero got caught up in the mess."

"Sounds pretty lucky, doesn't it? For Martin, I mean. Falling to his doom in one universe and instead getting rescued by a portal to ours?"

Martin could not see what was going on in the next room, but Basil rubbed the rope burns on his wrists before saying, "I'm beginning to suspect that we have been wrong on that front. Upon further study, Martin appears to be the luckiest man in any universe. I believe his continued survival more than ample proof."

Daisy smiled, though both men missed it.

"But how do you account for their demand that we hand over a Citizen? If Martin isn't part of the plan, then they couldn't have known he was here."

"It's no secret that taking a Citizen of Anatamenwar against his will is a violation of neutrality, though it is a secret that we couldn't possibly get one inside the Valley with the protection. I think whoever is behind this wanted to rattle you before his attack, so you would go off on a wild goose chase, wearing yourself out or possibly becoming injured. In this regard, Daisy, I see you have played into his hand quite nicely."

"All the same. If there is any way they could prove Martin

is a Citizen, then Anatamenwar would be justified in declaring war on our Valley, and no one in the Neutral Territories would come to our aid. I can't run that risk."

Martin Hathaway had heard enough. Walking back toward the kitchen, he considered all he had heard. Daisy was right. It might not be likely the clockwork men had anything to do with him, but that possibility was still there. If there were even the smallest chance that his presence could harm the Valley, he would much rather have died at Eagle's Peak.

Back in the parlor, Basil continued, "All this hinges on the idea that they catch Martin. Our plan is to drive them out. It seems to me—"

"Never mind, Basil," Daisy interrupted with a wave of her free hand. "Martin isn't listening anymore."

"You made me run through all that again so your bumbling bloodhound could play amateur sleuth?"

"Of course."

Basil sighed. Warming body and soul in front of the newly roaring fire, he suggested, "Seeing as how there's nothing to do but wait for tomorrow, what do you say to fetching Melody up here and the four of us playing board games for the afternoon? I even promise not to stun Martin when he surrenders his better judgment and lets you win."

THE AFTERNOON AND early evening passed in a lively and enjoyable fashion, but there are only so many times half a party can lose competitions to the other half before interest wanes. Melody and Martin had dozed off in the front parlor somewhere between one and two hours after Basil and Daisy had stormed off to the Library to consult *Glooscap's Guide to Games of Gentlefolk* about a question of the legalities of Daisy's last move. Emerging ultimately victorious, Basil woke his wife and the couple departed for their cottage. Daisy decided to let Martin continue sleeping where he was, though the ache in his neck when she eventually did shake him awake made him wish she had not.

Martin yawned, rubbed his neck, and looked about. The sky outside appeared lighter than he last remembered it, but not by much.

"What time is it?" he asked.

Daisy handed him a picnic basket. "Nearly dawn. Come on, I need you to carry this to the ship for me."

He followed her out the front door, trying to smooth his hair into some presentable shape with one hand and no mirror.

"Why do we have to take a basket to the ship before dawn?"

"Melody and Emma will be bringing the children and others who can't or shouldn't fight on board as soon as the sun rises. We have something to do first."

"Children and those who can't fight? You don't think . . ."

Daisy smiled and slid her hand inside his. "It's just the Safety Protocol. A failsafe in case a fight comes to the Valley or . . . The kids will love a chance to be inside the *Nephthys*. Poor Jameson spends half his time when we're at home chasing them away from her."

When they reached the ship, Martin found he was useful for more than the carrying of burdens, as Daisy required assistance getting on board one-armed. It was a markedly different arrival on the ship than the day he had stood beside Basil with Daisy's coffee. No one announced her presence or saluted her in the halls. Daisy crept onto her vessel like a ghost and moved through it just as silently.

Like that first morning, Martin followed the Captain to the Control Room. He assumed the basket he carried contained an array of breakfast foods for the crew assigned to the ship and started to ask Daisy where he should lay the spread when she approached the helm. She pressed a button concealed on the spindle, and the stairs behind them flattened and slid aside to reveal a large compartment.

"This is the Smuggler's Hold," Daisy explained as she entered and switched on a small, electric lamp on the wall. "We store contraband goods in here in case of raids or port inspections."

Martin was impressed that a space of this size could be so well concealed. He was able to walk into the Smuggler's Hold without stooping, and the compartment seemed to span the full width of the ship. Looking around he noticed the barrels of Dathúil's wine, several wooden boxes, a stack of books, and a hammock.

"What's that in here for?" he asked, pointing to the hammock.

Daisy took the basket from him and set it down beside the stack of books.

"It's for you. Emma Westfield is the only one who knows you'll be in here. She'll let you out when the coast is clear, be that when we win or when she gets the ship close enough to Fitzgerald House to deem it safe. There's food and drink in the basket if you need it. I brought your library books so you won't get bored. I added a few of my favorites, too. This one's *The Escapades of Paxton Cambridge*. I think you'll really enjoy it."

Though his career as her Personal Assistant had been brief,

Martin knew that the Captain was not one with whom one should openly disagree, but he could not help himself. Every fiber of his being balked at the idea of letting this delicate, one-armed angel fight on his behalf. In the tone he had only previously employed to shoot down requests for paper extensions, he asserted, "Daisy, no. I'm not hiding on the ship while the rest of you fight for the Valley."

"Paxton's a bit of a detective," she continued, flipping through the pages as if Martin had not spoken at all. "He means well, but half his cases are only successful through blind luck and a plucky resolve. A man who used to be on the crew wrote it, but—"

"Daisy! Put the book down and look at me. I'm not doing this. If anyone should be hiding out in here, it's you. You're injured!"

"I'll be fine." Daisy set *The Escapades of Paxton Cambridge* aside. Stepping forward, she reached into Martin's pocket.

"Hey now!" Martin cried.

Daisy pulled out the brass key and held it so that Martin could see the word Mendax clearly. "The rukh didn't attack me. It attacked you. Whoever this Mendax is, he wants you. I can't keep you safe in a battle, but I can if you stay here."

"I don't want you to keep me safe!" Frustrated, Martin paced around the Smuggler's Hold, which suddenly seemed a great deal smaller than it had on first impression. "Daisy, do you know why your mother hasn't spoken in twenty-two years? It's not because she misses your father. It's because she can't forgive herself for letting him die for her."

Placing his hand on her shoulder, Martin stepped closer and spoke softly, "It hurts me every day to see your arm in this sling and know that it's my fault. I will march right up to Mendax's lair and give myself up before I let you get so much as another bruise on my account."

"I know. That's why you're staying here. The door can only be opened from the outside."

"Daisy—"

"No! Don't you understand yet? I am Daisy Fitzgerald Mc-Namara, Captain—"

"Oh for Pete's sake!" Martin threw his hands in the air and turned from her as she recited her full title. "Everyone knows who you are!"

"—and Bane of Anatamenwar. Every man, woman, and child in a five-mile radius is under my protection. All 105 of you."

Martin looked back at Daisy and bit his lip. He stepped forward, sliding an arm around her waist and pulling her toward him.

"That's fine, Daisy," he whispered. "But I don't care if you take the whole world under your protection. You're still under mine."

After two long weeks' worth of existential crises, he finally knew exactly what he wanted from life on Arnica—or any planet, when it came down to it. Unfortunately, it was time to say goodbye. For the first and foreseeably last time, Martin Hathaway kissed Daisy McNamara. Her free arm hung limp at her side, but soon he felt it brush against his hip and slide slowly up his back. This was his moment.

Martin stepped back, tears in his eyes.

"I'm sorry, Daisy," he said as he raised the blaster he had just removed from her holster, aimed, and fired.

⚙ CHAPTER TWENTY ⚙

Hello Darling,

Well, I knew it would come to this someday. Here I am, stuck sitting up a tree for God knows how long, waiting to jump down upon armed animatronic antagonists. Sometimes I wonder if the room, board, adventure, and research funding are worth being the chief executor of Daisy's hare-brained schemes, but then I remember life without you in that god-forsaken little bakery back at Anatamenwar. It's enough to make me at peace with the squirrel who is currently nibbling on my favorite hiking shoes.

Let me tell you, darling, keeping fifty-eight people quiet in the treetops since dawn has not been easy. I finally had to gag Angelo. No amount of separating him from others was doing any good. I can't believe on this crew of savants I'm the only one who thought to bring a book. "Oh, we're going to sit in the treetops until the enemy decides to show up? Sounds riveting! I can't possibly fathom how I could ever tire of such an activity."

Oh for the love of . . . darling, you are never going to guess who just came wandering out of the Valley and is headed for the forest path. On second thought, I won't insult your intelligence. After this fortnight the answer should be obvious: Martin, that loony labrador. I had rather thought Daisy intended to lock him away somewhere until the threat had passed. I must say, I do resent that she did not inform me of the details of her presumably absurd plan to ensure Martin's safety. The very idea that I would give up his location if caught and tortured is ridiculous. Martin tortured me for an hour and I never once disclosed the Captain's location.

But I digress. The point is: here comes Martin. That imbecile Westfield tried to shout "Hello!" but I threw an apple at him before he completely blew our cover. If the Captain wanted Martin to know where we were, she would have mentioned it. And there goes Martin, blissfully unaware that 115 eyes are fixed upon him. I suppose Daisy's plan was to send Martin off on some ridiculous errand in the forest, though as she believes our mechanical foes to be coming from that very direction, I fail to see the logic in that choice. Oh, darling, I hope Martin's not off on some misguided attempt at heroics. I'm bound to be sent to go rescue him while the crew sits around yakking about how noble he is. That's the way of things, isn't it? Some poor sap sacrifices himself completely unnecessarily and is remembered in song and prose for eternity, whereas no one recalls the man in the tree doing his job like a sensible person.

Where the devil is Daisy? She should have met us out here by now. I hope she's not running around the Valley searching for her wayward terrier.

Must leave off here, darling. Something ticking this way comes!

Yours always,

Basil

To SAY THAT Martin Hathaway had a plan would be embellishing. Rather, Martin had conceived of two possible outcomes of his decision to head into the forest: he would run into Mendax and surrender or he would wander through the forest, missing the villain entirely. In either case, no one would find him in the Valley, which would leave no just cause to declare war. Martin felt that at the very least he could do no harm, and that was something.

He felt a pang of regret as he crossed the bridge over the river. Looking back, he could see the Valley spread out in all its cozy glory. He wished he had time to stay a while, to explore every corner and rest under every tree. It occurred to him that, standing on the other side of the river, he could still see the Valley, which must mean that it had found him to be an acceptable addition. Maybe he would be able to return someday. People had escaped from Anatamenwar before, or there would be no Free Peoples.

This warm idea carried him into the forest. He had thought he heard someone calling, but he credited such a notion to wishful thinking, since he could not see anyone. Practically an instant later, an apple dropped from the tree in front of him, making a hollow "thump!" as it must have bounced off a limb on its way down. Martin caught it and smiled. This was a lucky break. He had not yet eaten anything today. He munched on the apple as he walked, reflecting on how sometimes it's the little things that let one know when he is on the right path.

Finishing the apple and tossing the core aside, Martin realized he had no idea how far he should walk or which path he should take were he to come to a second one. This very problem soon presented itself, as the forest path split off in two directions in front of an immense pine tree.

Martin was saved a lengthy debate over the merits of turning right or left by the appearance of a purple light on the trunk of the tree. The light spread wider and formed the shape of a ring.

The light ring reminded Martin both of the solar corona and a doughnut, though one can guess which vision he admitted to in public recitations.

In an instant, the ring of light had spread far enough that Martin could see the full figure of a man standing inside it. The man stepped through, and behind him Martin noticed several more men and another path, which led off into the distance. Since there was no path through the trunk of the tree seconds before, Martin rightly conjectured that he had just witnessed the opening of a portal to some other realm.

The man addressed Martin. "I seek Captain McNamara of the A.S. *Nephthys*."

"She sent me." Martin held his chin high and assumed what he hoped was a heroic stance. "I am the Citizen. I will return with you if you agree to leave the Lost Valley in peace."

The man stepped forward and scrutinized Martin.

"Inconclusive," he declared. "Facial features register a 98.583463281 percent match, but specifications indicate you should be two inches taller and have significantly lower eumelanin concentrations."

"What?"

A second man stepped through the portal, carrying a stack of papers.

"Mendax authorized slight deviations from specifications if the Citizen presented himself," the second man said to the first.

"Wait. You guys know what I'm supposed to look like?"

"Affirmative. Captain McNamara does not think she can fool us with a decoy, does she?"

Martin assured them that she did not, and that he had come on his own free will. Glancing at the papers the second man carried, he saw that they were posters declaring him a wanted man. A drawing on the poster bore an uncanny resemblance to Martin, but the Martin in the drawing was dressed in a three-piece suit. His hair was also cut short and worn straight with a part on the side. The real Martin thought it odd that whoever he actually was, the Citizen must look exactly like Martin would if Martin were Basil.

Shaking his head in hopes of removing the disturbing image, Martin repeated his nature and purpose. The first man opened a compartment on his chest and removed a pair of brass handcuffs. In horror at such a sight, Martin Hathaway stumbled backward, but the second man caught him and the first bound his wrists.

"You are a prisoner of Mendax," the first man stated. "You are to be incarcerated and you will appear when summoned."

"Alright, alright!" Martin pulled himself out of the men's grips. "I'm coming with you. There's no need to get pushy. Let's go."

Martin Hathaway took a deep breath, closed his eyes, and stepped through the portal.

He was completely underwhelmed by his first conscious journey to another realm. The sensation was no different than if he had stepped from the door of the kitchen into the living room. With a sigh, he marched with his captors toward a hoard of other clockwork men.

Cold as an Antarctic winter, the first man told the others, "You have your orders. Leave none alive."

The men saluted and crossed through the portal.

"WAIT!" Martin screamed. "I surrendered! You're supposed to leave the Valley alone!"

"You asked us to leave it in peace. When we leave it, it will be so."

Martin kicked his captor as hard as he could. He cried out in pain, as kicking the man felt exactly like kicking a car. A heavy hand came down on the back of his head, and Martin Hathaway struggled no more.

THE SUN ROSE higher as midday approached. The air was warm. It was the sort of morning one knows he has to enjoy while he can, for the afternoon was going to be unbearably hot. Henry Jefferson leaned against the brass telescope that comprised the Ship's Eye, having recently relieved another from his watch. Ship's Eye was fixed on the forest, but nothing remotely interesting had happened. Jefferson wondered how Anne was coping with the twins below deck. Between the feedings and the changings and the crying . . . well, it would not hurt if he closed his eyes. Just for a moment. He had run the entire Valley while the Captain had been gone. She would understand.

Something cold nudged his nose. He swatted at it. His hand collided with something solid and rubbery. Jefferson gave a start and opened his eyes.

Mr. Underwood stood before him, covered in oil and brandishing a man's severed arm.

Basil said slowly and forcefully, "Where. Is. The Captain?"

Jefferson sputtered, "Who's arm is that?!"

"Need I remind you that Ship's Eye works best when your own are open? I walked across the entire Valley carrying an arm and now that I've boarded the ship you want to know where I got it? If you weren't a new father, I'd flog you within an inch of your life. Where is the Captain?"

"She's not with you?"

"If she were with me, what would be the point of climbing up to C Deck to ruin your beauty sleep?"

"Did you try her house?"

Basil looked as if he might forget Jefferson's new status and beat him with the arm anyway. "How long have you been asleep, man?! Of course I checked her house! I have scoured every inch of this Valley shouting 'Captain! Captain!' since the battle ended! Surely you didn't miss the battle?!"

"No, of course not. It was very exciting. Um . . . did we win?"

Basil threw all three hands in the air, turned, and climbed down the ladder to B Deck. Below, families were reuniting and friends were celebrating. All gave Mr. Underwood a wide berth as he stomped through. Tony and Jocelyn trailed him, the latter carrying a box of parts and the former still wearing his gag. They ran down the forward port stairs and stormed into the Control Room. The Westfields jumped to a professional distance apart at their appearance on the upper deck.

"This is utterly ridiculous!" Basil thundered. "She has to be somewhere! This is exactly why normal leaders tell their officers their entire plans!"

"Maybe we should ask Martin," Emma Westfield suggested. "The Captain might have told him where she was going."

"Ask Martin?! Has everyone around here gone mad? Martin's either been mauled by a bear or Reprogrammed by an actual Monitor by now."

"Oh, heavens, no. He's in the Smuggler's Hold. He was banging on the door about an hour ago. He tried to convince me he was the Captain, but Daisy warned me not to let him out under any circumstances until she got back from the forest. He does a fantastic impression of her, by the way. If we could convince Daisy it was all in good fun, we must have him do it for Comedy Night."

"Good god, Emma. You and Jake were made for each other." Basil ushered the Helmsman aside with the severed arm and pushed the button opening the Smuggler's Hold. The officers stepped inside to find Daisy reclining in the hammock with a copy of *The Escapades of Paxton Cambridge*.

"Basil! Excellent! I take it the battle went in our favor!" Daisy hopped out of the hammock. Tilting her head, she asked, "Why are you covered in oil? I thought the plan was to jump down and remove their keys."

"Plans change," he said, shaking the arm at her.

Glancing at her other officers, Daisy replied, "Yes, but why are you the only one covered in oil?"

"If you could have been bothered to make it outside today, you might know that already!"

"I am sorry. I did try, but Martin stunned me and Westfield followed orders above and beyond the call of duty. Now, report. How went the battle? Was anyone hurt? And whose arm is that?"

Basil sighed, clicked his heels together, and reported. All had gone according to plan. They had surprised the clockwork men in the forest, and by keeping three of the crew to one clockwork man they were able to keep them from blasting anyone long enough for the keys to be found and removed. There was significantly more of the enemy than had been anticipated, however. Some of the crew had been injured from being flung into trees or punched by the metal arms. Med Staff was attending to them. The arm Basil carried was one of the enemy's, and that was all Basil had to say about the matter.

"Excellent." Daisy walked through the crowd of officers and made her way out of the Smuggler's Hold.

"But, Captain," Jocelyn called after her, "what about Martin? Where's he gone?"

"I imagine he's gone to surrender to Mendax and save the Valley from attack."

"But the Valley was attacked. And we saved it!"

"At the expense of my brown suit," Basil added.

"Yes, I know. I'm very proud of all of you." Daisy took a seat in the Captain's chair and turned to Tony. "But the battle was only the beginning. Our quarrel is with Mendax. Now, Mr. Angelo, retrieve the *Nephthys*'s phone. We're going to rescue Martin."

"I knew it." Basil groaned. "Not that I particularly care at this point, but how exactly do you plan on finding your lost puppy?"

"We're going to track him within three feet. I planted my phone in his pocket when he . . . escaped. If we find Martin, then we find Mendax."

"Ah. Well, that's dandy, Daisy. If it's all the same to you, however, I want a cup of tea, a bath, and a nap before I rush headlong into danger for another one of your toys."

"That's fine, Basil. We'll get a lock on his location, plot the course, and then send for you. Mrs. Westfield, please have all non-flight crew members return to their homes."

Emma and Basil started up the stairs. In the doorway, Basil stopped and turned back.

"Out of curiosity, Daisy," he asked, "how exactly did Martin stun you? I understand that he got me via the element of surprise, but you planned on taking him into the Smuggler's Hold."

"He got a hold of my blaster."

"Ah. And he did that how?"

Daisy ran her fingers over her lips. "He did that by shut up, Basil."

"I see. Happy hunting, Captain. Basil out."

When he was certain Basil had gone, Tony removed his gag.

"Captain," he whispered, "we never should have won that battle without casualties. There were just too many of them. But Underwood went psychotic when it took too long to locate a key, ripped the man's arm off, and started beating half the army to death with it. Do you understand, Captain? They're metal. They can't die, but he killed them anyway!"

"Well," Daisy smiled, "let's all be thankful that he's on our side. Now, back to work, Mr. Angelo. If Martin is still in this universe, I want him found."

⚙ CHAPTER TWENTY-ONE ⚙

Martin leaned against the stone wall of his cell feeling absolutely wretched. The clockwork man had hit him in the exact spot where the bump he received from the skylight had recently healed. He was hungry, too. Hungry, alone, and clueless as to what was to become of him. Worst of all were the scenes of destruction with which his imagination continually plagued him. The Valley was under attack, and he had done nothing. He was a fool to think he could have helped; this was not his world. He did not understand how it worked. Daisy understood, which was why she made plans. All Martin Hathaway could do was react.

His sole happy thought was that, somewhere, Daisy was safe. If the all else failed, she would live to rebuild. He reminded himself that he was not the Keeper of the Lost Valley. He had wanted to protect Daisy McNamara, and that end he had achieved. She would hate him for it, of course. Hate him for preventing her from defending her people. Hate him for taking advantage of the one time she had let her guard down completely. That was not Martin's original intent, but he would never be able to explain what he did, even if he ever were to see her again.

Martin's unhappy reflections were interrupted by the appearance of two clockwork men. They each carried a person over their shoulder. Without a word to Martin, the clockwork men opened the cell door, flung their burdens inside, locked the cell, and returned from whence they came.

The men groaned and struggled to sit up. One of them said to the other, "Ok, Gibs. So pretending the control was working didn't fly. I say next time we just tell him we want to serve him. This is getting old."

"I know you!" Martin sprang forward and helped the men to as comfortable a position as one can attain in a stone prison. He would have been grateful to see any human face, and finding ones he vaguely recognized filled him with an unwarranted enthusiasm. "You were in Daisy's library!"

Gilly looked him over and replied cautiously, "You have an advantage on us, son. I don't recall your face."

"No, you wouldn't. I'm . . . new. But I was in the library when you came to tell Daisy there were Monitors in the Valley. I was laying down, and Melody was running a brain scan on me."

Gibson's eyes widened in interest. He asked for news of the Valley, but before Martin could satisfy his request, Gilly interjected, "You're very free with first names, aren't you, son?"

Martin narrated the story of his brief career with the *Nephthys* in as much detail as he thought the men would need to believe his veracity. Gilly remained skeptical, but when the tale turned to the preparations for the clockwork invasion his amazement could not be concealed.

"Thank the stars for Fitzgerald House," Gibson said, holding his head in his hands. "At least I know my Annabell will make it out of this mess."

"But she's going right into another one," Gilly said gruffly.

"Mendax isn't going to be satisfied until he gets the Captain. And the Captain's never going to rest until she gets the Valley back just the way it was. You'll see. She'll come for us yet."

The sarcastic tone with which Gilly had said "Mendax" gave Martin some hope that perhaps their foe was less than competent in person. Nonetheless, he could not share Gilly's assurance that Daisy would get them out of this prison.

"That's only if she can find us," Martin said with a shake of his head. "Mendax is using portals to transport his army. We're probably a long way away from the Valley. Hell, we might not even be on the same planet anymore."

This was a disheartening thought, and Gilly and Gibson reminisced over the aspects of life on Arnica that they missed the most to cope with it.

Martin was about to introduce his favorite part of Arnican existence into the conversation when he felt a vibration in his pocket. Were he at home, Martin would have known that this sensation meant he had received a text message. Not anywhere remotely like home, however, he was momentarily puzzled. He slid his hand inside his pocket and, sure enough, he felt his phone.

The pure, overwhelming joy of this discovery was only matched by the day he had not died on the rukh, and Martin responded in the same manner as he had then.

Gilly and Gibson were naturally disturbed at the sight of their new cellmate shaking with laughter, tears streaming down his cheeks—all for no apparent reason. Hesitantly, they inquired after his condition.

"It's Daisy!" Martin said, pulling his phone out of his pocket. "God, she's amazing. Can you believe it? She knew! She knew the whole time I was going to stun her and run away, so while I was stealing her blaster she dropped my phone in my pocket!"

The two men did not believe it, and not merely because they did not understand what a phone was.

Unaware of the disturbed stares his companions were fixing upon him, Martin checked his messages. #2 had sent him three, which read:

Don't worry, Martin. We're coming to get you.

If you are with Mendax, don't answer your phone. That would give away our plans. Basil also thinks it would be rude, and I concur.

Also, if you are not Martin and have stolen his phone, we are coming for you. He will be avenged.
—Captain Daisy Fitzgerald McNamara

"Look, see?" Martin showed the messages to Gibson and Gilly. "You were right. She is coming for us!"

"What is that?" Gilly asked.

"Right. You weren't there. This is a phone. We use them to communicate where I come from, and Basil and Jocelyn—"

"No," Gilly pointed to the picture that accompanied each message. "What's that?"

"Oh, this?" Martin tapped the icon to bring up a larger version. "It's a picture of Basil tied to a chair."

"GET HIM, GIBS!" Gilly cried and pounced upon Martin.

The three men knocked about the cell, Gilly hanging onto

Martin's neck and Gibson attempting to subdue his legs.

"No! Wait! You don't understand!"

"WHAT HAVE YOU DONE WITH MR. UNDER-WOOD?!"

Few people can claim to have been rescued by a villain, but Martin Hathaway was one. Gibson and Gilly had pinned him face down on the floor and were threatening to break his arm if he did not disclose Mr. Underwood's location when a guard arrived, picked them up, and set them to the side. Martin had just enough time to slip his phone back into his pocket unnoticed before the guard lifted him to his feet and announced that he had been summoned by Mendax.

"ALL THIS TIME," Daisy sighed, staring up at the mountain range that surrounded the Lost Valley on three sides. "It's genius. We look ahead to Anatamenwar, and the enemy makes camp in our backyard."

"Yes, so you've been saying." Basil reclined in a wicker chair in Daisy's flower garden, sipping what he considered to be a hard-won glass of lemonade. He had chosen this particular spot to wait out the afternoon as the garden was enclosed by high stone walls, which he had hoped would prevent Daisy from staring off into the distance. However, it seemed he had over-estimated the height of the walls and underestimated Daisy's ability to fixate. "And thus I continue replying, no amount of brooding in the direction of the Erigeron Hills is going to get us any closer to them. Sit down, have something to eat, and wait on Jocelyn's report like you chose to do this morning."

"Think of how many times we've flown over those mountains to explore some other part of the world, and we never looked at them. Not once. I've mapped all twelve islands in the Acantholepis Archipelago and I have no idea what's on the other side of the Erigerons."

"Well, consider this yet another wonderful learning opportunity."

"I knew an ancient race of Dwarves once lived in those hills, but I thought I knew enough about Dwarves. I wanted to see something new. Svadilfari's stronghold could be within ten miles of us. Mendax might have found his actual machine while I was out raiding supply ships."

"Daisy, is this one of those conversations where it doesn't make a difference if I participate or not? Because if it is, I think I'll pop off for another nap."

"Has . . . have we confirmed communication yet?"

"If by that you are asking whether or not Martin has replied to your three messages, then we both know he has not. Would you like me to check the phone—that has still not rung—again, in case one slipped by?"

Daisy turned on her heel and stomped over to a second chair. "I just don't see what's so difficult about sending a 'Thanks for not leaving me behind. P.S. I'm still alive' note. It took me less than thirty seconds to compose each of my texts."

"Perhaps he has more important things on his mind. Like resisting torture."

"You think Martin's being tortured?"

Basil pressed his fingers together and considered the question.

"Daisy, what happened in the Smuggler's Hold? I'm fairly certain I know, but you've used your feminine wiles to your advantage before with significantly less fretting afterwards."

"I'm not 'fretting,' Basil," she admonished, sinking into the chair.

The First Officer picked up the bulky brass object that represented several hours of his life's work and flicked the screen to on. "Oh, look, Martin finally replied!"

Daisy sat straight up, bright-eyed. "He did?!"

"Of course he didn't!" Basil snapped and slammed the phone back upon the end table. "Pull yourself together, Daisy! Perhaps you need to say whatever it was that happened aloud. Get it out of your system, or some other rot like that."

"Hello there!" Melody's singsongy voice called from the garden gate. "Mind if I join you two? You look so peaceful."

"You've never been more welcome," Daisy waved Melody over and poured her a glass of lemonade. "How are the injured?"

Melody sunk into a chair on Basil's right, exhausted. "We just got the last one treated and resting in Sick Bay. Thankfully, we were able to get most of them back to their homes to recover. I honestly can't remember a time when my boys were this busy. Will you be visiting them all, Daisy?"

"Yes, when the mission's complete."

The three sat in the sunshine and discussed the adventures of the day. Daisy did what she could to not appear as if she thought this afternoon was the most tedious waste of time she ever had the misfortune to weather. She did succeed in not checking the phone for messages while Basil was looking; Melody caught her at it twice.

Finally, after what seemed like an age, Jocelyn Heart arrived in the garden. She carried a small, misshapen lump of metal, which she dropped onto the table.

"What is that?" Basil said with unconcealed wonder.

"That," Jocelyn replied, "is an electronic brain."

"Impossible! No one could build something like that! It's so smooth, and they were so human!"

"I don't think anyone built it. I think this thing just is, like a human brain just is. And just like a human brain, I can report on what all the parts are, what they're made of, and what they do, but I cannot for the life of me tell you how it achieves consciousness."

Basil turned the electronic brain over in his hands. "It's simply marvelous!"

Daisy, however, was less impressed and more practical.

"So you can't build one?"

"Negative, Captain."

"Basil, can you?"

"I hate to give up the ship before it even sails, Captain, but I'm going to have to agree with Jocelyn. It's possible I could reassemble one, of course."

"Excellent." Daisy sprung to her feet. "If you can't build them, then Mendax can't either. That means he found them, and unless he's instituted some prolific metal breeding program, he has a limited supply of them. I'd be very surprised to find we did not clean him out this morning. Come on, Basil. We've wasted enough time. Let's go get this creep and bring Martin home."

"Alright. Just let me . . . wait. Why 'Come on, Basil' and not 'Come on, everyone?' Aren't we taking the ship?"

"Don't be silly. Mendax would see the airship a mile off. We're walking."

"Walking! Daisy, there are ten miles of mountain between us

and Martin's phone!"

"And ten miles back. The sooner we get started, the sooner we'll be home."

Grumbling something about needing to change his shoes, Basil rose to exit the garden. Catching his hand, Melody said softly, "Darling, when you run into Mendax, will you do something for me and the Med Staff? Kick him as hard as you can."

"I'll do my best, darling," Basil smiled, "assuming I can still stand when we get there."

WITH THEIR PHONE as guide, Daisy and Basil slowly made their way around the base of the nearest mountain. They clambered over stones, trudged through underbrush, and leapt across streams. All along their way, Basil informed Daisy of exactly how happy he was to be off rescuing Martin Hathaway.

"I've been thinking it over for the last three miles, Captain," Basil said, lumbering past a small tree, "and I've decided to name the largest of the blisters on my left foot 'Martin.' Perhaps you could assist me in coming up with appropriate eponyms for the rest. Obviously there's 'Marty' and—"

"Shh!" Daisy crouched behind a large stone. "Look, there it is! That has to be the ruins of Svadilfari's keep!"

Basil hunkered down beside her and looked over to where she pointed. Nestled between two mountain bases rose a single stone tower. Trees and other growth nearly obscured piles of stone, which Basil conjectured had once connected the tower to the mountain, forming a fortress that in its day must have been a sight to behold.

"There's a dirt path leading off from the tower," Basil whispered, "from which we can conclude the front door must be located on the west. As the only visible entrance, we can assume it will be guarded. I estimate the tower to be fifty feet in height, which would put that single window at forty-five feet up. The tower comes to a point, so I don't think it likely there's a trapdoor in the roof. That makes the window our best option, despite the 85.6384 percent likelihood that the villain occupies the room to which it is connected. Now, judging by the masonry, I believe I could scale the side with some ease, but Melody would never forgive me if I allowed you to do so in your condition. I could lower a rope if we had the foresight to bring one, which, I note, we did not. Therefore, I'll have to search for one when I get inside and . . . wait . . . Daisy! Where are you going?"

"Don't worry, Basil," Daisy said when her first officer had caught up with her, "I have a plan." While they walked toward the tower, she removed her sling, folded it carefully, and tucked it inside her belt.

"What are you doing? Melody's going to have a fit!"

"Melody doesn't have to know. You remember what Fionn mac Cumhaill says about directly engaging the enemy."

Basil sighed, "*Never admit to weakness.* But, Daisy, you really have to consider the long-term ramifications of . . . are we walking up to the door?"

"Yes." Daisy scrambled up the side of the hill on which stood the tower and stepped boldly onto the dirt path. She marched straight to the heavy oak door and sounded the iron knocker. Basil stood behind her, dutifully waiting for the brilliance of his captain's plan to manifest.

The door opened. Two men, both ticking audibly, stood behind it, blasters in hand.

"I am Captain Daisy Fitzgerald McNamara," she said with her chin held high. "And you have something that belongs to me."

The men glanced at each other. Turning back to the visitors at their front door, they raised their blasters and said simultaneously, "You are prisoners of Mendax. You will follow us."

Basil pinched the brim of his nose.

"Daisy, no more making plans while you're taking laudanum."

⚙ CHAPTER TWENTY-TWO ⚙

HANDS HELD OVER their heads, Daisy and Basil were led up the winding stone staircase and through the heavy door with the brass knocker. Near the center of the room they saw a cylindrical iron monstrosity. Though they had studied the ancient sketch of Svadilfari's machine in some detail, they were both astonished by its bulk. Basil made a mental note that someone had modified the machine, as he saw dials that were not a part of the original schematic.

One piece that had been clearly labeled in the Elven book was a long rod through which the string stimulation energy was focused and projected. This was pointed straight ahead at a large red curtain that obfuscated an eighth of the room.

"Three guesses as to what's behind the curtain, Basil," Daisy said upon entering.

"And they all begin with 'm': Mendax, Martin, or martyrdom."

One of the clockwork men commanded, "Silence! You will speak when called upon."

"I think you're wrong there, Cuckoo." Basil smirked. "It seems like I will speak whenever I please."

Clipped on the chin by the butt of a blaster, Basil decided he did not please to speak at this current moment.

Immediately to the right of Svadilfari's machine was a large round ottoman. On this Basil and Daisy were directed to sit, Daisy facing the curtain and Basil the door. The clockwork men bound their wrists and feet separately and their backs together. Basil said a silent prayer of thanks that they were at least tied in sitting position, the difference in lengths of their torsos nowhere near that of their legs. He remarked to Daisy that he had found a rope inside the tower as promised, and he was clipped on the other side of his chin.

Having sufficiently subdued the prisoners, the clockwork men exited, never to be seen fully assembled again.

Basil knew this was his moment to point out that, once again, Daisy had led him to certain doom. Pondering over the most cutting witticisms in his repertoire, he felt her head rest between his shoulder blades. With a long-suffering sigh, he said, "Comfy, Captain?"

Daisy confessed that she would not mind having her arm back in its sling even if they were going to directly engage the Devil himself. Basil turned his head to say something encouraging, but the door opened. He looked up to see a familiar man dressed in an unfamiliar manner standing in the doorway.

"Well, well," Mendax laughed. "Nearly a hundred people at her beck and call, but the great Captain McNamara would never dream of sending anyone but herself and her first officer to blindly race into danger."

"Good god," Basil chuckled. "Daisy, you're never going to guess who our formidable foe is."

Quietly, Daisy replied, "It's Will."

Mendax threw back his head and cried, "No, you fool! I . . .

oh, come on! You didn't know that! You remember my voice, right? That's why you know."

"No." Daisy sounded a trifle bored with this exchange. "I had it figured out last week."

"AAARRGH!" Mendax cried and ran around the ottoman to face Daisy, long black cape billowing impressively behind him. "Do you have any idea how annoying you are?"

"I believe clever is the term."

"No! Annoying! I would stay up weeks creating the perfect surprise ending for you, and you would read the first two chapters, hand the book to me, and say something like, 'They aren't monsters. They're the super-evolved descendants of the original crew, and the captain doesn't know he's been sleeping for two thousand years.' GAH!"

"You should have been there the time we tried to throw her a surprise party," Basil said sympathetically. "But seriously, Daisy. How did you know we were up against the awesome might of Will the Bard—"

"Mendax!"

"—and I did not?"

"Don't blame yourself, Basil," Daisy said. "I didn't give you all the puzzle pieces. It was simplicity itself, really. The clockwork monitors walked straight toward the Valley, so we know whoever sent them knows where the Valley is, making him one of us. But why go through all the bother of assembling a metal army to defeat me when it would be much simpler to poison me or stab me in my sleep? Ah, whoever it is can't get near me. If he once could get in the Valley but now cannot, then he must once have been one of us but now is not. That narrowed the list down considerably.

"But our foe has a clockwork army. Why not attack with it while we're unsuspecting, rather than give the two-week ultimatum, in which time we could find a way to counter them? And why bother messing about with a machine and pseudonym pulled from ancient literature? Clearly, we're looking for a disgraced former crew member with a flair for the dramatic and a penchant for poetry. Who else fits the bill other than our old Bard, Will?"

Mendax clapped his hands slowly. "Excellent, Daisy. Excellent." He laughed and bent down to look her in the eye. "But I'm not Will. Will is dead. I am Mendax."

"Yes, Mendax." Daisy nodded and smiled with the left corner of her mouth. "A name from an ancient poem, but not one from our world."

Mendax grinned, his teeth gleaming white in the dimly lit tower.

She continued, "A poem from Martin's world. Martin, the man who fell through Space and Time to land on my coffee table. That's quite a coincidence, isn't it? Except there are no coincidences in literature, are there, Will? Not in the hands of a skilled author like yourself. Oh, no. You know all about Martin's world, because Martin isn't Martin, is he?"

"Say, it, Daisy!" Mendax raced over to the curtain. He flung it open, revealing a man dressed in corduroys and blue sweater, gagged and chained to the wall.

"Is it Martin?" Basil strained to see over his shoulder. "Ha ha! I got it in two!"

"Basil doesn't understand, Daisy!" Mendax ran back and thrust his face close enough to hers that their noses nearly met. "He never cared much for the details, did he? But you do! Say it! Say his name!"

Firmly, Daisy said, "He's Paxton Cambridge."

"REALLY? MARTIN?" Basil cried in disbelief. "This really, actually was all about Martin?"

Daisy nodded. "That's why we had the two weeks. So that Martin would get attached to us. He would then offer himself as sacrifice to save the Valley, just like Paxton in the final Escapade. Will knew I wouldn't let that happen and would come to his rescue."

Basil's "Yes, but Martin?" was drowned out by Mendax's cry, "WILL IS DEAD! And you killed, him, Daisy! He loved you, and you cut out his heart and you ate it for breakfast!"

This time Basil made sure he was heard. "He loved you?! Daisy, please tell me that he is using this word in its subservient sense: 'We love the Captain. She gives us a cookie ration every night and hardly ever orders floggings.' I mean, you don't honestly expect me to believe that you..—"

"Shut up, Basil," Daisy snapped. She felt the first Officer moving behind her in a manner that felt as if his body could not decide if it wanted to giggle or shudder.

Ignoring this distress, she stared Mendax straight in the eye and laughed derisively. "Please. Spare me the hyperbole. You never loved me; you loved the attention. That's why you left me when I took on Basil."

"Alright. This is getting silly." Basil had given up straining his neck to see the pair behind him. "You clearly spent too long in the sun, Mendax. And Daisy, as soon as we get home I'm having Melody adjust your prescription."

"Shut up, Basil!" Mendax demanded. To Daisy, he said, "He didn't leave you. You replaced him."

"No," Daisy said firmly, "I made a friend, and you couldn't handle that. Then you killed Paxton to get back at me, so I dumped you on an island."

Mendax insisted, "He killed Paxton so you would see that he was the genius, not that pompous windbag you keep at your side."

"Well, that was pretty stupid of him, genius."

"Are you seriously telling me," Basil interjected again, "that I am tied to you as the result of an unresolved lovers' quarrel? And how did I not know you two were lovers?"

Mendax suggested that if Basil had spent more than three nights in the Bachelor's Quarters, he might have learned a few things. Daisy explained that it was not ever any of his business.

"But really, Basil." She sighed. "Airships don't need bards. It should have been obvious."

"Oh, but librarians are central to successful flights?"

"Of course. Who's going to keep track of the books?"

"SHUT UP, BOTH OF YOU!" Medax began to pace around the ottoman. "I wrote a monologue, and you two are going to quietly listen to it!"

Basil sucked in air through his teeth and muttered, "To listen quietly."

Unperturbed by this remark, Mendax began, "When you sailed away from that godforsaken island, Daisy, I swore I would have my revenge. I spent every day contemplating ways I could crush you. Finally, I was picked up by the A.S. *Tatenen*, whose one-legged captain was more than happy to aid me in my quest to overthrow a certain tyrannical trollop . . ."

Mendax had crossed in front of Basil, who lifted his legs and kicked him with all the force he could. Toppling to the floor, Mendax cried out, "HEY!"

"That's for Med Staff," Basil said satisfactorily. Kicking Mendax again as he tried to rise, he added, "And that's for impugning the honor of my Captain. By the way, I would recommend increasing the radius of your walk if you wish to continue your already tedious monologue. I can do this all day."

Crawling out of Basil's reach, Mendax rose and picked up where he had left off, "I had intended to direct the *Tatenen* straight to the Valley, but to my horror I discovered that I could not find my way back. The ship dropped me on the edge of the Erigerons, where I wandered, desperate to find the Valley again. I could not, but I did find this tower, and the machine. That's when I formed my plan. If you had cut me out of your heart, Daisy, then I was going to finish the job and remove yours, permanently. All I had to do was find the one man you could not help but love and then take him from you. I knew that given an infinite number of universes, one existed where Paxton Cambridge was real and exactly as I had imagined him. I vowed to boldly explore each and every one until I found him."

"You know, Mendax," Basil interrupted, "I can already conceive of five flaws in your master plan, and I have yet to turn my mind to the problem."

"WHO'S THE ONE TIED TO THE CAPTAIN, BASIL?"

"Point conceded. Continue."

"It turns out, I didn't have to explore any of them. The first portal I opened was directly underneath the common room in the clockwork men's barracks. One hundred of them came toppling into my room, awestruck by the power of the god who summoned them."

"Oh great." Basil rolled his eyes. "He's a god now, Daisy."

Mendax ignored him and continued, "The clockwork men were suited by the nature of their universe to follow commands. Utilizing their superior processing capabilities, I was able to develop more sophisticated controls than that ancient Dwarf could ever had imagined. I could now open a portal anywhere I chose, to anywhere I chose, and I could even zero in on any life-form I chose. Now, Basil, you'll love this part, so listen up: I sat down, and I converted every characteristic Daisy loves in a man into an algorithm, which I then programmed into my machine. It took a full week of scanning, but my machine found Paxton."

"Except it didn't find Paxton," Basil said, exasperated. "It found Martin. Honestly, Mendax, if you must attempt a contribution to the field of Mathematics I strongly recommend you restrict your efforts to the counting of metric feet."

"ARE YOU QUESTIONING MY MATH?"

"Normally I would never deign to stoop so low, but yes. Yes, I think this is the appropriate time to question the math."

"Maybe he's not the historical Paxton, but he is the man I wrote for Daisy."

"No, this is utterly absurd. Martin is a very nice sort of fellow, but the idea that out of all the dashing, intrepid men Daisy has spurned on her travels that she would go giddy over a Martin . . ."

Almost inaudibly, Daisy said, "Shut up, Basil."

"I mean, the man fell out of a . . . wait, what?" Basil craned as far as he was able. "Good God, Daisy, what happened in the Smuggler's Hold?! Now I knew you were acting a trifle overprotective lately, but I chalked it up to worry over the Valley. The whole point of assigning Martin as your Personal Assistant was so that he could annoy you with his affection, not inspire its return!"

"He's . . ." Daisy hesitated. The left corner of her mouth turned up as she decided upon the appropriate word for an independent airship Captain to employ at this juncture. ". . . sweet."

"Sweet! So's Cook's iced tea!"

Fionn mac Cumhaill's advice completely tossed aside, Daisy cried, "Alright, fine. He's everything I ever wanted. He's kind, and funny, and clever . . ."

"Now Daisy . . ."

"No! He is! This isn't his world, but he's keeping up and trying to think like we do. I call that clever. And he's a trooper."

"A trooper?" the First Officer repeated, suavely displaying a moderate fraction of the mirth he felt.

"Basil, we put him on a horse for the first time in his life in the morning and sent him to ride in a royal hunt in the afternoon all so I could get an Elf to read a book. You should be so easygoing."

Basil smirked. "And?"

Daisy rolled her eyes and stamped her feet. "And he's adorable. Alright? I said it. Are you happy now? Is everyone happy now?"

"Hmm." Basil considered this, seriously. "I think I'm more bemused than happy. How about you, Mendax? Are you happy? Or are you bemused as well?"

For anyone who is wondering, Martin Hathaway was happy. No one, however, thought of asking him, and it is a difficult thing to smile while wearing a gag.

Mendax, as usually is the way with villains, was not happy, despite achieving exactly what he had set out to do.

"Now do you see the genius in my plan?" he asked. "The math was perfect, but the pastiche was even better. I had my clockwork men develop a control so I could harness a rukh and send it to attack Daisy while she slept in her cabin, knowing my Paxton would come to her rescue, inspiring the love that only a hero can."

"Oooh, hate to take the wind out of your sails, Mendy, old chum." Basil shook his head. "But it was Martin who was attacked and rescued. By Daisy."

This did throw Mendax for a bit of a loop. The mind control had taken a great deal of time and effort to construct. Also, what was Martin doing in Daisy's cabin? Even he had never been in Daisy's cabin.

"It doesn't matter," he said, resuming his circling. "The result is the same. And then—"

"And then you sent the baobhan sith after us in the mountain," Daisy interjected, "leading to our prolonged exposure to each other in the cave-in. I still haven't figured out how you managed that."

"Baobhan sith?" Mendax was dumbfounded. "Look, Daisy, sometimes crazy things just happen to you. Now, as I was saying . . . and then—"

"Wait. What about my mother? She spoke for the first time in twenty-two years upon seeing Martin. I hated it, but I had to accept then that Martin was more charismatic than anyone I had ever met. How did you do that?"

"Ah," Basil said. "Let me field this one, Mendo. Thing is, Daisy, your mother actually speaks to everyone but you. The only thing different about Martin being with us was that she did it while you were still in the room. Apparently, she wishes she could talk to you, but you look and act a great deal like your father and it fills her with infinite sadness. Her words, not mine."

"When were you going to tell me this?!"

"I had hoped never. If it makes you feel any better, Martin did not know either."

Daisy leaned her head back to process this new insight into her own life. Mendax jumped in front of the ottoman and cried, "IF I MAY CONTINUE . . . and then I shall perfect this technology. When I am able to control the minds of humans, I shall sell my controls to the Principle. Then there will be no more Unpredictables, no more Free People, and no one to enjoy the Valley but me!"

Like a true McNamara, Daisy shook off her sadness and smiled. "Yes. Now we come to it. So your plan is to retire in luxury in my Valley? But you can't get in my Valley, not as long as I'm on Arnica. How are you going to kill me, Will? Cut out my heart?"

"WILL IS DEAD!" Entirely too quickly to not be disturbing, Mendax changed his tone from frantic rage to eerie calm. "Yes, Daisy. I'm going to cut out your heart. But I am not going to kill you. I'm going to kill Paxton."

"That doesn't make any sense. Even heartbroken, I'll still be here. You won't be able to get in the Valley."

Mendax uttered a chilling, rolling laugh. "Look at your eyes dart about, Daisy. You've figured it out, but you're still clinging to hope like a fool." He walked over to the machine and ran his hand over a lever near the focusing rod. "Do you know what this is, Daisy?"

"It's the power switch."

"Good. I see you've been doing your homework. I've set the coordinates of my machine for Paxton's world. Soon, very soon, Daisy, I am going to pull this lever"—he crossed over to Martin, grabbed a chunk of his hair, and pulled his head back—"and open a portal using the strings that currently constitute your precious Paxton. Then, after you've watched his atoms be scattered across Space and Time, I am going to shove you and your obnoxious officer through it, stranding you in a universe without your love for eternity."

"Why do I have to go?" Basil demanded.

"BECAUSE I HATE YOU!"

"That's hardly a reason. It seems to me . . ."

Basil was prevented from further critiquing Mendax's plan by the Captain, who leapt to her feet and hopped over between the villain and the power switch, dragging Basil over the ottoman and across the room.

"Daisy!" He groaned, his back bent nearly ninety degrees. "This is exactly as uncomfortable as I thought it would be. Good to know my imagination doesn't embellish."

"Wait," Daisy cried. "Wait, Will, please. I'm . . . I'm sorry."

Mendax stopped in his tracks and stared at her. "You're what?"

"I'm sorry. I'm sorry I made you feel less special than Basil. And I'm sorry I didn't know how to handle your being angry with me. I shouldn't have left you on that island. It was tyrannical of me, and you deserved better."

"Daisy." Mendax was practically breathless. "I don't think I've ever heard you apologize to anyone before."

Martin Hathaway caught Daisy's eye. She winked and looked back at Mendax.

"Are you . . .," she ventured ". . . are you still going to kill Martin?"

"Of course." Mendax laughed. "I'll enjoy it all the more, now."

"Oh." Daisy sighed. "Well, then I'm sorry about this, too."

It all happened in an instant. Daisy bent forward, pulling Basil into the air. Basil lifted his legs as he went and kicked the focusing rod, knocking it away from Martin. He then returned to his feet and flipped Daisy up high on his back. Her boots connected with Mendax's face with a force sufficient to send him flying in front of the focusing rod at the same moment that Basil's chin came down on the power switch.

There was a flash of purple light, a blood-curdling scream, and a portal to a sparsely decorated living room filled the Time and Space previously occupied by Mendax.

⚙ CHAPTER TWENTY-THREE ⚙

"BASIL!" DAISY CRIED upon landing back on her feet. "You killed him!"

Basil Underwood frequently felt as if his efforts aboard the *Nephthys* were not fully appreciated, but today took the proverbial cake. "The man was going to kill Martin, maroon us, enslave the Free People, and possibly destroy the universe in the bargain! I believe 'Thank you, Basil' is in order!"

"We don't kill people!"

"What did you want me to do, Daisy?!"

"Not kill him!"

"My mistake, Captain. Next time, let's be sure to go over our spur-of-the-moment plans in detail so we're both on the same page. 'Oh, Mr. Mendax, would you mind covering your ears while we discuss the morally ideal way to defeat you? Thanks ever so much.'"

"But Basil—"

"No. I'm sorry, but I can't hear you over the sound of Martin still being alive."

"Martin!" Daisy gasped and hopped over to where he was chained to the wall. As they do, moral crises gave way to immediate concerns. The world would certainly be a more tragic place if they did not.

Daisy inquired after Martin's spirits and whether or not he had been hurt, while Basil bemoaned her lack of care for his back. Martin did his best to assure Daisy that he was both unharmed and overjoyed, though all he could manage were exuberant nods of the head and muffled sounds that may or may not have been speech.

"This is no good," Daisy declared. "Basil, can you stand up?"

"With pleasure, Captain." Basil straightened out his back and breathed a sigh of relief. Lifting Daisy's weight was nothing compared to the strain of the angle to which he had previously been subjected. Now at eye level with Martin, Daisy leaned her head forward and removed the gag in his mouth with her own.

"Umm . . . ok," were the first words of a vocally free Martin Hathaway. "That was . . . really hot . . . and I might have just forgotten all the things I had wanted to say."

Daisy giggled. Basil bellowed, "Oh, for God's sake! Captain, we've ascertained that Martin's fine. Can we focus on getting ourselves unshackled now?"

"Nope!" Martin said quickly upon the First Officer's inquiry. "I remember! Daisy, that was amazing. All of it. The whole two weeks of figuring out his game and playing it and beating him at it. You're fantastic. And I don't think you're a tyrant. You have people to protect, and you love them and just want what's best for them and that's awesome and—"

"Martin!" Basil bellowed over his speech. "Can you please do this later? When we're untied? And preferably when I am not around?"

Unmoved by Basil's plight, Martin continued, "But . . . did you mean what you said? About me, that is."

The corners of her mouth turned up, Daisy replied, "Of course. Why would I have said it if I didn't mean it?"

"No, really, you two," Basil insisted, "let's do this later."

Martin whispered, "I love you, Daisy."

Daisy laughed. "Oh, Martin. I love you!"

Basil pleaded, "Later! Let's do this later. Or never. That would be ideal. But right now, there is an unstable machine holding open a portal to another universe and we need to free ourselves and shut it down before it decides it's tired of working properly and takes us all out with it. Now it seems to me, Captain, that our best course of action would be to . . ."

It suddenly occurred to Basil that something did not seem quite right. It was too quiet. He was filled with an intense desire to hear both Martin and the Captain talking at once.

Peering around his shoulder, he asked, "What are you . . . ? OH. GOD. WHY?!"

First Officer Underwood had officially been pushed to his limit.

"Right, Daisy," he said, hopping away and pulling her from Martin. "You've now forfeited the privilege of being tied to me."

"Basil!" Daisy admonished, legs kicking in the air. "What are you doing?"

"I'm making a command decision, Captain. We're going through that portal to look for something or someone to cut us loose."

"Through the portal?!" Martin cried. "But it's unstable! What if it closes and you can't get back?"

"Don't worry about us, my boy. If you are a standard candle for your universe, I wager Daisy and I could conquer it by the end of the week."

Helpless to intervene, Martin Hathaway watched as the two people he cared about the most in this world jumped into another one. He rattled his chains and hoped they would return soon. Looking about, he noticed steam issuing out a gap between one of the bolts near the top of the machine. Racking his brain to recall if the steam had always been there, he hoped Basil and Daisy would return very soon.

THE DAYS AFTER Martin's disappearance had naturally been stressful for Hailey. For some reason she could not fathom, everyone and the local news had designated her Martin's official spokesperson, and as a result she had to field phone calls between his family, his friends, his work, and his search party. The most trying aspect of the entire ordeal was an annoying student of his who kept turning up everywhere "investigating the possibility of foul play" and insisting that Mr. Hathaway never would have disappeared intentionally without leaving a sub list. Having put her own life on hold for far too long, Hailey spent the afternoon at home attempting to catch up on the work she had neglected.

"That's so true." A master of the multitask, Hailey proceeded to leaf through contracts as she chatted with Nadya over the Internet. "And my life coach, therapist, and spin instructor all agree as well. I am a river, and I need to allow myself to flow. I've been trapped in a stagnant pool for far too long, and I need to channel my grief into energy to break through the dam."

Nadya had many encouraging aphorisms to share, but their wisdom was lost when Hailey suddenly heard voices in her living room. Not accepting Nadya's assurance that she had probably just left the television on, she whispered that she would call Nadya back, shut her laptop, and reached for her phone and Martin's baseball bat.

Creeping from the bedroom into the hallway, Hailey discovered a man and a woman in her kitchen tied together by an almost comical amount of rope. To her horror, the man had one of her knives.

"Well, Captain," Basil said, exasperated, "if held still, I would not have had the opportunity to cut you."

"Never mind, I got my hand free."

Hailey screeched, "ALRIGHT! I don't know how you got in here, but you need to get out right now or I am going to call the police. And don't even think about . . . whatever you're thinking about . . . because I am armed and went to a very expensive self-defense class."

"Oh dear!" Basil looked up at the ceiling. "Daisy, we've found Martin's still shockingly indecent girlfriend. You better handle this one."

Hopping around 180 degrees, Basil bent over and set Daisy down.

"Oh, hello," Daisy ventured. "I am Captain Daisy Fitzger—"

Hailey swung the bat wildly and screamed, "WHO ARE YOU PEOPLE? AND HOW DO YOU KNOW MARTIN?"

"Well, as I was trying to say, I am—"

"WHAT ARE YOU DOING IN HERE? I'M WARNING YOU . . ."

With a disgusted roll of her eyes, Daisy drew her blaster and fired. Hailey slumped to the kitchen floor.

"Ah, Daisy." Basil chuckled as he finally broke the rest of their bonds. "You are nothing if not the paragon of diplomacy."

"She wouldn't stop screaming." Daisy held her left shoulder and rotated her arm slowly. Melody was going to kill her when they got back. "Thank god that's over. Now, Basil, you carry Hailey to the couch while I go and get Martin."

"I beg your pardon?!"

"You heard me. It's bad enough to present Martin with a stunned girlfriend. I won't have him finding her crumpled up on the kitchen floor."

"Why does he have to find her at all?"

"This is his home. We . . . we can't keep him. We have to let him go back. Now hurry, so we don't get stuck here as well."

"Captain, I can't pick up an unconscious, half-naked woman. I am an officer and a gentleman." Basil blushed and leaned closer to whisper, "And a married man!"

"And a big baby!" Daisy called over her shoulder as she stepped past Hailey and entered the bedroom. Retrieving a blanket from the bed, she wrapped Hailey up like a particularly fluffy burrito. "There. Is that better?"

"Infinitely."

Daisy ran off through the portal. As ordered, Basil lifted Hailey and set her on the couch in the most lifelike pose he could arrange. He then decided to look about the apartment to ascertain if there was anything worth appropriating. He was surprisingly pleased with Hailey's taste in end tables and thought this a good sign for the rest of the abode. True to his nature, however, he grumbled throughout.

"Oh, yes, Captain," he muttered, opening the kitchen cabinets. "You run off and release Martin. Poor little puppy has no idea you're about to kick him to the curb. God, I can see it now. They're probably frantically kissing—thus prolonging the normal time it should take someone of Daisy's ilk to un-shackle another from a wall—but then she shoves the trusting sap away with some needlessly noble assertion that whatever they're doing isn't right. It isn't, of course, but nor is subject-ing your forbearing First Officer to your depravity. Didn't stop you then, did it, Captain? But she'll press on, insisting that he belongs back in his world with his little harlot even though he's made it very clear that he's forgotten all about her. Oh, no! Martin doesn't understand. Don't you love him, Daisy?! Now, she'll have to spell it out for him and . . . hello, what's this?"

Basil had found a package of Oreos on the counter and popped one in his mouth. Delighted with this new taste sensa-tion, he tucked the package under his arm and wandered off to explore the bedroom.

". . . and she'll reference some idiotic but heroic thing she said to him a week ago like, 'I promised I'd get you back to where the stars are right again,' to which he will respond with some romantic rot like, 'The only stars I need are the ones in your eyes.' Oh, God, I think I just made myself sick with the sweetness of it all."

Still muttering to himself, Basil re-entered the living room carrying a large cardboard box just as Daisy and Martin emerged from the portal holding hands.

"Basil!" Daisy cried breathlessly. "Martin's staying with us!"

"Of course he's staying with us. We're the best thing that ever happened to him. Well, Martin? I suppose you feel some chivalric urge to set things right with your former flame before you do, though?"

Martin Hathaway replied that it was the right thing to do. Basil said something as he stepped through the portal back to

Arnica about hoping Martin would be comforted that he had done the right thing when the universe exploded, but no one was listening to him. Daisy and Martin ran over to the couch and attempted to revive Hailey utilizing the ancient medical art of slapping her in the face and shouting.

The front door opened.

"Hey, Hales, I got the wine you wanted, but I couldn't remember the weird name of the cheese so I . . ." The grocery-laden speaker stopped in the doorway, keys dangling from his hand. "Martin?!"

"Zac?!" Martin Hathaway sat back and scratched his head. Daisy McNamara kept her hand on her blaster, just in case.

"Oh, look!" Sometime while their focus had been on Hailey, Basil had returned to the universe. "The little floozy's moved on. Who's surprised? Not me." With that, he exited again into his own world.

Zac sputtered several half-finished questions at once, the most pressing of which being how the giant, purple-rimmed hole in the living room wall got there and whether or not it would affect the security deposit. Overlooking the fact that he had been the one to make that deposit, Martin explained his adventures in Arnica as simply as possible.

Setting the groceries aside and slowly edging toward the couch, Zac responded, "Dude, we thought you were dead. Or run off or something. I mean, nobody could find you. Not the park rangers or the police or the news chopper or anyone."

Martin nodded slowly. "Are . . . um . . . those my keys?"

Zac colored slightly. "Yeah. You left them behind, remember?"

"I remember."

"And . . . well, then you remember I promised to take care of Hailey if you died, right? And she was really cut up about your disappearing, man. No wonder she fainted when you got back. Are . . . you aren't mad, are you?"

Martin shook his head. "No. It actually makes things easier. A lot can happen in two weeks, I guess."

"Dude, it's only Wednesday."

"What?! Wednesday! Why you little . . . !"

Sensing the change in the direction of the conversation, Daisy raised her blaster. The gesture was enough to remind Martin Hathaway of his priorities. He laughed and took her hand.

"It's ok, Daisy. Let's go home."

MARTIN AND DAISY ran back through the portal and over to Svadilfari's machine. One hand atop another, they held the power switch and readied to shut it off when Daisy remembered something crucial.

"Wait! Where's Basil?"

"Over here, Captain!" Basil waved from the ottoman where he was munching on Oreos and writing in his notebook. "Glad I'm still a factor in your happy ending."

Martin grinned and said, "Tell Melody I said 'hi'!"

"I would think very carefully before you pull that lever, Martin. I've already killed one of Daisy's paramours today. I might develop a taste for it."

Whether he had done so carefully remained to be seen, but Martin Hathaway had already thought quite enough about the universe in which he wanted to live out the rest of his days. Pressing his lips once more to Daisy's, together they pulled the power switch and closed the portal.

Then, Martin remembered something crucial.

"Ahh! How stupid!" He groaned. "We were in my apartment! I should have grabbed a change of clothes or a toothbrush or something!"

"No need for lamentations, lad." Basil jumped to his feet and picked up a large cardboard box. Handing it to Martin, he said, "I found this box in the bedroom closet. It's labeled 'Martin,' so I took the liberty of rummaging through it. I think you'll find an ample supply of clothing and other necessities in there."

"You went to look for my clothes? While I . . . while we—"

"Someone has to think of these things. There was the most hideous velvet jacket in there, however, and I did leave that behind. I assure you that it won't be needed here."

Martin was overwhelmed with gratitude. Setting the box aside, he did the unthinkable. Martin Hathaway hugged Basil Underwood.

"What?! What is this?!" Basil cried. "Daisy! Control your boyfriend!"

Daisy started to laugh, but her merriment was cut short when Svadilfari's machine issued a disquieting hiss. All heads turned to see the machine sputter and shake.

"But . . . we turned it off," Martin said.

Basil began to back away from Martin and the machine, believing both to be equally unstable. "Ah. It appears the two-thousand-year-old parts have had quite enough of our shenanigans. On the off-chance it explodes without destroying the universe, I suggest we run."

It was a plan after Captain McNamara's own heart. The three

raced out the heavy wooden door with the brass knocker and down the winding stone staircase. Martin had taken the time to gather and bring his box with him, and as they leapt out the front door and rolled to the bottom of the hill, he noticed Basil also carried a burden.

"Is that my coffee table?!"

"Yes. It's very lovely, and now justice has been restored to the universe."

The trio huddled together at the bottom of the hill using the coffee table as a shield. Each prayed in their own fashion that the universe would survive to appreciate Basil's efforts on its behalf.

There was a deafening roar. The room at the top of the tower burst apart, sending stones and hot iron flying through the air. A purple light shot through the mountain range, and the tower crumbled. Debris fell on all sides of our heroes, including a single metal hand.

As the dust settled, three heads slowly poked up from behind the coffee table.

"We're not dead!" Martin cried, and the party fell into peals of laughter.

Ever alert, Daisy rose and drew her blaster.

"Something's moving the rubble!" she warned.

"Impossible!" Basil insisted. "I can see enough parts for two clockwork men scattered on this hill alone!"

Nonetheless, something was moving. Daisy walked forward slowly. A hand emerged, followed shortly by a familiar head.

"Captain!" Gilly exclaimed. "I knew you'd come for us! Gibs! The Captain saved us!"

Daisy holstered her blaster and ran to help Gilly and Gibson.

"Of course I came for you." She laughed. "I could never leave my men behind."

Martin and Basil stood on the hill, shaking their heads.

"She forgot all about them, didn't she?" Martin asked.

Basil slapped a hand on his back. "Today, we learn perhaps the most important of life's Truths: this is Daisy's world. We only exist to ensure it stays that way. Now, come on, you great Pomeranian, let's go give her a hand with those stones."

WHEN THE COMPANY had finally made their way back to the Lost Valley, all five members were exhausted. Gilly and Gibson trudged off for their cottages with a thankful wave to the Captain. The remaining three collapsed in Daisy's parlor, each supported by the thought that it had been a day well spent.

"Now that we can call this mission concluded, Captain," Basil said from his chair, "shall we summarize what we learned?"

Her head resting upon Martin's shoulder and her arm back safely in its sling, Daisy replied, "It's more important to learn how to accept an apology than how to give one."

"Nicely put. I was going to go with 'All artists are crazy,' but yours is much pithier."

"Wait, what?" Martin looked back and forth between his friends. "I don't . . . that's not what you should have taken away from all this."

"Yes, it is," Daisy insisted. "If Will had accepted my apology, he would still be alive."

"But . . . no . . . you're supposed to learn that forgiving in the first place is better than punishing and making someone become evil."

"If I had forgiven him in the first place, I wouldn't have you. And you wouldn't have me. That's a two-for-one."

"And I wouldn't have these delightful sandwich cookies," Basil added, "which I need to bring home to Melody before I finish them all and deprive her of a present from another universe. So, Captain, if I may be dismissed, I think I'll replace your library coffee table and then mosey on home for dinner."

After Basil exited table in hand, Martin nudged the box of his clothing with his foot and said, "I wouldn't mind getting settled in either. Where . . . um . . . where can I put this?"

Quite matter-of-factly, Daisy replied, "With your other things. In the Bachelor's Quarters."

"Oh. But I . . . I mean, I kinda thought . . . it is a big house and all . . ."

Daisy rose and crossed over to the window seat. "Martin, if that was a proposal, I suggest you work on it and try again later. Until then, you will report to the Breakfast Parlor with coffee every morning at 0700 hours and you will be dismissed no later than 1800 hours as long as we are in the Valley. Is that understood?"

Martin mumbled a weak "Aye, Captain" and pondered over the course of the next few years of his life. He was not the first, nor is he likely to be the last, to realize that dating one's boss is a complicated matter in any universe.

Looking out the window, Daisy observed, "It appears to be another of those nights where it is entirely too hot to remain indoors." She picked up Martin's clipboard from where he had left it the day before, crossed the room, and handed it to him. "I think I'll take my dinner in the garden tonight."

Martin took the clipboard and fell back into his own thoughts.

"Did you write that down?" the Captain asked.

"Hmm? Oh, right. Yes, dinner in garden. Got it."

"Excellent." Daisy smiled and walked back to the window seat. "Then it's official."

Martin was busy wondering what difference it made if Daisy took her dinner on the moon when Basil poked his head into the room and whispered, "Keep up, Martin."

Though the gears in his mind turned slowly, he soon broke into a grin. "Oh, right! You know, I think I'll stop by the kitchen and see if Steuart can't make something special tonight. Since it's so hot and all."

Happily, Martin Hathaway ran off to put everything in order for his first official date with Daisy McNamara.

Basil leaned in the doorway and crossed his arms. "Well, Daisy? In the last twelve hours I have defended your Valley, released you from captivity, rescued your Personal Assistant, disposed of your archnemesis, replaced your coffee table, and begun training your new boyfriend."

Clicking his heels together and saluting, he said, "First Officer Underwood formally requests tomorrow off."

FROM THE NEXT INSTALLMENT IN THE MISADVENTURES TRILOGY

SHIPWRECKED OFF HERAMATHEA'S COVE

Martin Hathaway had quickly learned that he was, in all reality, in love with two women: Daisy and the Captain. One thought he was the best sort of man possible, and the other mildly tolerated his presence. Watching her pop up the collar on her green, felt trench coat before stepping out into the snow, there was no question in his mind as to which of the incarnations was before him. Martin grabbed his clipboard, shut the door, and trotted dutifully behind the Captain.

"When did they arrive?" she asked Gibson on her right.

"Last night, Miss. Just before the storm hit. Must be something awful important to get the Anatamenwarian Ambassador out this time of year."

"No doubt. Why didn't the patrol call me when their fire was spotted?"

Gilly looked askance at Martin and replied, "We tried, Miss. We left four messages. Thought it best to alert you in the morning."

She stopped walking and turned on her heel. Never prepared for the Captain's abrupt changes of direction, Martin walked into her.

"Well?" she demanded.

Sheepishly, Martin put his hand in his coat pocket and withdrew his cell phone.

"Four missed calls, Captain," he reported. "Three from line four and one from line three. Probably a watch shift change accounts for the last one. Do . . . um . . . do you want me to check the messages?"

"Why are there messages, Martin?"

"Well . . . I . . . guess . . . we . . . couldn't hear it ring in the parlor. What with it being in my coat in the closet and all."

"Mr. Hathaway," she spoke calmly. Martin knew he was in trouble now. "What exactly was the point of asking Engineering to build machines that enable communication between myself and the patrols if you can't be bothered to keep one on your person?"

Martin bit his lip and kicked at the snow. It had taken him two months to convince Daisy to let him have his cell phone back, and then she had only capitulated on the condition that he answer any calls, "Captain's line. Martin speaking." It was a hard-fought battle, and he did not relish the thought of losing ground. It was time to employ Strategic Misdirection.

Leaning forward, Martin kissed the Captain on her nose.

Fifteen seconds later, he climbed out of the snowdrift into which Daisy had sent him flying and brushed himself off.

Works every time, he thought merrily, jogging to catch up with the rest of the party.

ON THE FAR northern edge of the Erigeron Mountains lay a natural overhang onto which Wistar McNamara long ago had built a small, cedar cottage. For generations since, the overhang generally and the cottage specifically were known as Communication Point, and it was there that anyone who wished to conduct business with the McNamaras would wait until they were noticed.

This morning, Martin counted twenty canvas tents erected close together about the base of the mountain, their presence indicating the officialness and importance of the visitors waiting in the cottage. Martin shook his head as he climbed the stone steps behind Daisy and pitied the poor souls forced to sleep outside on a night like the last.

Having dismissed Gilly, Gibson, and the rest of the patrol, Daisy opened the cottage door and revealed its occupants. The two men inside looked as if they had passed a night only slightly better than that of their entourage. They wore long, thick, fur coats and huddled near the stone fireplace. Daisy nodded to Martin, who went off to prepare coffee in the primitive yet functional cottage kitchen.

The taller of the two men stepped forward as Martin exited. From the kitchen, Martin could hear the exchange of forced pleasantries.

"Captain McNamara. How wonderful to see you so well recovered from our last visit. I see you've dispensed with your overzealous First Officer."

"On the contrary, Ambassador, Mr. Underwood is at this moment leading a mission of the utmost importance. He will be sorry to miss you, however. It is not often he meets a chess player of your caliber."

The conversation continued in a similar vein until Martin returned and served coffee. The presentation of warm beverages signaling the start of any Arnican business exchange, both men took their seats and looked expectantly at the Captain.

Always one for theatrics, Daisy waited until Martin had assumed his mark behind her chair before inquiring, "Well, gentlemen? What brings you from the warmth of your homes to the edge of my Valley?"

The Ambassador spoke quickly, "We are here on a matter of grave importance to the citizens of Anatamenwar and the Principle himself. It is the Principle's express wish to engage your crew on a highly classified mission."

"Highly classified, meaning you will not give details until after I accept."

"Captain McNamara, you cut straight to the heart of things."

Casually, Daisy glanced over her shoulder and asked Martin how her schedule looked for the foreseeable future. Martin knew fully well that Daisy never consulted him about her schedule when there was anything on it, which meant his role was to flip through the pages on his clipboard and frown.

"Your annual visit to the Blessed Isle is long overdue, Captain," he replied, "and you've agreed to assist the Waitzian Warlocks with their quest for the Cup of Zaluzania."

Daisy sighed and sipped her coffee. "I'm sorry, Ambassador, but as you've heard, my company is already in great demand. Please give my condolences to the Principle for his loss."

The Ambassador countered, "We are prepared to pay you handsomely for your troubles. Five thousand anatamens in advance, and another ten thousand upon your successful return."

Martin had no idea if the quoted amount was a reasonable payment or not, but he decided the Ambassador must have undervalued Daisy's services, since she burst into laughter.

"What care I for your anatamens? If I want anything from your merchants, I will take it." Daisy rose from her chair and started for the door, calling to Martin, "Come along. These men summoned me from a comfortable hearth merely to amuse themselves and waste my time."

"Name your price!" the second man cried. "The Principle will pay it."

Her back to the visitors, Daisy smiled in a manner that Martin would have described as sinister if she had not also winked at him.

She turned and declared, "My price is this: two hundred thousand potted orchids in the deepest shade of purple your gardeners can cultivate, one thousand yards of silk the color of the summer sky, and one thousand yards of silk the green of newly sprouted grass. Bring me hunter green, and you shall rue the day."

The men from Anatamenwar stared at her momentarily and bent their heads to whisper amongst themselves. Their negotiations concluded, the Ambassador confirmed, "We will deliver the silk by the end of the week, and the orchids upon receipt of positive news."

"Excellent." Daisy resumed her seat, smoothing her skirt and striking a genteel pose. "It appears we have reached an accord. Now, Ambassador, perhaps you can enlighten me as to what would constitute 'positive news.'"

The Ambassador began his explanation by introducing the small, mousy man who had accompanied him. "This, Captain McNamara, is Mr. Oisin of the Publishing House."

Daisy smiled politely and informed Mr. Oisin that his products were always a delight to discover when raiding Anatamenwarian cargo ships.

"Mr. Oisin and the Principle have been working closely together of late"—the Ambassador ignored Daisy's allusion to the thorniness of their relationship—"on a project that we hope will one day benefit all citizens."

He pulled a roll of paper from inside his coat and spread it across the table. Leaning over Daisy's chair, Martin saw that it was a map of the known Arnica. The Ambassador pointed to a large island that looked exactly and nothing like Madagascar.

"This is the island of Hyoseris. You are familiar with it?"

"I am familiar with its location," Daisy nodded, "but I have never traveled to it."

"Few have. That is one of the reasons the Principle consulted Mr. Oisin. With the aid of the Publishing House, the Principle has dispatched Fionn mac Cumhaill to explore and map Hyoseris."

Martin had been taking careful notes on his clipboard and interjected, "I'm sorry, who?"

"Fionn mac Cumhaill," all three replied.

"Finn McCool?"

Daisy pronounced the explorer's name slowly and deliberately.

"So, Finn McCool?" Martin repeated.

"Yes, Finn McCool." Daisy gave up and said to the Ambassador, "I fail to see where the *Nephthys* factors into the Principle's plans, then. He already has an explorer-for-hire."

"But he's lost!" Mr. Oisin squealed. "He always sends back regular reports for publication, but we haven't heard from him in months!"

"I see," Daisy nodded. "The Principle has lost his explorer, and the Publishing House has lost their star author. You want my crew to risk their lives to prove that he has not lost his."

"In a nutshell," the Ambassador confirmed. "Fionn mac Cumhaill is missing. Find him."

"Sounds like as good an excuse to sail south for the winter as any. Wouldn't you agree, Mr. Hathaway?"

Mr. Oisin's spirits perked up considerably upon hearing Martin's name.

"Mr. Hathaway?" he said with great import. "Not Martin Hathaway of Eagle's Peak?!"

"Um . . ." Martin looked to Daisy for guidance, completely unused to being recognized outside of the crew of the *Nephthys* and the Elves of the Blessed Isle. Daisy raised her eyebrows and appeared quite as taken aback by Mr. Oisin's exclamation as Martin was, though perhaps she was a bit more amused than he. For lack of a better answer, he replied, "Well . . . yes."

"Your fame as a poet precedes you," Mr. Oisin said, rising to shake his hand. "No need to be modest, young man. I make it my business to know whenever promising talent presents itself. What do you say to a contract? We could have your words available for purchase in every civilized nation on Arnica."

Martin was flattered, but he was also honest. "I only recited for the King. The words weren't really mine."

"Tut, tut. No one scruples such things these days. We could publish the lot under the title *Poems of Eagle's Peak*, if it makes you happy. Then we can release works of your own after you've honed your chops. I could front you an advance on royalties today, unless you also wish to be paid in fabric."

Martin shrugged and said to Daisy, "We could get a cake."

"No need. Basil 'won't' bake us the most wonderful cake

you've ever tasted." To Mr. Oisin, she smiled, "What Mr. Ha-thaway means is that he'd be delighted to negotiate a contract, but it is poor form to broker one business deal before another is cold. If you would follow us, Mr. Oisin, you and Mr. Hathaway could speak further in his quarters."

"Don't be a fool, Oisin," the Ambassador warned, rising and making for the door. "She means to lose you along the way to her Valley and laugh as you wander about in the snow for days, wondering where you are."

"Ambassador, you know me far too well. I look forward to the day of your retirement."

"As do I, Captain McNamara. Come along, Mr. Oisin."

Disappointed, Mr. Oisin followed the Ambassador out of the cottage. Before taking his leave, however, he handed Martin his card with the promise, "Anytime you want to live up to your potential, you send me word. The Publishing House will set you up for life. Just ask Fionn when you meet him."

"WHY DID YOU DO THAT?" Martin asked from the kitchen as he cleaned up the evidence of the business meeting.

Daisy stood in the main room, watching the caravan from Anatamenwar prepare to depart and contemplating the mission to which she had agreed. "Do what?"

"Dismiss Mr. Oisin like you did."

"Because he's an odious, little man."

"But he was talking to me."

"He left you his card. What's wrong, Martin? Not living up to your potential?"

Daisy had spoken in jest, but at Martin's mumbled reply

she turned from the window and walked tentatively into the kitchen.

"I am sorry, Martin. I had no idea you really wanted to be a poet."

"I don't want to be a poet," he sighed. "But . . . I don't know. It's not really a proper job, is it? Being your Personal Assistant, I mean. Basil only gave it to me to annoy you."

"But you've made it a proper job," Daisy wrapped her arms around his waist. "I thought you enjoyed it."

"I do. It's the best job I've ever had."

"But?"

"But I don't have anything to offer you. Everything I have, you gave me. My proposal last night was basically me asking permission to move into your house."

"I don't care about what you have. Why would you think you need to offer me anything?"

Martin shrugged. "I don't know. I guess I've been thinking about what Basil said. You know, about how he has a home and I have a hammock."

Daisy laughed, "You do know that I gave Basil his home, don't you?"

"I know," Martin slowly began to smile. "Sometimes I forget that things here aren't exactly like they are on Earth."

"Are all marriages on Earth pecuniary transactions?"

"Maybe they are," Martin traced his index finger along Daisy's cheek. "But are you sure you really don't want me to be more than the guy who follows you around all day?"

Daisy said something that every one of Martin's former loves had said to him before. The only difference this time was that, when Daisy said it, she was not trying to leave him.

"I want you to be happy." She squeezed him tightly before taking his hand and leading him out of the cabin. "Whatever that entails. I suppose we could train you to be a second on some of the other jobs on the ship if that would make you feel better."

Martin agreed that it might, and Daisy considered that matter resolved. Stepping into the sunshine, she felt no reason to further contain her good humor.

"Just think, Martin," she cooed with glee, "we've got the best of Basil this time. We can get married as soon as we get back from Hyoseris, and there's nothing he can say to stop it, because we acquired everything he wanted."

"You know, for as good of friends as you are, you two sure seem to enjoy getting the other's goat a lot."

"Basil doesn't keep goats. But, if you mean I delight in defeating him, then you've got something there. Don't worry about Basil, though. He's going to be so excited when he finds out we're meeting Fionn mac Cumhaill. I just enjoy *Warfare and Other Human Relations*, but Basil has first editions of all his works, and every time we go anywhere remotely civilized, he looks for a bookstore to see if anything new's been published."

Daisy insisted Martin keep the details of their mission to Hyoseris a secret in order to better surprise Basil when they find his hero. Martin agreed, but added what he felt might be an important piece of information.

"He's one of mine, by the way. Finn McCool."

"You've read his works?"

"No. I mean, he's from my world. Finn McCool was a folk hero. He wasn't real like Reginald McNamara, but he was about as famous."

Furrowing her brow, Daisy asked, "He was a hero? Nothing sinister like the last one?"

"Oh, no. He told a lot of tall tales and bragged too much, but that's the worst of it."

"You will let me know if anything else pops up during this mission that parallels your world, won't you, Martin?"

"Of course, Captain," he grinned. "I learned my lesson with Mendax. You decide what's important and what's trivial."

"Excellent."

⚙ ACKNOWLEDGMENTS ⚙

I would like to thank everyone who lent their support to getting Martin Hathaway off the ground. It is truly amazing and slightly baffling to learn how many people have blind, unwavering faith that I know what I'm doing. Specifically, this novel owes much to my sister Patty Glen, brother Thomas Glen, and friend Katelyn Thompson, who acted as eager beta readers and tireless sounding boards. Its polish and shine can be attributed entirely to my fabulous editor and first organic fan Laura Zats. For its existence in print, I very humbly thank Captain Luc Baker-Stahl of the A.S. *Oakenshield*, Captain Raymond Ontko of the A.S. *Shakespeare*, and Captain Patty Glen of the A.S. *Holmes*. I would be remiss not to also take this opportunity to acknowledge the storytellers who came before, whose characters, truths, and styles are forever woven into the fabric of my imagination, as well as my parents, Tom and Annie Glen, who forced me to go outside as a young child but always accepted reading as a proper activity to be conducted in trees. Finally, I would like to thank Orlando Bloom, for had he not looked good in tights this book may never have been possible.